THE FIRST EULGARIAN TALE

Into the Wind

ABIGAIL JEANNE
COVER ART BY EMMA BEAN

All characters in this book, aside from the Protector, do not exist outside the imagination of the author and have no relation to anyone bearing the same name. Neither are they even remotely inspired by any individual known or unknown to the author, and all incidents are purely fictional.

Into The Wind
The First Eulgarian Tale
Copyright © 2022 by Abigail Jeanne

ISBN: 979-8-9864588-0-9

TABLE OF CONTENTS

Pronunciation Guide Of Names And Places 1

An Introduction To The Continent 3

Year Ninety-Five 5

Chapter One 10

Chapter Two 19

Chapter Three 25

Chapter Four 37

Chapter Five 43

Chapter Six 53

Chapter Seven 69

Chapter Eight 79

Chapter Nine 96

Chapter Ten 106

Chapter Eleven 124

Chapter Twelve 135

Chapter Thirteen 149

Chapter Fourteen 157

Chapter Fifteen 167

Chapter Sixteen 186

Chapter Seventeen 195

Chapter Eighteen 205

Chapter Nineteen 214

Chapter Twenty 223

Chapter Twenty-One..235

Chapter Twenty-Two..245

Chapter Twenty-Three 255

Chapter Twenty-Four 266

Chapter Twenty-Five..278

Chapter Twenty-Six 287

Chapter Twenty-Seven..297

Fifteen Years Later..306

Excerpts From *Debster's Dictionary* 310

Bibliography 314

Acknowledgments..316

About The Author 318

To my Savior,
You gave me the most expensive gift ever when You sent Your
Son to die for me!
Thank You, first and always, for my salvation,
and for Eulgaria.

"And who knows whether you have not come to the kingdom
for such a time as this?" Esther 4:14b

PRONUNCIATION GUIDE
OF NAMES AND PLACES

Abihail: ꞌa-bə-hāl
Acaidia: ə-ꞌkā-dē-ə
Azal: ə-ꞌzāl
Chionia: chē-ꞌō-nē-ə
Caldonia: kal-ꞌdō-nē-ə
Dumah: ꞌdü-mə
Ekro: ꞌek-rō
Eulgaria: loo-ger-ē-ə
Hosie Vine-agar: ꞌhō-zē ꞌvi-ni-gər
Izhar: ꞌiz-här
Jamain: jə-ꞌmān
Jattir: jā-ꞌtär
Kannauj: ꞌkən-nə-jēm
Keilah: ꞌkē -lə
Kelian: ꞌkē-lan
La-kaodai: lə-ꞌkā-ō-dī
Lo-debar: ꞌlō-de-bär
Maon: ꞌmā-ȯn
Mark-hai: ꞌmärk-hī
Mushi: ꞌmü-shē

1

INTO THE WIND

Mahli: ˈmal-ē
Prokaryota: prō-ˈker-ē-ō-tə
Saidi: ˈsā- ə-dī
Shaphir: shə-ˈpär
Thebes: ˈthēbz
Zephyr: ˈze-fər
Ziph: ˈzif

AN INTRODUCTION TO
THE CONTINENT

A land filled with rolling plains, stunning moun-
tain vistas, endless deserts, and pure, glassy
lakes; a land inhabited by fearless warriors—this is The
Continent.

The Continent, a vast country spanning almost the
entirety of the largest known landmass on the world
of Hereth, is approximately 3.8 million square miles.
Hundreds of Tribes and Clans inhabit its borders.

Each Tribe is governed by a Chief and Chieftess, with
assistance from that Tribe's most prominent warriors, or
head warriors. The most extraordinary Tribe is called the
Tribe, and though it is counted among the smaller Tribes,
it makes up for that greatly in the skill of its warriors and
craftspeople.

Each Clan is governed by a ruling body known as
the Grand Council. The Grand Council is comprised of
all the Clan's elders, together with the Chief and his heir.
Women have but a small part in governing the Clan. Of
all the Clans that fill the Continent, the Clan is the largest

and fiercest, and the Clan's greatest ambition is to control the whole of The Continent.

The Tribe and Clan have been enemies for long ages of time. The Clan has not, however, ever brought its full military might down upon the Tribe, perhaps respecting the long tradition of mutual rivalry that has only been broken by brief spurts of partially-friendly relations.

The Continentals are a simple people, not wishing to disturb their beautiful land but to grow with it and around it, and it is in this that they find great beauty. They may be on good terms with the countries around them but have a long history of not looking outwards for help in times of crises but inwards to their own people.

The Protector, the creator and sustainer of life on Hereth and all the other worlds, blessed some with a Gift, the ability to control one aspect of nature. These are Fire, Water, Ice, Wind (or Sound, as some name it), Rock, Light, Earth, and Nature.

In the Early Days, before Settlers from the Far Countries began to inhabit the lands surrounding The Continent, many were given Gifts. In time, the Gifts came but rarely, and it was a precious thing indeed to be given a Gift.

Some began to say that if you were given a Gift, you must be chosen by the Protector for a Great Deed…

YEAR NINETY-FIVE

he seventeen-year-old girl stood by her father, Chief Mark-hai, who stood at the head of three freshly dug graves. On the other side of the Chief stood the girl's cousin, a somber-looking young man.

She reached out gently and touched Chief Mark-hai on the arm. He looked down and offered a faint smile. "I love you, Zephyr."

A low, plaintive melody drifted towards them from the center of the village. Zephyr turned her eyes from her father, but she could not see the funeral procession yet. In a flash, she was transported to a day fourteen years ago.

"Mammy!" Zephyr called, a delighted smile on her tiny lips. "Look!"

"At what?" Lasha, Chieftess[1] of The Tribe, turned from the fireplace, speaking in the sweet tone she always

---

1 The title for the female ruler of a Tribe or Clan. Despite the claims of some scholars it is spelled with a *T*.

used with her only daughter, no matter how tired she might be.

"Watch me," the three-year-old said. Zephyr's brow furrowed in concentration, and she pointed her hand at the hand-carved wooden blocks with which she had been playing. One of the blocks shook and then slowly lifted, borne upwards on a sudden gust of wind.

The block continued rising upwards for a few inches, then hung in space uncertainly before sliding backward and settling on top of the tower Zephyr had already built.

Lasha dropped her wooden spoon and rushed forward, scooping her daughter up into her arms. "Oh, Zephyr! We have been blessed indeed. A Gift! *The Protector has given you a Gift! Oh, my daughter, only wait 'til we tell your Father!"*

Zephyr shook her head, shaking off the vivid memory. There were snatches of other memories from before her sixth year, but that was the only memory that endured so clearly and completely in her heart.

The funeral procession was in sight now. Zephyr's heart clenched as the first of the three caskets came into view. Young warriors bore the earthly remains of Zephyr's mother and Bark's parents on their shoulders.

The lament grew louder, coming from the throats of fifty women who walked behind the coffins. There was a deep sadness in the wordless melody, but also beauty.

It was a tune that spoke of grief coupled with hope and faith in the Protector's good and wise pleasure.

Zephyr shifted her weight slightly, just enough to see Bark on the other side of the Chief. His face was contorted with grief, and tears gathered in his eyes. What must it be like to lose both parents in one day? To not even be able to sit by their sides as they left this world for the Protector's throne?

It was a child's most sacred duty to sit at the side of aged parents and do all one could to ease their last pain-filled moments, and Zephyr's heart ached for the pain her cousin must now feel.

The procession entered the graveyard. A sense of unreality pervaded the day for Zephyr and, she suspected, for her family as well.

"Zephyr!" Lasha ordered sternly. "Put that duck down right this instant."

"Yes, Mammy," the six-year-old said, ducking her head sheepishly, as she waved her hand and allowed the duck to float to the ground. She had been practicing levitating things without holding her arm out.

Lasha rubbed her hand over her face. "Come here, and sit down."

Zephyr obeyed, locking the duck pen gate behind her before joining her mother on a bench outside their rack-leen.

"What did we talk about yesterday?" Lasha said, sternly yet gently.

"I don't remember."

"I do not remember." Lasha corrected. "You are not to use your Gift on animals, people, or anything that is not yours. Do you understand?"

"Yes, Mammy," Zephyr said quietly.

Lasha sighed. There was no guarantee that Zephyr would not forget as soon as she ran away to play with her friends. "Darling, the Protector does not give Gifts very often now. You are special," Lasha hugged her daughter close. "I knew that the moment you opened your eyes, but now everyone knows it. The Protector has some special task for you, and you cannot be ready for that task if you spend your time misusing your Gift."

"I understand," Zephyr said, and, looking deep into Zephyr's eyes, Lasha knew that she really did.

Zephyr blinked, forcing her mind back to the present. She watched as the warriors carefully lowered the coffins into the ground. Swift Arrow, one of the pallbearers and Zephyr's guard, met her eyes and gave her a long glance. Zephyr smiled at him and wiped tears off her face.

Chief Mark-hai began to speak. He spoke of the three now-departed ones. Bark's father had been a scientist. He had wanted to study the flora and fauna of the North, even inventing the words used to describe his area of study.

Bark's mother and Chieftess Lasha were sisters. They had been as close as any sisters could be, but the attributes and accomplishments of those who had died were not what occupied the main thread of the Chief's discourse.

He quickly turned to the hope they all shared. The hope of rewards after standing before the Protector's throne and returning those rewards to the One who gave them. The hope of a future day of glory in which all would be made right.

It was a fitting end to the day.

CHAPTER ONE

The raging clouds sent wave upon wave of unrelenting rain into the sides of the six-sided rackleens.[2] Thunder pealed like brass bells, and lightning lit up the sky like the largest display of flashworks ever seen in Hereth.

The door flap on the central rackleen flew open, pushed inside by a sudden gust of wind, and a young man stumbled in. A lithe girl hurried to tack the gazelle leather back in place.

"Get back outside," she scolded as she paused mid-flight to scoop up the door tacks. The angry roar of the wind sank into a quiet purr for a moment, and one could almost imagine the wind slinking back like a naughty kitten.

"Bark, you are nearly drowned!" She exclaimed, turning her attention to her cousin. "Get out of those wet clothes before you catch a chill."

---

2 Rackleens are the six-sided buildings used on The Continent. The word is borrowed from the Eulgarian words *rack* meaning *live* and *leen* meaning *family*. Thus the word literally means *a place for our family to live.*

"I am fine, Zephyr." Her cousin dismissed her concern as he dropped his storm poncho to the ground. "Besides, if I had not gone, what would have happened to the animals? The yard was almost flooded, but now the ducks and your llama are safe in their pens, and," he added with a shrug. "Chief Mark-hai had no business going out in the storm with his cough."

Zephyr had picked up Bark's poncho, put it inside a tightly woven basket and pushed him behind a curtain while he was talking. "Put your clothes in there." She pushed the basket behind the curtain. "I put dry clothes on top of your trunk."

"Thank you, Zephyr." He said.

Bark reappeared a minute later. "Did you put your clothes in the basket? I do not want to ruin the floor panels."

Bark nodded. "Of course I did."

"Right," Zephyr pressed a mug of warm nettle tea into his hands, "because you never leave a mess in the rackleen."

"Never," he agreed with a grin, sinking to the ground beside his unlac.[3]

Zephyr leaned against the wall and looked down at the two men seated on the floor. "One more thing,"

Bark looked up expectedly.

---

3 Means *uncle*, it is a common term of respect given to family friends as well. Pronounced *Un-lac*.

"Your llama? Really? You named the poor thing and cannot even bother to use her name. Ella will be very offended when I tell her."

"Whatancta,"[4] Bark shrugged. "I am not in the habit of worrying about offending llamas."

"Really, Bark," Chief Mark-hai said, amused. "Stop teasing your poor cousin. She, and her llama, deserve your respect for keeping this rackleen running. Honestly, I think she does more work in the Tribe than you do." He shook his head in mock disappointment.

"You do know that she is leaving, right?" Bark muttered into his tea.

The Chief slapped Bark playfully on the back of the head, causing Bark's head to jerk and his nose to take a dive into his tea. "It is my lungs that are bothering me, not my ears, m'lad."

Zephyr giggled and joined the men on the floor. She leaned her head on her father's shoulder. "Thank you for letting me move."

Chief Mark-hai looked tenderly down at his daughter. "You are most welcome. I thought that you could do with a bit of freedom and fun before you marry, but I have not given up the search for the perfect husband for you."

---

4 Another borrowed Eulgarian word meaning *whatever* or 'I'm done discussing this topic, but I don't want to be rude so I'll say, *whatever*." Pronounced *wha-chatcha*.

12

"I know that you will find the right man," Zephyr said trustfully. Unbidden, a face sprang to her mind, and she mentally shook her head. *Where did that come from?* She wondered.

Chief Mark-hai kissed the top of her head. "I do not take that trust lightly."

A loud thunderclap shook the rackleen. The Chief looked up and sighed. "You are not moving tonight, my daughter."

Zephyr sighed. "I knew. That wind was too strong."

Chief Mark-hai smiled proudly. "Of course, the Princess of the Tribe is in tune with the winds."

Zephyr smiled. "I only hope that Cornflower and Sunblossom did not get caught trying to move when the storm broke."

Cornflower, a healer, and Sunblossom were Zephyr's closest friends, and the threesome were moving into a rackleen together.

It could not have been better timing. No sooner had the words left Zephyr's mouth than they heard a sharp, loud knock on the door frame. Both cousins scrambled up, but it was Zephyr who reached the door first. She pulled the door tacks out, and two young ladies, a warrior, and a wolfurnut,[5] along with plenty of rain, entered the rackleen.

---

5 Pronounced *wolf-ur-not*. See *Excerpts from Debster's Dictionary*, page 310.

Bark and Zephyr wrestled the door flap back into place and turned to view their unexpected visitors. Cornflower and Sunblossom stood in the middle of the rackleen, along with Swift Arrow and Sunblossom's pet wolfurnut, Betsy.

"What are you all doing here?" Zephyr asked, confusion etched on her face.

"With the storm so rough, I went to check on the girls," Swift Arrow began. "Unfortunately, the crew who built the rackleen did not ensure that the ceiling panels were properly tied on. They had collapsed inwards, and the rackleen floor was flooded with three inches of water. Betsy was trying to use a trunk as a boat."

Wolfurnuts are notoriously water adverse.

"Well, the first thing to be done is to get you out of your wet clothes," Zephyr said briskly. "Bark, find clothes for Arrow. I have something for you girls, I am sure." She pulled a curtain down that spent most of its life rolled up on the ceiling and deftly tied it to a small ring on the floor.

Sunblossom and Cornflower stepped behind it to change. Zephyr popped open her trunk and sorted through it until she found two pairs of clothes. "You are a little bigger than me, Flower, so you can wear this outfit from my dowry, and Blossom, you can wear my extra clothes." Zephyr tossed the clothes to her friends and walked across to the fire.

"I will dry you off as soon as I can, Betsy." She added, as the wolfurnut rubbed herself against Zephyr's legs and whined.

Zephyr refilled the kettle with water and hung it over the fire before adding more nettle leaves to an earthenware bowl. "The rain barrels will be full in the morning." She said cheerfully, going about her tasks and effortlessly beginning a conversation simultaneously. When Sunblossom and Cornflower finished changing, they attempted to help Zephyr, but she waved them to seats on the floor beside the warriors.

Chief Mark-hai watched her with tender eyes. Zephyr was the mirror image of her mother in that moment, moving from task to task with ease, as though the demands placed upon her as woman and hostess were of no account, joyfully doing what needed to be done for no other reason than that the task was there and needed to be done.

As she walked in front of Swift Arrow for the sixth time, he reached up and deftly grabbed her hand, pulling her down to sit next to him. "I think you can sit now."

"Was I blocking your view of the flames?" Zephyr asked, cocking her head and smiling.

"Not at all," Swift Arrow responded earnestly. "It always makes me dizzy when you pace."

Zephyr laughed and scooched over to join the girl's conversation.

"I did not realize how tall Jerusalem artichoke plants can grow," Cornflower was saying in disbelief. "For something that grows underground, their height is really incredible. Two of them are up to my waist!"

Sunblossom laughed. "I thought the Elders gave you the field because you know all about Jerusalem artichokes."

"No, no, Blossom, you are mistaken." Zephyr grinned. "Cornflower said she knew all about *eating* them."

"In the words of Last Spring," Cornflower said with a gleam in her eyes, referring to a woman in the Tribe. "'As long as Cornflower does not cook the Jerusalem artichokes, we will be fine.'"

The girls maintained their serious expressions for precisely three seconds before dissolving in giggles. It was well known, far and wide, that letting Cornflower in the kitchen was to ask for a fire.

The giggling faded, and Sunblossom nodded toward Chief Mark-hai. "Is he alright?"

Zephyr did not even have to look at her father. "It has been two years exactly since the Terrible Hunt and the—" she faltered, "and the funerals." Her voice was barely above a whisper. "It is a hard time for all of us."

"I overheard some women yesterday saying that Chief Mark-hai would do well to take another Chieftess." Cornflower hesitated, as if unsure how to proceed. "I do not agree with them, but I do wonder, how your father is holding up without someone in whom to confide?"

"He did not confide in anyone for many months, and then he began talking to some of the warriors, Bark and La-kaodai mostly. I wish he would talk to Swift Arrow instead of La-kaodai."

Sunblossom made a face. "La-kaodai is not worthy of any position of leadership, howsoever he may appear to most of the men. He is a—a—" she floundered, looking for the right word.

Cornflower's face lit up with an idea. "A rude—"

"Girls," Zephyr admonished softly. "We must not gossip."

"Even if it true?" Cornflower asked.

Zephyr gave her a pointed look before saying softly, "No matter La-kaodai's character, it is not our place to speak ill of him."

Bark broke into their conversation by announcing to the rackleen at large, "I do not know how the rest of you feel, but I am ready to sleep."

"You boys should take the beds and let us girls sleep on the floor," Zephyr suggested.

"You girls should sleep on the beds," Swift Arrow gallantly argued.

"But there are only two open beds," Zephyr pointed out, logically enough.

Chief Mark-hai resolved the difficulty when he roused himself from his silence and said, "Nonsense! I will sleep on the floor with the boys."

"Are you sure, Father?" Zephyr asked, uncertainty tinging her voice.

"Absolutely." The Chief assured her.

Zephyr glanced at Cornflower and shrugged as if to say, *I cannot argue, can I?* Zephyr rose and crossed the room to one of the trunks and opened it. Cornflower and Sunblossom began pushing trunks into groups of four to create beds.

Zephyr layered the trunk-beds with thick blankets while the other two girls arranged extra blankets and furs on the floor for the men. Bark began gathering the tea things while Swift Arrow looked on in surprise.

Such work was considered strictly a woman's task, and Chief Mark-hai was a man who adhered tightly to tradition, so seeing his nephew doing "women's work" under his nose came as a bit of a shock.

The Chief made no move to rebuke Bark, so Swift Arrow rose and banked the fire. Unlike some warriors, Arrow had no problems with helping the ladies. Straightening up, he met Zephyr's pleased smile. "Thank you, Swift Arrow." She smiled.

He smiled back, treasuring her pleasure. "You are most welcome."

CHAPTER TWO

In the soft gray of the pre-dawn of the following morning, Chief Mark-hai stood outside his rackleen, taking in deep breathes of fresh morning air.

As was usual and fitting for the Chief, he was the first awake. He treasured these early morning moments, when the village was quiet, and he was gifted an opportunity to think and mull over the issues involved in running a Tribe.

He and his wife, the late Chieftess Lasha, had spent this time together in years past. He talking through the problems confronting him; she listening and, at times, offering advice.

The first day after the funeral, Zephyr had woken early and joined Chief Mark-hai outside. They had stood side by side, Zephyr holding on tightly to his arm. After that first terrible morning, however, she had respected his need for quiet, something that he had not even had to voice to her.

This particular morning, the Chief was mulling over who would marry his daughter. As Chief, and the young lady's father, he had a double right to choose whomever he wished.

It was a heavy responsibility, and Chief Mark-hai felt the loss of Lasha keenly in that moment. Women always knew more than men about the characters of the people who lived in the Tribe. That was the way it had always been, and that was the way it would always be; however, the Chief felt sure that he could handle picking a mate for his daughter.

Several candidates came to mind, each a young and distinguished warrior, but how to choose? Chief Mark-hai began to pace.

The man he chose needed to be strong and healthy, smart, cunning, wise, and able to rule with a firm hand. He must be a man who would treat Zephyr right, with the respect and love she deserved. Such a man would be able to provide for and protect not only his family but the whole Tribe.

The list of men that the Chief considered suitable had already been narrowed down to two or three. He dismissed one as too young. That left two.

Chief Mark-hai stopped pacing and rubbed his hand over his chin. *A weighty choice indeed*, he thought. Weighing the two men carefully, he knew that they were almost equal, except for the fact that both men had been offered a position leading the Tribe's warriors. One of those men had turned the offer down. The other had not, and Chief Mark-hai had yet to regret his choice.

"Yes," he murmured aloud. "I think he will do nice-ly."

A sudden memory accosted the Chief, stopping him in his tracks.

A forest clearing. Sun shining brightly through the branches. The birds had just resumed their singing, but Mark-hai was oblivious to the beauty of his surroundings.

He knelt on the forest floor, Lasha's head on his lap, her breathing coming in ragged gasps. "Take care of Zephyr," she murmured.

Mark-hai picked up her hand. "It will be alright, my love."

"Choose a good husband for her."

"I will, I promise." Tears pricked at his eyes as he watched his wife.

"La-kaodai—don't—" her words trailed off. One more breath and she was gone.

Mark-hai's heart clenched, and he cried.

He had never cried before. It was unbecoming of a warrior, much less a Chief, but this was a grief he had never known.

And so he cried.

Chief Mark-hai closed his eyes and clenched his fist at the painful memory. He did not want to remember what had happened after. The silent ride home. Having to tell Zephyr that her mother was dead and then holding the girl while she sobbed. Receiving the news that his brother and his wife's sister were gone as well—-

"Father?"

Mercifully, Zephyr chose that moment to open the door flap, and stick her head out.

The Chief turned. "Yes, Zephyr?"

"What do you want for breakfast?" It was such a mundane, simple question that he almost laughed.

"Porridge is fine," he assured her.

"Yes, but what kind?" She shifted. "Cornflower and Bark want plum and date porridge, but Swift Arrow and Sunblossom want molasses."

"What do you want?" Chief Mark-hai asked. He didn't know anything about porridge. He simply ate what he was given and was thankful.

"Cacao porridge," she said immediately.

"Make that then."

She smiled. "If only you would always agree with me," she laughed.

"What did he say?" Bark asked from inside. "I am hungry."

She turned her head. "Well, if one of you sleepyheads would bestir yourselves enough to walk me down to the storage rackleens, then I could make breakfast."

"I am coming," Swift Arrow said, coming up behind her and cinching his kameiz[6] belt at his waist. "I would not expect Bark to be awake until you are serving breakfast."

"Well, of course not," Zephyr said reasonably, starting down the path. "He is just like his mother."

A trace of a shadow passed over the Chief's face. Zephyr and Bark did not often refer to their deceased parents, and it did Chief Mark-hai's heart good to know that he was not the only one who held their memories close.

They were seated on benches around the fire pit on the side of the Chief's rackleen. Bark had made an appearance before breakfast if only to prove Swift Arrow's words wrong.

"Zephyr," The Chief began. "Before you and the girls begin work on your rackleen, I need you to deliver a message for me." He paused, waiting for her response, even though he didn't have to. He was her Chief *and* her father.

"Of course, Father."

"Invite La-kaodai to dine with me tonight."

6 A long, curved dagger—all experts agree that it was given to the Chief of the Tribe by the Settlers and spread from there.

"Yes, Father." She paused. "What do you want to eat?"

"Whatever you decide to make will be fine."

Zephyr may have been moving out, but until she was married or another woman asked to take over the task, it would still be her responsibility to see that her father was fed.

After everyone was finished, Zephyr, Cornflower, and Sunblossom began clearing the dishes. "We will clean the rackleen, Zephyr." Sunblossom offered. "While you and Swift Arrow deliver the message to La-kaodai."

Zephyr smiled her pleasure. "Thank you, girls."

"Any time," Cornflower smiled. "Only—I do not want to hear later that you and Swift Arrow had fun without me."

Zephyr laughed. "Do not ask me to promise the impossible, Flower."

"If I must," Cornflower grouched, but there was a smile lurking on her face.

Another day begun, Chief Mark-hai thought, as he watched a small group of warriors come up the path towards him. He sighed contentedly. He was as happy as he could possibly be.

CHAPTER THREE

hree years ago, after the Battle of the Fallen Timbers, La-kaodai had been placed in charge of all the Tribe's warriors. It was indeed a great honor and a sign of Chief Mark-hai's respect that such a young warrior now led of men with so much more experience than him. It was a bittersweet honor for La-kaodai; however, because he had not been the Chief's first choice.

There was another warrior, who had saved Chief Mark-hai's life on the field of battle, who had been offered this position first. That other warrior, however, had turned the Chief down. He was happy with his current assignment, he had said.

Not that La-kaodai doubted him. If he had accepted the position La-kaodai now held, La-kaodai would have quickly asked to become one of Princess Zephyr's guards.

All this was hard for a man like La-kaodai to swallow, and it was harder still to see that other warrior parading around the village behind the Princess. What was worse, every man under La-kaodai's command would have been much happier if the other warrior had accepted, but, they all had to obey him, and that was no small balm to his soul. He was quite happy as long as he didn't have to face that other warrior. Unfortunately for him, his happiness was to be short-lived on this morning.

"Ready!" La-kaodai shouted. A row of warriors raised their bows and fitted arrows to strings.

"Draw!" The warriors drew their bows.

"Fire!" A storm of arrows flew toward their targets, almost every single one hitting its mark. "Good, good." La-kaodai paced down the row of targets. Then he stopped.

Deliberately, he bent and picked up the only arrow that had not hit its mark. "Fast Rain," he barked. The young warrior stepped forward. "I want you to practice with that bow and arrow until you can hit a target twenty-five times in a row. Do you understand me?" He asked in a low tone.

"Yes, sir." Fast Rain's voice was subdued.

"Gather your arrows," La-kaodai snapped at the rest of the group.

"Peace be on you, La-kaodai," a feminine voice said from the edge of the practice field.

La-kaodai turned with a cheerful smile, only to find himself face to face with that other warrior.

"La-kaodai!" Swift Arrow added his greeting to Zephyr's, unaware of the emotions battling for control inside the other man. "Peace be on you." He turned to the

Princess. "I am going to go see if some of the warriors can help me repair the rackleen later."

Zephyr nodded, and Swift Arrow strode away.

"Peace be on you, Princess Zephyr." La-kaodai bowed, not even bothering to try and greet the other warrior. Glad to have the princess to himself, La-kaodai forgot to listen to Zephyr's words, instead enjoying the way she looked.

She was dressed in traditional Tribe garb, made from soft gazelle leather. Her leggings peaked out from underneath the edge of her skirt. The long sleeves of her blouse were decorated with images of the wind. Her blue-black hair was pulled into a neat bun at the top of her head, into which she had tucked a small cluster of maple leaves, and her feet were neatly shod in moccasins.

La-kaodai tuned back in just in time to hear her say, "So will you come?"

"It will be my pleasure," he said smoothly.

"Wonderful," Zephyr smiled. "Chief Mark-hai will be pleased to hear it. Arrow, are you ready?" She called.

La-kaodai inwardly flinched at her careless use of Swift Arrow's nickname.

"Just coming," Swift Arrow walked over. "May peace follow you today, La-kaodai."

"And you," the other warrior managed through a tight-lipped smile. As the princess and her warrior walked out of earshot, he turned quickly to a warrior standing behind him. "What did I agree to, Running Eagle?" He demanded.

"Supper in the Chief's rackleen tonight." Running Eagle said promptly, having paid more attention to Zephyr's words than how she was attired.

"Do not look so smug." La-kaodai snapped, turning back to the warriors and barking commands, trying to ignore the way Zephyr had said something to Swift Arrow as they walked away and how he had stepped closer to hear and respond.

"We need to find my father," Zephyr was saying.

"Do you know where he was going this morning?" Swift Arrow asked.

Zephyr scoffed. "Hardly. Somedays, *he* does not even know where he will be." She stopped. "Crab Apple, do you know where Chief Mark-hai is?" She called to another young woman.

Crab Apple nodded. "He went to the Gathering Rackleen to supervise the repairs."

"Thank you," Zephyr said, dipping her head before continuing onward with her guard. They passed a group of warriors repairing a llama pen, and she waved to Bark.

"Will the rackleen need much work, do you think?" She asked.

"The ceiling panels need to be retied, but I do not know if any need to be replaced, if that is what you are asking."

"It is," Zephyr confirmed. "The girls will be there before us, I am sure, and Cornflower has a good eye for such things."

"She does, indeed," Swift Arrow agreed. They had arrived at the Gathering Rackleen, and he scanned the crowd, looking for the Chief.

Life on The Continent was by no means easy, and the days were taken up in many tasks that needed to be done for the good of the whole Tribe. Noon meals were eaten all together in the Gathering Rackleen, so that one group of women could spend the morning cooking, and the rest could attend to the various tasks that needed to be done.

"There is the Chief," Swift Arrow pointed. The twosome made their way over to Chief Mark-hai and waited for him to finish speaking to a pair of women.

The Chief smiled when he saw his daughter. "Just what I need," he proclaimed. "A ray of sunshine."

"Is everything alright?" Zephyr asked, leaning closer.

"Of all the ridiculous things I have had to deal with as Chief," he said, dropping his voice to just above a whisper, "that one might take the balankn.[7] It was two women arguing about whose infant was whose."

"Why would they do that?" Zephyr raised her eyebrows.

---

7 A small, cake like dessert.

"It seems one of the children had died," Chief Mark-hai waved his hand to dismiss it. The death of a child was an unnatural, horrible thing, as were all deaths, but they were so common that those outside the family could not allow themselves to mourn unduly over it.

Zephyr clucked her tongue sympathetically. "I shall have to go speak to the grieving mother."

Chief Mark-hai squeezed her shoulder. "And that, my dear, is what will make you a fine Chieftess one day. Now, what did you need?"

"Ah, La-kaodai accepted your invitation," Zephyr said, stepping back and speaking louder again.

"Very good, very good." The Chief nodded. "I suppose you are off to repair your rackleen now?"

"Yes, Father," Zephyr nodded. Then she hesitated. "Unless you need me?" Saying the words almost hurt, so badly did Zephyr want to move into the new rackleen.

"No, not today." Chief Mark-hai said. "I was just wondering."

Zephyr bowed her head. "Thank you, Father."

Swift Arrow and Zephyr hurried to the Princess's rackleen, both eager to begin. "Shall we start repairing the floor panels?" Zephyr asked, once they stood in the doorway, surveying the damage.

There was still standing water on the floor, while ceiling panels hung from the roof poles and draped over the trunks. Cornflower and Sunblossom had arrived a few moments before Zephyr and Swift Arrow.

"Everything in the trunks is still dry." Sunblossom offered from behind.

"It is a good thing that Bark made those trunks, or we would have lost most of our things." Cornflower observed, shooting a surreptitious look Sunblossom's way.

"Swift Arrow helped." Zephyr pointed out, slipping out of her moccasins, setting them on a bench, so she didn't have to wear wet shoes.

"Plenty of warriors can build trunks better than Bark and I," Swift Arrow said, objecting slightly to the praise.

"But they did not build *our* trunks," Zephyr said with a gleam in her eye, "so we would not know that, now would we?"

Swift Arrow rolled his eyes good-naturedly and began to shimmy up the side of the rackleen.

"I wish I could do that," Cornflower murmured.

"Well, you cannot," Sunblossom said briskly, "so help Zephyr and I move these trunks."

The girls worked steadily all morning. Thankfully, the floor panels needed nothing more than to be dried out. A few of the ceiling panels were ripped, but most needed nothing more than to be re-hemmed.

By the time dinner time came around, they had all the ceiling panels ready to be reattached. After dinner, several of Swift Arrow's warrior friends came down to the rackleen to help. It would take them most of the afternoon to get every single floor and ceiling panel securely in place.

La-kaodai's mother, Last Spring, nervously watched her son, late that afternoon. He looked supremely confident, a sure sign that he had some new scheme up his sleeve, which almost always led to trouble of some sort for *someone.*

"Please, La-kaodai," she begged, "do not overstep again."

La-kaodai had his back turned to his mother, and rolled his eyes. "Really, Mam, Chief Mark-hai never seems to mind, and besides, last time I 'overstepped,' as you call it, a subversive warrior was banished."

In the corner, La-kaodai's younger brother, Fast Rain, rolled his eyes in turn. "If you call not polishing his bow your way *subversive.*"

"He was a thief and a liar." La-kaodai said, whirling around.

"Keep telling yourself that, if it makes you feel better," Fast Rain shot back, angry at the way he had been treated at the practice field. Fast Rain sank back in his seat. "Do not worry, Mammy. He will spend the whole evening staring at the Princess." Although the words were addressed to Last Spring, his eyes were on La-kaodai.

"There is a reason that you are not a full warrior yet," La-kaodai shot back. "I do not care if the Princess is there or not."

"Coe,"[8] Fast Rain said wryly, "which is why you could not take your eyes off her earlier."

"I will have you know—" La-kaodai began threateningly, at last becoming angry.

"Boys!" Last Spring exclaimed, holding onto her remaining vestiges of authority over her oldest son. "Please, do not just—"

"If you are quite finished," La-kaodai cut in coldly. "I do not want to be late." At that moment, he looked so much like his father that Last Rain shrunk back from scolding him.

As he walked proudly out of the rackleen, Last Spring knew that he would never listen to her again.

The Protector painted the skies purple and pink before Sunblossom, Cornflower, and Zephyr finally stood outside their finished rackleen. Swift Arrow had checked that each ceiling panel was in place.

Bark and Swift Arrow stood behind the girls, finding pleasure in their enjoyment of the finished work. Betsy crouched between Sunblossom and Zephyr, looking

---

8 Means *clearly*, a very common word throughout the known world. According to Dr. Brain's excellent work *Words and Where They Came From, Probably* (Spoon of Power Publishing House, 0097) it most likely originated with the Settlers. Pronounced as spelled: *co*.

dubiously at the rackleen as though she were waiting for the water to return.

"Come along, Betsy," Sunblossom laughed as the girls stepped over the threshold.

"It is beautiful." Zephyr breathed, spinning in a slow circle.

The ever-practical Cornflower surveyed the rackleen. "It is like all the other rackleens."

"Yes, but this rackleen is ours." Sunblossom smiled. Betsy padded over to the fireplace, clawed at the floor, and then laid down and went to sleep.

Zephyr whirled faster and giggled. "I am as free as a bird!" Her anklet[9] jingled, causing Cornflower to laugh.

"Not quite," she pointed at the anklet.

Zephyr collapsed onto the pillows that were arrayed in front of the fire and smiled. "But now, I can do the work whenever, and in whatever order I choose. I can sing and dance in my own rackleen if I want, without offending tradition."[10]

Cornflower and Sunblossom joined her in front of the fireplace. "I had forgotten that such things bother you so," Sunblossom said.

---

9 Unmarried women and girls wore anklets given them on their thirteenth year, to show that they were under the authority and protection of their fathers. After the signing of a marriage contract the husband would give his wife a new anklet.

10 A common phrase on The Continent. Refers to the act of rebelling or ignoring tradition.

"Sometimes, I feel so stifled," Zephyr said, with a frustrated growl to her voice. "I must do this task and that task, and nothing else in the mornings. I must eat at such and such a table at dinner, and in the afternoon, I must do only that task and this task. Then when evening comes, it is only proper for me to say and do certain things."

"We may not run in the woods and certainly not join hunting parties or do anything that a boy would do for fun," Cornflower added, a wistful note in her voice.

"No climbing trees, no jumping streams, no clambering up the face of a cliff." Sunblossom finished.

"I suppose we should not complain. No, I know that we should not complain," Zephyr said firmly, as though correcting herself. "The Protector has a plan, even if I do not agree with it."

Somebody cleared his throat behind the girls, and they turned hastily around. "Oh, peace, Bark, Swift Arrow," Sunblossom said a little too brightly. "I had quite forgotten that you were back there."

Swift Arrow tried to hide a smile, as Bark answered uncomfortably. "We can see that."

Zephyr was studying the wall closest to her with rapt attention and Cornflower looked everywhere but at the boys.

Swift Arrow rescued them all by saying, "Remember, Bark and I are in the next rackleen should you need anything."

"Thank you," Sunblossom smiled sweetly. After the boys exited the rackleen, Sunblossom tacked the door flap back into place.

She turned around and met Zephyr's eyes. They giggled.

"Well, that was embarrassing, now, was it not?"

Zephyr smiled. "Only mildly."

"Only mildly?" Sunblossom shook her head. "I did not know that you had such an interest in rackleen walls."

"We need to go to sleep." Cornflower reminded them. "Harvest begins tomorrow!"

Sunblossom groaned. "As if anyone could forget."

Zephyr laughed and tossed a pillow that she had just pulled out of a trunk at her friend. *"Those who complain work twice as long."* She quoted in a singsong tone.

"Oh dear, she is using my own grandmother's sayings against me!"

Cornflower tossed Sunblossom's nightclothes into her face and shrugged. "Life is hard, m'dear."

Sunblossom made a face at Cornflower's back before turning to make up her bed.

Cornflower banked the fire once the other two girls were in bed, and soon darkness and quiet fell over the rackleen.

CHAPTER FOUR

La-kaodai was very pleased with himself as he knocked on the door frame of the Chief's rackleen. Chief Mark-hai let him in, and La-kaodai's eyes swept the room. Zephyr was nowhere in sight.

"Where is Zephyr?" La-kaodai asked as casually as he could manage.

"She moved into the Princess's rackleen today." The Chief looked surprised that La-kaodai had not known this.

"Ah, yes, of course," La-kaodai said, as though it had simply slipped his mind, but inwardly he was seething. To ever have any hope of being Chief, La-kaodai would have to convince both Zephyr *and* Chief Mark-hai that he should marry the Princess, but he could not do that if Zephyr was not even present.

"I have a proposition for you." Chief Mark-hai said, ladling a bowl of stew and handing it to his guest. "Panther stew. Zephyr made it, so it is sure to be good."

La-kaodai took the bowl. "What kind of proposition?"

"I have chosen you to marry my daughter, unless you have already chosen a bride?"

La-kaodai studied his Chief. *'Unless you have already chosen a bride?' Is this a test?*

"In all truth, Sire, I have not yet begun to think on such matters." It was not entirely the truth. La-kaodai had not thought about marrying a girl; he had thought about marrying one girl in particular.

"It is a weighty matter," Chief Mark-hai agreed, taking a sip of water.

"Why me, Sire?" La-kaodai asked as humbly as he could manage.

"I believe that you will make a good Chief. In fact, you remind me of my father."

La-kaodai raised his eyebrows. "Is that good or bad?" The former Chief Lo-debar had been hated and loved in equal measure.

"A good thing, I believe. The downfall of Chief Lo-debar was that his wife died in childbirth and was not there to help him."

"It is a great honor, Sire," La-kaodai said thoughtfully. *It will not be becoming to appear overeager,* he thought.

"You do not seem pleased." Chief Mark-hai sounded dissatisfied.

"Not at all, Sire. I am simply—overwhelmed." La-kaodai said swiftly. "How does the Princess feel about your offer?"

"She does not know yet."

La-kaodai took a bite of stew while he nodded. The lady in question did not need to be informed while her father was arranging her marriage, but with how close the Chief and Zephyr were, it would not have surprised La-kaodai one jot to learn that she already knew.

"She will, of course, be pleased that I have chosen a husband."

"What young lady would not be?" La-kaodai smiled.

"So, will you offer your contract to my daughter?" It was the traditional phrase, and it was at that moment that La-kaodai knew Chief Mark-hai was deadly serious.

"I will," it was said smoothly, confidently. "It would be my honor." He bowed his head.

The Chief smiled and rose from his seat, walking towards a shelf and removing a scroll from it. "I am not going to give this to Zephyr until after the Harvest, but here it is."

La-kaodai dipped his quill pen into a pot of berry ink and wrote his name across the bottom of the scroll. "It is done," he smiled.

"It is done," Chief Mark-hai agreed. "I understand that you are supporting your mother and younger brother?"

"Yes, Sire."

"That is good that you already have a rackleen and household. It smooths the way considerably, does it not?"

La-kaodai smiled. "It does, indeed."

Chief Mark-hai saw La-kaodai out the door later that night and then retired to his own fire. He was satisfied. He had made the best possible choice.

No other warrior had proven his leadership. No one else would make a good Chief.

At least, that is what Chief Mark-hai believed.

Zephyr would sign the contract in a month's time. When Chief Mark-hai died or was ready to relinquish the role of leadership, La-kaodai and Zephyr would become Chief and Chieftess.

This was the way it was supposed to be.

The Chief went to bed with a contented heart. It was always good when he was right, and everyone else agreed with him.

Last Spring was waiting when La-kaodai returned home, puffed up with his own success.

"How was supper?" She asked, a bit timidly.

La-kaodai sent an annoyed glance her way. "Fine. The stew was delicious."

Fast Rain was lying on the floor by the fire. "What about the Princess?"

"She was not there." There was a note of triumph in La-kaodai's voice.

"I bet that made you furious," Fast Rain sat up and grinned.

"Fast Rain," Last Spring murmured. "Show love."

La-kaodai narrowed his eyes in Fast Rain's direction. "That is none of your concern."

Fast Rain shrugged. "Maybe I just want to see my brother happily married so that he will have less time to badger me." He dropped back down and put his hands behind his head.

La-kaodai rolled his eyes. "Well then, *brother,* you will be glad to learn that I will be married."

Last Spring's eyes slid shut, and a flood of conflicting emotions assaulted her. She felt despair over how much her son sounded like his father, yet happiness over the thought of having a daughter to share the burden of housework. There was sadness over who her oldest son had become, and fear that her youngest son would become the same. It did not help that worry over the future was clouding her thinking, too.

"Who will you marry?" She finally asked when she found her voice.

La-kaodai sent her an appraising look. "I shall not tell you. I believe it is her father's responsibility to tell her. I would not want her to find out from the village gossips."

Something inside Last Spring snapped. She had put up with too many years of her husband's biting tongue and derogatory accusations. This was her son, and, yes, he was by law her provider and protector, but that did not mean she would sit by timidly while he insulted her!

"I do not make a habit of speaking with gossips." She said.

"You do not? Well, that is a surprise to me." La-kaodai turned to face his mother.

Fast Rain sat up, his mouth hanging open.

"I am sorry that you know so little of my character." Last Spring stood her ground for once.

"Maybe your character has changed." La-kaodai shot back.

Last Spring stared calmly into his eyes for a moment. He was just like his father, and he would always have to have the last word. Well, very well then. She would not prolong an argument that she knew she would not win.

Last Spring turned away. "Fast Rain, will you bank the fire, please?"

"Women's work." La-kaodai scoffed, turning away.

Fast Rain's jaw bunched in anger. Last Spring laid a gentle hand on his arm. "Do not," she whispered. "There is no point."

CHAPTER FIVE

arvest finally came to an end after a grueling month in the fields and over the cooking fires. Once again, there was time and space to devote to matters other than food. As the Tribe took a deep breath, the more observant members noticed changes.

Last Spring looked different, and that was the only word for it. Not a single woman in the village could get Last Spring to divulge what had happened within the confines of her rackleen, although wild theories abounded.

Fast Rain went about his duties with a set jaw and, though he was still young and it was unusual for the younger son to provide for his aged parents, was already talking of building a rackleen, claiming a wife, and providing for his mother.

La-kaodai himself was being flat-out rude to Swift Arrow and his friends. La-kaodai seemed triumphant, as if he had won something that no one else could take from him, which was more than enough to give some warriors, including Swift Arrow, pause and concern.

The second day after the First Frost was one of six days of celebration in the Tribe. To celebrate, Zephyr, Cornflower, and Sunblossom were hosting some young people in the Princess's rackleen.

Bark, Swift Arrow, Strong Oak, Crab Apple, and Dancing Wave came from the Tribe. Since it was a holiday, both the Forest Tribe and the Clan had sent pairs of representatives, so Saidi, a young man from the Clan, and Ivey Flower, the young Chieftess of the Forest Tribe, were there also.

The rackleen was full to overflowing as the afternoon meandered towards evening. The girls had placed baskets of nuts by the fireplace for roasting and made large quantities of various types of tea, along with several loaves of bread into which they had mixed dried fruits.

Zephyr and Ivey Flower were huddled together in one corner. "Tell me, how have you been? I have not seen you for an age." Zephyr said, pressing herself tighter into the corner. Strong Oak and Dancing Wave, Bark and Sunblossom, and Cornflower and Crab Apple had decided they needed to dance.

Ivey Flower smiled, glad for a chance to talk to her old friend. "Laughing Brook is nearly six now. She is so full of joy and energy she nearly drives her father and I to distraction. The boys are all getting big too."

"But how have *you* been?" Zephyr persisted, determined to get an honest answer.

"Exhausted, actually. I am not the youngest married woman in the Tribe, far from it, but I am the youngest Chieftess ever. As Chieftess, I am supposed to be the wise leader of all the women in the village, but I find myself needing advice just as often as I am called upon to dispense it."

Zephyr smiled in sympathy at her friend. "I can imagine. Ever since my mother died, some women have expected me to fill her shoes. I am grateful that that number is few indeed. It cannot be easy for you to live in the shadow of the last Chieftess, either."

The Chief of the Forest Tribe had been married once before, and his wife had died giving birth to her only child, a boy named Far Sight.

Ivey Flower sighed. "I remember her well. She was a wise woman. It seems so strange to be married to the Chief now that she is gone, and poor Far Sight has struggled with my presence since the first day. I keep working at it, however, and last week he called me 'Mammy.'"

Zephyr smiled with her friend over this small victory. Ivey looked as though she could not believe it still.

"How is your family?" Ivey asked, determined not to talk about herself all night.

"My father is well. He seems to have adjusted to living in an empty rackleen well, although he often says how much he misses Bark and I. Bark and Swift Arrow moved into the rackleen next to ours and—"

Cornflower collided with Zephyr. "Sorry, Ze." Cornflower pulled herself up.

"May I suggest something a bit calmer?" Zephyr asked, reaching up to fix her hair.

"Like what?" Cornflower asked.

"I do not know," Zephyr said, an edge of annoyance creeping into her voice. "Charades or History in One Minute. Anything that does not take up the whole of our rackleen will be much appreciated."

"Sorry, Zephyr," Cornflower said again, this time sheepishly. "Dancing was not my best suggestion."

"No, it was not." A smile danced at the corners of Zephyr's mouth.

"What were you saying about Bark?" Ivey Flower asked, once Cornflower had walked away.

Zephyr thought a moment. "He led his first hunt this year." There was a note of pride in her voice now.

Leading his first hunt was the first step to becoming a head warrior for every young warrior in the Tribe. It required focus, skill, knowledge, and wisdom: four traits Bark had proved he possessed.

Ivey smiled. "What an accomplishment! Though he will be a young head warrior, will he not?"

"He has many trials yet to complete before he is made a head warrior. Since he is the Chief's nephew, he may attain rank sooner than others, but he has no wish to hurry that day."

"A wise philosophy," Ivey Flower said.

"Swift Arrow is of the same mind. He was offered a promotion a few years ago but did not take it as he did not feel old enough. Unfortunately, the position was given to another warrior just as young."

"We heard something about Swift Arrow doing just that, but of course, the warriors of my Tribe cannot fathom it. I do wonder, was there any other reason he turned down Chief Mark-hai's offer?" Ivey Flower asked innocently. She knew full well what position Swift Arrow held.

The festive gathering was interrupted by a loud knock on the doorframe. Grateful that she could dodge Ivey's question, Zephyr hurried to open the door flap.

Fast Rain stood outside. He had a strange expression on his face. "Princess Zephyr, Chief Mark-hai requests your presence immediately."

Zephyr glanced around at her guests. "One moment, please, Fast Rain." She turned and spoke quietly to Sunblossom and Swift Arrow, who had come up behind her. It being a chilly night, she then reached for her shawl before she stepped outside to follow Fast Rain.

They walked across the village in silence. Sounds of other celebrations filled the cool night air. "I am sorry to take you from your festivities." Zephyr finally said.

Fast Rain shrugged. "It was just Mammy and me."

Zephyr raised her eyebrows but chose not to comment.

"Peace be on you, Father," Zephyr said when she entered the Chief's rackleen, bowing her head.

"Sit down, sit down, daughter." Chief Mark-hai said, too excited to respond to her greeting. Zephyr moved gracefully across the room and sat on a cushion before the fire.

Chief Mark-hai produced a scroll and stood over her, excitement radiating from him. "Do you know what this is, Zephyr?"

She shook her head. A hundred possibilities darted through her mind, each to be rejected in turn as implausible.

"A marriage contract!" *That* was the one possibility she hadn't even considered. She had hoped to marry for love, as her mother had before her, but she knew such marriages were uncommon.

Whoever her future husband was to be, she would learn to love him, just as Ivey Flower had.

She took a deep breath to steady her voice. "From whom?"

"La-kaodai." Zephyr could not stop the involuntary gasp that escaped. So deep was her trust in her father that this poor decision of his came as a great shock.

Yes, it was true that the warriors did not speak of the failings of each other. Yes, a man always consulted his wife before arranging his daughter's marriage, just in case the wife knew something that the husband did not; and, yes, it was most certainly true that her father did not have his wife, but *La-kaodai*?

Arrogant, rude, self-centered, merciless La-kaodai? Zephyr had heard Last Spring speak with a slight tremble in her voice of how her son resembled her late husband. She had participated in the general outrage when La-kaodai had managed to get a man banished unfairly. She could think of a dozen reasons that she should not marry La-kaodai and not a single one that said she *should* marry him.

"Zephyr? You are pleased, yes?" Chief Mark-hai broke into her tumultuous thoughts.

"I cannot sign this contract." Zephyr finally managed.

Chief Mark-hai frowned. "But this will be good for the Tribe. A strong leader is vital to the wellbeing—"

Zephyr let her father go on about duty to the Tribe and duty to family. She had heard it all before. It was a long speech, and not one that made her more inclined to sign that contract and so become La-kaodai's wife.

When he finished, Zephyr spoke firmly, yet respectfully. "La-kaodai may appear to fulfill all the proper qualifications for a suitable husband, but he does not in truth possess them. He would not care for the people as is becoming for a Chief to do so. I have seen many instances of his pride and selfishness. He is rude—"

"Stop," the Chief said firmly. "For you and La-kaodai to wed is my wish. This is what is best for you and the Tribe. You have no proof of what you say. I know you wished to marry for love, but it is *my* job to see you safely wed, and you will not cross me." He held the contract out to her.

She took it, unrolling it slightly to look at the bottom. As she had feared, La-kaodai had already signed it, his bold hand cutting across the lower half of the scroll. Words her mother had spoken long ago came to mind. *Do you know the most valuable lesson your father has taught me? To never waver from the right. If I know something to be wrong, I must not do it. You will be Chieftess one day, Zephyr, and you would do well to remember this.*

Zephyr resolutely rolled the scroll back up and thrust it at her father. "I refuse this contract." Her voice held a note of finality, but Chief Mark-hai was not prepared to give up so easily. He firmly believed this to be right.

A knock on the doorframe cut off the reply he was preparing to make. "Who is it?" The Chief called, with barely concealed annoyance.

"The Chief and Chieftess of the Forest Tribe are leaving, and they wish to say their goodbyes," a voice called.

The Chief turned back to his daughter. "It is important to maintain good relations with our allies, so go and make our farewells; however, this discussion is not finished."

Zephyr sedately exited the rackleen, bid farewell to Ivey Flower and her husband, and returned to her own rackleen without once betraying that anything was wrong.

Arriving at her own rackleen, Zephyr passed Swift Arrow talking to Strong Oak. Swift Arrow watched her with something akin to concern as she entered the rackleen without meeting his gaze. Inside she was disappointed to find that Saidi still lingered. Cornflower and Sunblossom were pointedly clearing away the food and drink.

Bark was sitting by the fire, whittling something small, and listening to Saidi's monologue about being the son of the Chief. Desperate for quiet and a chance to talk to her friends, Zephyr did something that she had only ever seen her mother do once, force a guest to leave.

She walked up to the fireplace. "Excuse me, Saidi, Bark, but I must speak to you, Saidi." She took a step towards the door, and Saidi followed. "As I know that you are well aware, the eldest child of the Chief has more duties to attend than can be easily counted, even when away from home. Although it goes against all I have been taught about hospitality, I must say it. If I am so tired, then you must be so as well, so we will have to do without your company now."

Saidi nodded, flattered to be spoken to heir to heir like that. "Of course, of course. May peace rest upon you, Princess."

Zephyr sighed in relief as she secured the door flap behind the unwanted guest. Bark clapped. "Well done, cousin!"

Zephyr dropped wearily unto the cushions by the fire. Sunblossom and Cornflower exchanged concerned looks. Outside, Swift Arrow imitated the call of a sparrowbat, as he always did to let the girls know that he was coming in. He entered and asked, "Are you alright, Ze?"

Zephyr leaned her face on one had for a half-second."I need to talk to you all."

CHAPTER SIX

hree days after the First Frost, the sun still shone brightly, if not strongly. It glinted off the delicate tracings of ice that covered bare branches. The wind rattled the dead, brown leaves of the small, hardy bushes that covered the forest floor.

Swift Arrow leaned against Zephyr's rackleen, staring sightlessly into space. High above him, above the very treetops, three sleek, dark dragons glided over the forest in formation, carrying the messages that linked the far corners of the known world.

Swift Arrow could not find an easy way out of her situation for Zephyr. She only had two choices: give in or stand firm and accept whatever punishment her father decided to give her.

Tribal law forbade a young lady from marrying without her father's consent, so if both Zephyr and Chief Mark-hai remained stubborn, then she would not marry until her father died.

Swift Arrow and Bark had been more than a little stunned at last night's revelations. In fact, they had been downright incredulous at first. The more Sunblossom,

Cornflower, and Zephyr had talked, however, the more they had come to see that their perceptions of La-kaodai were altogether wrong.

Swift Arrow had gone to Chief Mark-hai and offered his own contract, early that morning. The Chief had been stunned but firm. He would accept no contract but the one he already had in his rackleen.

It was not until that moment, walking away from the Chief's rackleen and knowing that he could do nothing more to help Zephyr, that he had realized he loved Zephyr. It was with startling and disturbing clarity that he finally understood his feelings.

Swift Arrow pushed himself off the rackleen as he heard the door tacks being pulled out of the inner door-frame. If he could do nothing to save her from this fate, the least he could do was support her in whatever decision the Princess made.

"I spent most of last night thinking, and I wonder if you have thought through all the aspects of this," Sunblossom said. *This,* of course, being La-kaodai's contract.

Zephyr stopped folding up her bedding to give Sunblossom her full attention.

"First, what must you have in a husband? Second, how does La-kaodai meet or not meet those requirements?

And last, what will you do if your father refuses to let you marry anyone else?"

The first question was easy. "My husband must be a godly man who seeks to follow the Protector's laws with all his heart and mind. He must be compassionate, merciful, slow to anger, faithful, wise, and selfless. It would not hurt if he was handsome and strong as well." Zephyr finished with a smile.

The second question was more difficult. Zephyr turned back to her bed and continued work for several moments while she thought. "La-kaodai is strong and handsome, but those are surface things. Many would say that he is wise, but what is wisdom without godliness? He does not care for those who are weak: he is merciless, quick to anger, shifty, and self-centered."

"And if your father does not relent?" Cornflower asked softly.

Zephyr looked up, and the tears hovering in her eyes showed her friends that she had already faced this problem. "Then I shall never marry."

The girls continued their daily preparations in thoughtful silence. Cornflower broke it when she said quietly to Sunblossom. "Swift Arrow matches her description."

Sunblossom shook her head and held her finger to her lips. "She does not need to be thinking of that right now."

Zephyr turned around. "I already am." She said, her voice so soft that her friends almost missed it.

"Would you have chosen Swift Arrow if your father had given you a choice?" Cornflower blurted. Sunblossom elbowed her in the side.

Zephyr smiled even as she tried not to sob. "Yes." She closed her eyes and took a few deep breaths while her friends stood in frozen silence. "I am ready for breakfast if you are." She finally said with forced cheerfulness.

Blossom and Flower started and followed her slowly to the door. "Swift Arrow!" They heard her say brightly. "Will you walk me to the storage rackleens?"

The other girls could not hear Swift Arrow's reply, but as they exited the rackleen, they saw Zephyr and Swift Arrow walking down the path.

"How can she be so controlled?" Cornflower asked.

"It is beyond me," Sunblossom said, her eyes fixed on the retreating couple. "Zephyr would probably say that it is because she has to."

"Probably," Cornflower watched as Sunblossom walked over to the boy's rackleen and pounded on the door frame.

"Bark!" Sunblossom hollered. "Wake up. I need to sweep out the rackleen!"

"How do you do that every morning?" Cornflower asked.

Sunblossom shrugged. "It is just Bark. I could not do it to everyone, but Bark is—" She frowned, unsure of the right word.

"Different?" Cornflower asked.

"Yes, I suppose he is," Sunblossom said thoughtfully, "but I know not why."

"I do," Cornflower murmured under her breath as she turned around.

Cornflower stoked the fire, and Sunblossom swept out both rackleens and the clearing. Bark chopped wood while Cornflower began boiling water.

Swift Arrow and Zephyr returned then with dried berries and grain. Soon the porridge was ready, and the fivesome sat down to eat.

"Did you girls have a chance to talk this morning?" Bark asked.

"We did," Zephyr said quietly. "I am only more sure now. I may not marry La-kaodai."

Bark spoke decidedly. "Swift Arrow and I agree with you. No matter what, if La-kaodai never reforms his ways, you must not marry him."

Swift Arrow said nothing. Zephyr nodded seriously. She well understood the difficult path that she had begun walking down with her refusal. Sunblossom touched her on the arm. "We will stand by you, no matter what anyone else says." She motioned to the friends gathered together. "We all will."

As winter slowly revolved around Hereth, and the spring sun began to melt the deep winter snows, Zephyr remained steadfast in her purpose, despite the best efforts of her father, La-kaodai, and indeed, most of the Tribesfolk.

The older members, the elders, could not understand the disobedience of their Princess, and they deplored it for the example she was setting. Chief Mark-hai constantly harangued her whenever he saw her. La-kaodai used all his charms. It was rumored that once, he even tried to threaten her, but that Bark and several of his friends quickly stopped him. The rumor was given substance by the fact that these friends were banished on charges of theft soon thereafter.

Among those who were secretly sympathetic to Zephyr's plight, the women were the most understanding. They knew who La-kaodai was.

Through all that long winter, Zephyr's friends remained her one island of refuge, protecting her from the snide comments and mean looks of her people.

"Stay, Ella." Zephyr touched the neck of her llama to reinforce the command, then went back to loading the large washtub.

It was a Prokaryotan[11] invention that had only of late made its way to The Continent. A large wood box held a round metal tub. The tub was set on a metal turntable, attached via ropes and gears to a wooden wheel outside the box. A llama was harnessed to the wheel and turned the tub when the animal walked in a circle.

Pipes carried water from the river, and a valve allowed Zephyr to control the water flow. After the clothes had been washed, the water would be allowed to drain into the fields, and the tub would continue spinning. The clothes would be dried with the help of a fire built underneath the tub.

The Tribe owned three of these tubs, and the women shared their use. Zephyr added some vinegar to the tub before securing the lid.

"Ella, hup." Ella began walking ponderously around the worn dirt circle. Zephyr turned the water valve and counted to five before turning it off.

Betsy sauntered up the path and leaned against Zephyr's legs. "Peace, Betsy." Zephyr laughed and leaned down to pet the wolfurnut's silky fur.

"Well, peace be on you, Princess."

11 Prokaryota is a small country to the northeast of The Continent.

Zephyr stiffened and looked up at La-kaodai. He was leaning on the second washing tub, smiling disarmingly.

"Peace," she was acutely and gratefully aware of Bark's presence behind her.

"I am told that you were invited to your father's rack-leen. How was your conversation?"

"I believe the result was, both to my father and yourself, unsatisfactory." She replied flatly.

La-kaodai slammed his hand down on top of a tub, his face contorted in a mask of anger. "Why not?" He was all but yelling at her, although he was careful not to let his voice carry. "Why do you not save the both of us a world of misery and sign my contract?"

Zephyr did not so much as flinch. "I will not sign a contract that will condemn my people to suffer." Bark took a step forward to stand beside his cousin.

"I will not give up until you marry me, woman!"

"I do not and I cannot trust you. My father will come to his senses."

Bark squeezed Zephyr's elbow slightly. La-kaodai saw the gesture and rounded on Bark. "Stay out of my affairs, or I will banish you just as I banished Strong Oak and the rest." An unpleasant smile came to his lips.

"Do not threaten me, La-kaodai. I am the Chief's nephew." Bark said coldly.

"Are you threatening *me*? I will be your Chief one day, and it would behoove you to remember it."

"Ha! I doubt that very much." Bark said contemptuously. "Zephyr is a good bit more steadfast than either of us."

"*You laugh at me?*" La-kaodai was angry.

"Bark," Zephyr began.

"Yes, *Tree* Bark. Listen to your cousin." La-kaodai grinned derisively.

Now Bark was angry. "I will not be made fun of, La-kaodai!" He said threateningly.

"Bark!" Zephyr physically interjected herself between the two warriors. "That is enough," her voice was stern. "You two are grown warriors, and you are acting like infants - insulting each other, threatening each other. Is this how the Protector has called us to act?" She seemed to stand even taller, if such a thing were possible. "I will *never* sign your contract, La-kaodai. I hope you are clear on that point."

She did not give either a chance to respond but turned on her heel and moved away, calling over her shoulder for Bark to follow her.

"Coming, Princess," Bark scrambled to catch up with Zephyr as she strode regally away.

"You should apologize to him," she said softly.

"What? Apologize to La-kaodai? Never." Bark's face was a hard mask.

Zephyr sighed, but she didn't press the point.

As they moved through the center of the village, they passed a group of young men swarming over the roof of a rackleen, repairing it. Zephyr waved to Swift Arrow and nearly ran into her father.

"Zephyr, you have impeccable timing. I wish to speak to you." Chief Mark-hai said.

Zephyr pounced on the opportunity she had been handed. "I must needs speak to you, also, Father. It is of utmost importance."

"Of course, my daughter. What do you wish to say?"

"He has gone too far. He threatened Bark."

"Who?" The Chief asked anxiously.

"La-kaodai."

"La— Zephyr." Her name came out like a sigh. "What will I do with you? I know you do not wish to marry La-kaodai, but you will, in time, come to love him as he loves you."

Zephyr's mouth opened in shock. "You think I am lying?"

"Was anyone else present?" Chief Mark-hai asked somewhat sharply.

"No," Zephyr said slowly. "Just Bark and myself."

"Then I have no choice but to dismiss your accusations as unfounded."

"Unfounded! When have you ever known me to lie?"

Chief Mark-hai shook his head. "Enough. We will speak of this another time." He walked away from Zephyr and Bark.

"Did that truly just happen?" Zephyr asked, disbelief and sorrow etched across her face.

Bark nodded somberly.

"I wish to go home now," Zephyr said quietly. "Will you tell Swift Arrow that I need to talk to him after work assignments are over?"

Bark nodded.

The day of the Tribe was so structured that the men completed their work around the village in the morning, spent the afternoon practicing their warrior arts, and then doing as they pleased.

Swift Arrow finally walked up to the rackleens, having stopped to eat a hasty meal in the Gathering Rackleen. Zephyr had come to prefer being hungry for a time while she prepared a meal in her own rackleen over enduring a meal of hostile glares, and she and the girls were washing the dishes from the noon meal.

Swift Arrow seated himself on a bench next to Bark and waited for the girls to join them. When Zephyr, Sunblossom, and Cornflower sat down on the bench opposite the men, Zephyr wasted no words.

"La-kaodai is going to attempt to have the two of you banished."

Swift Arrow stared back steadily at Zephyr as she continued. "I do not know what he will try or even if he will succeed, but my father has banished other men on La-kaodai's advice." She rested her face in her hands. "I know not why Father would even listen to him."

Sunblossom rubbed her hand up and down Zephyr's back.

"What happened?" Swift Arrow asked. Bark explained what had happened by the washtubs.

"What happened to the clothes?" Cornflower asked suddenly.

Zephyr couldn't help the giggle that escaped. Cornflower always knew when she needed a laugh.

"No, I was serious," Cornflower said.

"I got them," Sunblossom explained.

"Back to the topic at hand," Swift Arrow said. "You are right, Zephyr. Our banishment might be right around the river bend."

Zephyr looked up, sorrow clouding her eyes. Bark saw it. "We will be alright, Ze."

"I know that *you* will be alright," Zephyr said faintly. "It is *me* I wonder about."

Sunblossom leaned against her friend. "You will be alright too," she murmured. "Cornflower and I will still be here, and remember, the Protector will never leave you."

"Zephyr," Swift Arrow said firmly. "Listen to me. If La-kaodai goes so far as to banish all of us and even Betsy and Ella, you must not give in. Not if he never mends his ways. Do you understand?"

Zephyr stared into his eyes. "Do you think it will come to that? All four of you being banished?"

Swift Arrow shrugged. "I do not know. Perhaps the Protector has something else in our future."

Zephyr smiled through the tears that threatened. "What did I ever do to deserve friends like you?"

Bark couldn't resist. "Absolutely nothing."

Several weeks passed quietly. La-kaodai seemed to have dropped the whole issue, and even Chief Mark-hai only summoned Zephyr a few times. Swift Arrow and Bark, however, were not so easily convinced that all was well.

One evening, the five friends were gathered in the Princess's rackleen. They had wedged a large, rectangular metal pan in the top quarter of the fireplace and were roasting nuts on it. Zephyr sat enthroned on a pile of cushions and was floating the nuts to her friends with a flip of her wrist as they were done.

They heard a knock on the doorframe, and without looking up, Zephyr said, "I have got it." She waved her hand, and the door flap flew aside.

A warrior stood outside, not at all perturbed by the fact that the door flap had opened seemingly by itself. "Princess Zephyr," he waited till she looked up. "Chief Mark-hai requests your presence.

"Hurry back," Swift Arrow began. Zephyr shot him a warning glance, knowing full well that anything said now would more likely than not end up in the ears of the Chief or La-kaodai.

"Because this is so much more fun when you are throwing nuts at us," Bark said smoothly.

Swift Arrow laughed. "Exactly."

Zephyr laughed too. "I will hurry." She promised.

"I finally understand why you continue refusing La-kaodai's contract." Chief Mark-hai said triumphantly. Zephyr and her father were sitting in the Chief's rack-leen.

Zephyr allowed hope to sprout within her for a moment. "You do?" She asked eagerly.

"Those *friends* of yours are a bad influence on you." The Chief smiled as if such a pronouncement would not bother his daughter in the least.

"You cannot be serious."

"Is it not true," Chief Mark-hai began sternly. "That they are the only members of the Tribe who have not encouraged you to sign the contract?"

"Yes, but only after I made it clear that I would not marry La-kaodai." Zephyr could sense the direction the conversation was going. "That makes them loyal friends, not enemies of the Tribe!"

"Whatever your opinion may be, I see that they are only making it more difficult for you to obey."

"The Protector does not require obedience when it is wrong," Zephyr said quietly.

"That is beside the point. If you do not sign the contract within two weeks, I shall banish Swift Arrow."

Zephyr stood and responded more calmly than she felt. "Do what you feel you must. I must obey the Protector."

Chief Mark-hai could not believe his daughter's stubbornness and conviction. *The Protector must have great things for her, if only she could get over her stubbornness,* he thought. What those things would be, no one could have guessed.

The stars sparkled like diamonds against a midnight blue setting. Moonlight illuminated the edge of the forest beyond the reach of the torches held by sober Tribeswarriors. Swift Arrow stood between two lines formed by many small stones that had stood for generations.

There was a long-standing tradition in the Tribe involving those two lines. Some banishments, like Swift Arrow's, took place because of a failure of obedience. They were meant to be a form of correction, and the banishments were not permanent. If the person in question chose to comply with the Tribe's laws and step over the line closest to the village, then he or she could rejoin the Tribe.

If the person continued to defy the Chief, then he or she stepped over the line closest to the forest and accepted banishment.

Tonight, the hard choice was Zephyr's, made doubly hard by the fact that it was not her but another who was being banished in her stead.

Chief Mark-hai's voice broke the still night air. "Warrior Swift Arrow, you are charged with subverting the decrees of your Chief." He could have been more explicit because everyone knew why they were gathered. "You are hereby banished until such time as those decrees are fulfilled."

Swift Arrow could see the silent tears streaking down Zephyr's face in the flickering torchlight. She had come to a conclusion of her own in the past few weeks, and he could read it on her face. Zephyr loved the man who was accepting banishment without a single complaint against the woman causing it.

Swift Arrow stepped back and melted into the tree line. A few warriors grimaced; he hadn't given the Princess half a chance to obey her father. For several minutes they could see the gleam of moonlight on the few arrows he had been allowed to take with him.

The Tribesfolk quickly dispersed, but Zephyr lingered until the last torch had died out and the skeeterflies came out.

CHAPTER SEVEN

The raid was over almost as quickly as it had begun. A band of heavily armed men had ridden swiftly and silently into the village. They had chosen the time of their raid well, as most of the warriors were away on a hunt.

They waited until every raider was in position before letting loose their war cries. The loud, barbarous shouts roused the whole Tribe.

Women's screams filled the night air, accompanied by a cacophony of llama alarm cries, wood being heaved onto empty rackleens, and hand-to-hand combat.

When the last raider had ridden screeching away, each with a prisoner riding before him, the villagers were left with a raging blaze that they scrambled to douse.

The brutal raid was over almost as soon as it began.

Chief Mark-hai stretched the kinks out of his back after hours of firefighting. The sun was, at last, coming up over the horizon as he looked around and frowned. Warriors slumped to the ground exhausted, while wide-eyed and silent women moved around distributing water and food.

Mark-hai's frown deepened. Where were Bark and Zephyr? Neither was known to shy away from honest work.

"La-kaodai!" The Chief called sharply. "Where is Zephyr?"

"I—I do not know." Real fear showed in the other warrior's eyes.

Without another word, the two warriors moved off as fast as they could for the Princess's rackleen. When they reached it, only two figures were present. Sunblossom jumped up from where she was huddled on the ground and ran towards them.

"Praise the Protector! I was afraid to leave him. Hurry, please. Bark is wounded." She turned, as if to go back to Bark's side, but La-kaodai grabbed her arm.

"What happened? Why is Cornflower not attending to him? Where is Zephyr?" He demanded roughly.

Sunblossom dropped her eyes. "They took them both. Three of them came to our rackleen. Bark had heard the shouts and was outside to defend us, but — he could not. They pushed their way into the rackleen and grabbed Zephyr and Cornflower. There was no reason: they just grabbed them and left me." Her eyes closed in pain. "Then they left."

She pointed to a figure on the other side of the clearing. "That is one them. Bark wounded him, but the others just — left him. I — I could not help him." A sob caught in her throat.

Chief Mark-hai felt his eyes mist. Sunblossom's was a pain shared by women all over the village.

La-kaodai just restrained himself from snapping at the distraught woman. Deciding instead that it would be in his best interest to curb his impatience, he began pacing the clearing.

Chief Mark-hai laid a gentle hand on Sunblossom's shoulder. "Who were they? Could you see?"

Sunblossom finally met his eyes. "Swamp Raiders."

The Chief's eyes closed in anguish. La-kaodai growled and slammed one fist into his open hand. Slaves taken by the Swamp Raiders never escaped and were never rescued, so deep did the Raiders live in the swamps, and so fierce were they. Their slaves only lasted a few months, at most, before they succumbed to the harsh conditions to which they were subjected.

"La-kaodai," The Chief said quietly, his voice thick with emotion. "Go find two warriors. Have them make a stretcher and come for Bark. Then see to getting everyone organized, and—" he hesitated, "find out who else we are missing."

La-kaodai bowed his head in submission, though inwardly he seethed at having to help the man who had just become Chief Mark-hai's sole heir and moved off.

The Chief knelt beside Bark. Sunblossom had done her best with the healing supplies in the rackleen, but she was no healer.

"After this, Cornflower is going to teach everyone she knows a little about healing." Sunblossom attempted a smile, standing at Bark's feet. Neither added, "if she comes back at all."

Chief Mark-hai sighed. "It is not right that men so wise and knowledgeable should turn their minds to such brutal acts." He shook his head. "With that fire, we have no chance of catching them."

Sunblossom looked at him quickly, new hope shining in her eyes. "Swift Arrow is out there, and the other warriors with him."

Chief Mark-hai shook his head as though despairing not only over the situation, but also over what he saw as Sunblossom's misplaced hope. "Why would exiles—" he began.

Sunblossom cut him off, something she had never dared to do before. "You forget which exiles of whom we are talking. Those warriors will not allow a hair on Zephyr's head to be harmed, if they can prevent it. We will lose nothing to try."

When the Chief only continued to stare down at his nephew with dull despair in his eyes, Sunblossom rose. As much as she hated to admit it, La-kaodai was Zephyr's only hope.

The Swamp Raiders are a confident bunch, are they not? Zephyr thought. So self-assured were the Raiders, in fact, they had forced all their prisoners to get off the llamas and walk.

Zephyr struggled against the ropes that secured her wrists together. She was surrounded by a couple dozen women from the Tribe. Despite Cornflower's earlier efforts to staunch the wound, a cut on Zephyr's temple continued to drip blood down her face.

Cornflower stumbled in the early morning half-light, and suddenly she was walking beside Zephyr.

"Stop that," Cornflower hissed. "It will only make them angry." She risked a glance at their captors. One of the men was glaring at her. One of the guards reached out and jerked the two ladies apart while issuing an angry command that none of the captives had any hope of understanding.

Zephyr sighed. *It seems this is it.* At the very least, she would enjoy her final walk through the woods. Birds sang merrily, and to herself, Zephyr identified each one: *quail-dove, love bird, blue jay, osprey, golden jay, sparrowbat—sparrowbat? Sparrowbats do not hunt at this time of day.*

Zephyr frowned and listened harder. Sure enough, once again she heard the insistent call of a sparrowbat.

A sparrowbat? Zephyr thought to herself again. *Why would a sparrowbat be out—oh, wait. It is Swift Arrow!*

Zephyr laughed without meaning too. The sheer ridiculousness of how long it had taken her to understand what was happening combined with her pure relief, and it all came out as a delighted laugh. One of the Raiders scolded her again, but Zephyr didn't care anymore.

Swift Arrow was coming.

Swift Arrow moved through the trees swiftly and silently. Above and around him ran the other warriors who had been banished. Swift Arrow halted and pointed through the dense trees. He could see the mass of Swamp Raiders moving through the trees ahead.

Now the former Tribeswarriors moved with even more caution until they were abreast and then ahead of the Raiders. Swift Arrow pulled himself up into a tree. Beside him knelt Strong Oak, the best archer Swift Arrow knew.

Swift Arrow could see Zephyr in the middle of the group of slaves. He gritted his teeth. She was hurt. Taking a deep breath, he imitated the call of a sparrowbat. He watched as Zephyr looked around, confusion filling her face.

Swift Arrow repeated the call three more times before understanding dawned on her face, and she laughed, actually laughed, earning her a rebuke from one of the Raiders.

"Now," Swift Arrow whispered. An arrow flew from Strong Oak's bow, and one of the Swamp Raiders fell with a shriek. Swift Arrow watched as the Tribeswomen cried out in terror and huddled together in the center of the space made by their captors.

He saw Zephyr calming the terrified women with tranquil certainty. "Shoot an arrow next to the Princess's foot." Swift Arrow ordered next, not trusting his aim to be that accurate. Just as Swift Arrow had hoped, Zephyr understood what she was to do, snatching the arrow up and cutting first her and then Cornflower's bonds before shoving the arrow into Cornflower's hands.

Swift Arrow grinned when Zephyr looked directly up at him and motioned with her hand. He sent an arrow flying at her. Zephyr raised her hand, and a strong breeze stopped the arrow mid-flight. It hung in the air for a minute before falling harmlessly into her hand.

Swift Arrow continued to fire arrows into the mass of Raiders, all the while keeping one eye on Zephyr. She seemed to be giving instructions to the women. He watched as she looked around and then settled her gaze on two young men, boys really, who stood behind her and to the left.

Zephyr thrust out both her hands, and a sudden guest took the Raiders by surprise, sending them tumbling over backward.

The Tribeswomen surged forwards, trampling the men and scattering into the trees. Zephyr tried to move with the rest, but she ended up in the rear, and it appeared that the long night had finally caught up to her.

Swift Arrow looked on with set jew as a Raider five times Zephyr's size reached out with snake-like speed and grabbed her arm. Zephyr was caught, along with three or four other women.

"We need to help them," Swift Arrow said to Strong Oak, already fitting a new arrow to his bow. Swift Arrow growled as the Raider lifted Zephyr off the ground and boxed her ear with his free hand before dropping her to the ground. The Swamp Raider hauled her onto a llama, and Swift Arrow drew his bow. "I do not think so," he murmured.

When the strong hand clamped down on her arm, Zephyr's first reaction had been one of surprise. Then when she was lifted off the ground, she felt only frustration. *Truly?* She thought. *I did all that only to be captured again!*

The Raider delivered a stinging slap to her ear before dropping her on the ground. Zephyr cried out as her arm connected with a sharp rock. *Swift Arrow!* She cried out mentally.

The double blows had left her dizzy. The world suddenly tilted, and she was set roughly on a llama. "Krakenkine, kongo kino kofta!" The Swamp Raider yelled as he hauled himself up behind her.

Zephyr didn't know if he was yelling at her or the other Swamp Raiders, and she really didn't care. She was tired, her head hurt, her arm hurt, even her ear hurt. An arrow hit the llama that she was riding. As they fell to the ground, she realized that she should run.

Smaller than the Raider, Zephyr managed to extract herself from the llama's dead weight first and hurl herself into the trees. She tripped on a root and went sprawling.

Fear pounded in her chest as she scrambled upright. Darting around a tree, she ran straight into another strong arm. Zephyr groaned and fought with all her might, but this new adversary held firm.

"Zephyr, Zephyr!" La-kaodai repeated, giving her a little shake. Zephyr stopped struggling and tilted her head up.

"La-kaodai? What on Hereth are you doing here?"

"Sunblossom thought that there was a chance we could still catch you, so I followed you." He tried to tuck a strand of hair behind her ear, but she jerked away.

"Do not do that, please." She said firmly.

La-kaodai frowned. "I will have the right to do that one day."

"But you do not now," she said resolutely.

"Fine, as you wish," La-kaodai growled. "Where are the other women?"

"They scattered into the trees when…when the Swamp Raiders were attacked."

"Attacked?" La-kaodai's head perked up. "Attacked by whom?"

But Zephyr would not say another word.

CHAPTER EIGHT

"No, I will not do it."

"But you must. If you do not, she will never sign my contract, and then what will happen if we are attacked again?" La-kaodai's tone was urgent.

"La-kaodai—" Chief Mark-hai stopped just shy of rebuking his head warrior for contradicting him. La-kaodai did make a good point. If they were attacked by the Swamp Raiders or anyone else before Zephyr was married, she would be vulnerable.

Besides, he firmly believed that La-kaodai was the man Lasha had wanted Zephyr to marry. Surely he could trust La-kaodai's judgment?

"He is only now able to guard Zephyr. I do not think he will be able to fend for himself." The Chief said.

"All the more reason to do it now. She is so compassionate that she will be unable to stand idly by and watch him banished as she did with Swift Arrow."

Chief Mark-hai's brow creased. Another good point. "Are you sure?" La-kaodai was the one who was in love with Zephyr. He *must* know what he was talking about.

La-kaodai knew how to convince someone to agree with him. "There is no doubt in my mind." He sighed. "I will, of course, acquiesce to whatever you believe is best. I only want Zephyr to be safe."

The Chief thought for another long moment. "Very well, I will do as you say."

Zephyr was bent over the small garden behind her rackleen, weeding, when Sunblossom's hurried steps broke the calm stillness. "They have banished Bark!"

"What?" Zephyr shot upright, dropping her hoe and nearly impaling a passing flowercat.[12] "It is the middle of the day." She picked up the hoe and returned it to its shelf.

Cornflower suddenly joined them, worry evident on her face. "The Chief needs you right away. You are to hurry."

Zephyr sighed. "This was La-kaodai's doing. I only wish I understood why my father listens to him so." She brushed her hands off against her pants. "Stay with Blossom, Flower. Finish the gardening; hard work will make you feel better."

---

12 Flowercats look quite like regular cats, except for the fact that they have four eyes and that their coats appear to have flowers printed on them and that their teeth can retract into their gums.

She rested her hand on Sunblossom's shoulder for a moment before taking off, running with long graceful strides. *I refuse to lose my balance so easily.* She thought to herself.

When she reached the Chief's rackleen, she did not bother to knock, and he spoke without preamble. "Sign the contract, and I will unbanish them."

"Firstly," Zephyr began calmly, sitting down. "*Unbanish* is not a word. Secondly, my answer must still be no."

Chief Mark-hai was clearly taken aback by his daughter's calm, measured response. This was supposed to be easy, not turn into another debate. He stammered for a moment in a way that was not quite what one expected from the Chief of such a large Tribe.

Finally, he found his voice. "I am surprised at you, Zephyr, allowing your cousin—"

"No, father, I am surprised at *you*." She said angrily. "You are the one who banished him, not me." She immediately caught herself and lowered her eyes. "Forgive my anger, Father."

The Chief ignored both her outburst and apology. "I see that you are determined to be stubborn; however, you will find your stubbornness is matched by my firmness. If you have not signed La-kaodai's contract in two weeks, I will banish Sunblossom and Cornflower. After that, you will have two more weeks to sign the contract, after which time you will be banished."

"I wish you would ask some of the women about La-kaodai," Zephyr whispered.

Chief Mark-hai ignored her again. "Of course, if at any time you decide to accept the contract, I will bring everyone out of banishment." He carefully avoided the word *unbanish* this time.

"And who will become your heir after you have banished all of your family?" She asked sadly.

"Yes, yes, you do understand! La-kaodai will become Chief, so you should save yourself and your friends the pain of banishment and marry him." He said earnestly.

Zephyr stood, eyes blazing, although she kept her tone respectful. "Who was it who taught me to never do anything that would hurt the innocent, even if it brought pain to myself? And who was it who refused to join the Clan in her war against the River Clan even though he knew it would embroil our Tribe in a different war?

"It was you! Did you say, 'well, we must fight anyway, so let us fight with the stronger Clan?' No! You stood for the right, and our people blessed you for it. You have taught me to always do what is best for my people, and I will do it. Even if they are willing to have this evil come upon them, I am not, and it will not come through any action of my own."

Zephyr shook her head and stepped back. "If you and La-kaodai go so far as to banish my llama, I still will not sign the contract."

"You will really allow your friends to suffer?" Chief Mark-hai asked incredulously.

Zephyr smiled sadly. "When this all began, they told me to do what was right, and that they would stand by me, whatever I chose."

Quiet filled the rackleen for several minutes until Zephyr spoke again. "May I be excused?"

The Chief stirred, as he had been deep in thought, and nodded his head. Zephyr left then, but he did not move for a long time, staring at the place where his daughter had been.

Zephyr paced back and forth in her rackleen. Betsy crouched nearby, following her movements with her head. Zephyr had watched as Cornflower and Sunblossom were banished and seen La-kaodai banish his brother, Fast Rain. She felt that all discipline was slipping from her father's hands and into the hands of her would-be husband-promised.

Zephyr understood that it was customary for the son or son-in-law of the Chief to take over some aspects of ruling the Tribe, but Zephyr and La-kaodai were not married nor was La-kaodai Chief Mark-hai's heir. She simply could not understand why her father trusted and loved La-kaodai so much.

With all her close friends gone and a warrior she did not know well assigned to guard her, Zephyr felt more stifled than usual. Zephyr stopped and petted Betsy's head automatically, her gaze focused on some distant point and her thoughts far away.

"I want you to keep Betsy." Sunblossom had said a few days before her banishment. "She will keep you company when we are all banished."

The long afternoons stretched without anyone with whom to pass the time. Dinner she always ate by herself, preferring that to the hostile glares of her people, which seemed worse now that her friends were gone. Breakfast and supper were more difficult choices to make. If Zephyr caved to the deSire for human companionship and ate with her father, she would spend the entire meal defending herself against her father's verbal sallies.

"Are you alright in there, Princess?" Her guard called. Zephyr pulled herself out of her reverie. It was time to get out of the rackleen when her guard began to wonder if she was alright.

"Yes, Running Eagle, I am fine." She said as she exited the rackleen. "Come, Betsy. I am going to visit Crab Apple."

Zephyr started down the path, Running Eagle a short way behind, and studiously avoided all comparisons between Running Eagle and Swift Arrow.

When she reached Crab Apple's family's rackleen, she found her friend lazing on a bench outside.

Zephyr joined her. "Peace be on you, Crab Apple." Running Eagle dropped to the ground underneath a tree and closed his eyes, presumably to give the girls some semblance of privacy. Betsy lay at Zephyr's feet.

"And peace be on you, Princess." Crab Apple replied amiably. She was an unmarried woman, slightly younger than Zephyr, and as sweet as possible, but she had never been one of Zephyr's close friends.

Crab Apple glanced at Zephyr. "How are you since the attack?"

Zephyr sighed. "I am not sure, really. Sunblossom, Flower, and I never really had a chance to talk it over."

"We could talk about it," Crab Apple suggested. "If you want to." She added hastily.

Zephyr glanced around and then made a decision. "I do need someone to talk to, but what I am telling you is confidential."

Crab Apple nodded seriously. "You can trust me."

Zephyr dropped her voice to just above a whisper as she confided in her friend. "I love Swift Arrow, and he rescued me from the Swamp Raiders, and I have no idea if he is hurt or even alive. My father gave me up for dead, and it was La-kaodai that came to my rescue. Everything is all mixed up." Zephyr sighed and rested her head in her hands.

Crab Apple laid a gentle hand on Zephyr's arm.

"As if all that is not enough, La-kaodai seems to have decided that if he does not marry me as soon as possible,

I might die, and then he will have lost his chance to be Chief." Zephyr laughed, a dry humorless sound. "The Swamp Raiders did not even achieve *their* purpose. The full affair seems pointless."

Crab Apple pursed her lips and thought for a moment. "Well, it cannot have been pointless. The Protector does not allow anything to happen outside of His will." She cocked her head. "I can think of several things that have come out of the raid."

Zephyr raised her head. "What?"

Crab Apple spoke with remarkable insight. "The Tribe will now better guard its borders and not send all of her warriors away at once. La-kaodai will, as you said, no longer be patient, but perhaps now Chief Mark-hai will better value his family as well. Perhaps, even, the result with the greatest impact is not even one we can see."

"What do you mean?"

Crab Apple shrugged. "I do not really know. I just mean that the Protector works in ways that are not ours."

Zephyr was quiet a moment. "You are right." She said at last.

"Oh, I know." Crab Apple said quickly. "You taught it to me in the first place."

Zephyr laughed.

"Do you find your rackleen to be smaller now?"

Zephyr sighed. "Yes. I do not think I have ever been so lonely before."

Crab Apple dropped her voice again. "I did not mean to remind you of your loss again, but I am proud of you, my Princess. I do not know that I would have the strength of character to do as you have done. Of course," she acknowledged. "I do not have an entire Tribe to consider when making decisions."

"And there is the rub," Zephyr said. "I made a decision to do what is best for my whole Tribe, and they all want me to do the opposite."

"We do not know what is good for us, I suppose." Crab Apple laughed. "Although we do not openly speak of it, I do believe that all of the women support you."

Zephyr smiled gratefully. "We know who La-kaodai is. Oh," she sighed, "this never would have happened if my mother were still alive. I have never understood why the Protector chose to take her when He did, but now…" she trailed off.

Crab Apple remained silent, feeling she had already offered the words Zephyr needed to hear.

"I know that He has a purpose in all this," Zephyr said quietly. "I pray that one day I might understand what it is."

The tension in the air was palpable. Everyone in the Tribe knew that today was Zephyr's final chance to sign La-kaodai's contract before she too would be banished.

Likewise, many had heard her firm declaration the night before that she would not sign it.

Yet there was a whole long, empty day to get through before the banishment, before Zephyr's torment would finally be over.

"You will sign his contract now, will you not?" Fast Spring asked as the women moved across a field weeding.

Zephyr straightened, stopped La-kaodai's mother, and looked her in the eyes. "No, I will not. Surely you understand that."

Last Spring sighed. "I do, and as much as it would be nice to have another woman in the rackleen to share the labor and—other things, I would not wish it on any woman. His moods are so hard to read and therefore hard to serve, as it is my duty."

She pressed her lips into a thin line and, saying no more, returned to her work.

The day marched slowly on. Zephyr traced the sun's passage through the sky, willing it to move faster. Finally, the sun was setting, and the Tribesfolk gathered on the edge of the forest without needing to be called.

The torches were set on long poles behind the assembled gathering. Zephyr took her place between the stone lines. Betsy leaned against Zephyr, sensing that something was terribly wrong. La-kaodai stood next to Chief Mark-hai, arms crossed, looking rather smug. He was sure that he had won.

A feeling of uneasiness settled over everyone. Would the Chief really banish the Princess? Such extreme measures felt implausible and impossible, as if they were all moving in some horrendous nightmare.

"Princess Zephyr," Chief Mark-hai's voice rose above the silent Tribesfolk, startling a sparrowbat that was sitting on a branch behind Zephyr. "Make your choice." There was no need to elaborate. Even the youngest member of the Tribe understood what was happening by now.

Zephyr let her eyes drift over the people of her Tribe. She took in the warmth of the cooking fires, the delicious aroma of supper, and the relative safety and comfort of the village. Then she turned her head and studied the forest. It was dark and cold, but her friends waited for her, somewhere within its recesses, as did someone who loved her.

She turned once more and faced her father. This might be the last chance she would ever have to speak to these dear people, and she planned to make the most of it. In a loud, firm voice that could be heard by all, she said, "I choose to consider the wellbeing of the Tribe before my own comfort. I choose to do what is right, and I choose to refuse the contract of a man who will not rule my people wisely.

"I choose banishment for my Tribe." Her confidence encouraged the women and planted seeds of doubt in the minds of the warriors. La-kaodai glared, and Crab Apple and Last Spring smiled encouragingly.

Zephyr turned and walked with her head held high into the forest, Betsy trotting at her heels. She never saw the look of total grief on Chief Mark-hai's face nor the way his mouth opened as if to call her name.

They were too close to the Tribe's village to risk a light, so Swift Arrow and Bark knelt in the branches of a yna tree, scanning the rough path below them for movement.

A dark shadow flitted from tree to tree. A single shaft of moonlight glinted off something on her ankle.

"There she is," Bark murmured.

"Zephyr," Swift Arrow called as loud as he dared, which wasn't very loud. Zephyr heard him anyway and looked up. He waved.

Zephyr came swiftly toward the tree and reached for a lower branch. She pulled herself up with surprising skill, considering that girls weren't allowed to indulge in "male sports."

"Impressive," Swift Arrow said as he pulled her up the last few feet. "Most impressive."

She shrugged as she settled on the branch between the two men. "I have watched you and Bark often enough. Climbing down could be a bit of a problem." She peered down between her legs at the ground, which now seemed very far away.

"You will not have to worry about that part for a while," Bark assured her.

"Why not?" She looked curiously at her cousin.

"Because you might as well have your first lesson in tree-walking now."

"Tree-walking?"

Swift Arrow explained. "We have learned that it is safest to hunt and live deep in the woods where the underbrush is thick, and the easiest way to travel through those areas is to go through the trees."

Even in the dark, Swift Arrow could see Zephyr's huge grin. "I get to learn how to climb trees?"

Swift Arrow chuckled. "Yes, and move from tree to tree without falling."

"Well, then, one of you has to go get Betsy. "

"I will get her." Bark slipped off the branch and out of sight.

Swift Arrow took a deep breath and picked up Zephyr's hand. She turned to look at him. "Zephyr, will you sign my contract?"

Zephyr's eyes grew wide. "I would love to Swift Arrow, yes, but my father—"

He stopped her. "We are banished now, darling. We do not have to abide by Tribal law."

"This is not how I ever imagined this happening," she whispered, "but it's perfect. Yes, Swift Arrow, I will sign your contract and become your wife."

Swift Arrow hugged her then, his strong arms surrounding her and pulling her close. "This is nice," he murmured.

Zephyr pulled back gently. "Perhaps we should go now?"

Bark spoke from behind. "I am ready if you two are." Betsy sat beside him on the branch. Bark had taken a length of sturdy vine and formed a rough leash to keep the wolfurnut from falling. "Are you ready for your first lesson?"

Zephyr nervously eyed the dark trees beyond her cousin. "In the dark? Are you sure that you can handle two students? Betsy has been known to be a bit testy at night."

Betsy barked and wagged her tail as though refuting Zephyr's statement.

Swift Arrow stood up and held his hand out to her. "Do not worry, Ze, I will not let you fall."

Sunblossom and Cornflower sat around one of the many fires that dotted the clearing which housed the exile's camp. The pleasant murmur of conversation rose and fell around them, but the girls sat quietly.

Finally, Sunblossom stirred. "Do you really think the Chief will go through with this? I cannot imagine him banishing Zephyr."

Cornflower shrugged. "Fast Rain made it pretty clear that La-kaodai is calling the shots when it comes to banishment."

Sunblossom shook her head. "I do not understand why the Chief listens to La-kaodai so."

Cornflower tilted her head toward her friend. "Last Spring told me that Chieftess Lasha's last words to Chief Mark-hai were 'Take care of Zephyr' and then 'La-kaodai.'"

Sunblossom lowered her head and looked at Cornflower in disbelief. "Surely the Chieftess did not want La-kaodai and Zephyr to marry!"

Cornflower sighed. "We only have La-kaodai's word on it. She might have said more."

Sunblossom frowned. "Do not say anything to Zephyr."

Cornflower nodded. "I will not." She turned and peered intently into the forest. "Is that them?"

Sunblossom stood up and cupped her hands around her eyes to block the glare from the fires. "Is Zephyr with them?"

Cornflower shook her head. "I cannot tell. The clearing is too bright, and the woods too dark."

It was not long before they could clearly make out the forms of Swift Arrow, Zephyr, and Bark. Sunblossom and Cornflower ran to meet them.

"We were worried that Chief Mark-hai would not banish you," Sunblossom said, hugging Zephyr.

"He did not seem to have a problem with it." Zephyr did not sound bitter, only sad, even as she hugged her friends.

"I cannot believe that," Cornflower said decidedly, linking arms with Zephyr. "He loves you."

Zephyr looked back and forth between her friends. "Oh, I have missed all of you." She seemed determined to ignore Cornflower's comment.

"Peace, Betsy," Sunblossom said, bending to pet her wolfurnut. Betsy wagged her tail politely but remained at Zephyr's side. "I think she is yours now," Sunblossom said ruefully. "You have her, though, and welcome. Bark promised me a pup as soon as Strong Oak's wolfurnut has a litter." She pulled Zephyr to their fire. "Look what Bark has given in the meantime." She extended her anklet so Zephyr could see.

"Ooh, Blossom!" Zephyr squealed. *Someone* had replaced Sunblossom's anklet charm. Before, she had worn a small metal sun, now she proudly wore a simple wooden tree.

"I always knew that you and Bark would marry." Zephyr smiled happily. She sat down on a rough wooden bench. "What did you do with the old one?"

"I kept it. I cannot return it to my father."

Zephyr nodded. "I suppose you could do nothing else."

Swift Arrow sat down beside Zephyr. "Here is yours," he said simply, holding out his hand.

Zephyr gasped. Chief Mark-hai had given her a cloud on her thirteenth birthday. Swift Arrow was holding a beautiful arrow charm. It was made of a gray metal, and its tip was covered in tiny purple gems that sparkled in the firelight.

"Oh, Arrow, it is beautiful." She breathed. She carefully unclasped and removed her old charm. Swift Arrow knelt in front of her and carefully added the new charm.

"Come on, Sunblossom," Bark smiled. "Let us go fetch the contract for Swift Arrow and Zephyr."

CHAPTER NINE

A breeze was blowing steadily through the trees the following morning. Zephyr stood on a branch, one hand resting on the trunk as she balanced, and her face turned into the wind.

"Ze?" Zephyr turned her head carefully and smiled at her new husband.

"Good morning, Swift Arrow." She said.

"You are up early. Everything alright?" He slipped his arm around her.

"Everything is wonderful." She leaned into his arms. "I am sure that I have been happier than this, but I cannot recall when. I have got the wind in my hair, and I can go climb every tree in this forest, if I choose. There are no more stifling, unspoken traditions weighing me down."

Swift Arrow laughed. "You know the only things that have truly changed are that you can do your chores in whatever order you please, wear what you like, and climb trees, correct?"

Zephyr laughed too. "Yes, but it still feels different." She glanced down at her clothes. "I think I might ask the leatherworkers to dye me some purple leather and make myself some new clothes."

"Something to match the yna trees?" Swift Arrow sounded satisfied.

"That, and purple is the color that the Eulgarians assigned to my Gift." She smiled.

"Come with me, Ze. I want to talk to you."

The morning light filtered through the leaves as Swift Arrow and Zephyr wandered among the trees at the edge of the clearing, deep in quiet conversation.

". . . and that is how we found Bark." Swift Arrow pulled his wife to a seat on a fallen log. "All of the warriors here have been talking, dreaming really, about gathering all the exiles in this forest together to form a Tribe. Those who have already moved to our clearing enthusiastically approve the idea, and—" he hesitated. "They have asked me to be the first Chief."

"Of course they did," Zephyr smiled. Then her brow furrowed. "Will not other Tribes and Clans feel they can wage war on us if we are a Tribe?"

"Perhaps, it is the way of the world to be ever fighting, but then we will be able to defend our land. As it stands, if the Tribe decides she wants this clearing, we can do nothing; but if we are organized into a Tribe, we can arrest them for trespassing." Swift Arrow grinned.

Zephyr chuckled.

"Not to mention, Swift Arrow added, "the resources of this land will be secured for our children."

"You think that we will be exiles so long?" Zephyr asked soberly.

"I do not know if your father will ever see Lakaodai's true nature. I cannot assume he will, though. If I do, we will never settle down or create a life for our family, and the Swamp Raider attack showed me that if the Tribe's village is not even safe, we will certainly not be safe here."

Crab Apple's words from a few days before flashed through Zephyr's head. *"But maybe the result with the greatest impact is not even one we can see."*

"What?" Swift Arrow asked, seeing the look on her face.

Zephyr explained the conversation that she had had with Crab Apple.

"Crab Apple has always been a wise woman." Swift Arrow said.

"As you are wise." Zephyr leaned against him. "I love the way you included our future children in your planning. This is something I have always admired in you. You do not plan for today alone." She cocked her head. "Now tell me the name of your new Tribe."

"I was thinking, 'Wind Tribe.'"

"Why Wind Tribe?" Zephyr asked curiously.

"Why, do you not control the wind?" He returned innocently. Zephyr's delighted laugh rang throughout the forest.

That very afternoon, half of the former Tribeswarriors had headed out into the forest to find as many exiles as they could and invite them to the first Tribal Meeting of the Wind Tribe.

Now, several days later, Zephyr gazed out in wonder from a tree branch as hundreds of people streamed into the clearing, a few curious hermits lurking at the edges. "They cannot all be from the Tribe, can they?" She asked Sunblossom, who stood beside her.

"Some are from other Tribes and Clans, but you must remember that Chief Lo-debar banished very many people," Sunblossom said.

Zephyr's grandfather, the late Chief Lo-debar, was infamous for his many banishments for the slightest offense.

"I remember, though my people seem to have forgotten." It was so softly said, Sunblossom thought she had imagined the words for half a beat.

Sunblossom turned and studied her friend, suddenly realizing the reason for Zephyr's deep conviction. Swift Arrow startled them both when he suddenly said, "Forgotten what?"

"The banishments of Chief Lo-debar," Zephyr said without turning.

Swift Arrow wrapped his arms around Zephyr. "Ah, people don't always like to remember bad things. Sometimes it's easier to forget."

Sunblossom surreptitiously backed down the branch a ways.

"But we should remember, so that we do not repeat the mistakes of the past," Zephyr said quietly.

"Just remember, Ze," he bent down to whisper in her ear. "That these are your people now, and they need you."

Zephyr turned halfway around and rested her head on his chest. "You always know just what I need to hear." She murmured.

Swift Arrow leaned down and pressed a gentle kiss to her lips.

"If you two are quite finished, Bark is looking for you, and I would like my eyesight back," Sunblossom called.

Zephyr looked over. Bark was standing next to his wife, watching his cousin with a cheeky grin, while covering Sunblossom's eyes with his hand.

A small smile came to Zephyr's face. She turned back to her husband.

"Shall we go?" He asked.

"We shall," Zephyr said, pulling her head up and smiling.

They departed the tree and walked toward the center of the clearing. The exiles nearly overflowed the small camp as they waited patiently for Swift Arrow to speak.

"How are they all supposed to see us, let alone hear us?" Swift Arrow asked, frustration tinging his tone.

Bark pointed up at a nearby tree, its lower branch offering an unobstructed view of the gathering. "I will make your voice louder," Zephyr said.

Swift Arrow looked down at her for a moment. There was not a doubt in his mind that she could do what she said. Zephyr, Bark, and Swift Arrow ascended the tree while Sunblossom went to stand with Cornflower.

As Swift Arrow began speaking, Zephyr waved her hand, and a strong wind picked up his words and carried them. His first few words were startling loud, causing Bark to wince, Zephyr allowed the words to become slightly quieter, once they had everyone's attention.

"We are all exiles. Some among us were banished unjustly. Others have been exiles for decades, more than paying for your crimes. Some even have children now. There are many of us, and if we were to live together, we could help each other.

"We could defend each other against Swamp Raiders and wild animals. We could make sure that no one goes hungry. I have recently been reminded just how dangerous it is to live on The Continent." Swift Arrow glanced at Zephyr.

"However, we are at the mercy of the Tribes and Clans around us. If any one of them decided they wanted our land, we would have no choice but to give it up or be killed. I do not want us or our children to live as forced nomads. I want them to have a place to live.

"The only way to do this is to form a Tribe. It will be called the Wind Tribe, and anyone who wishes to join will be more than welcome. We will not exile anyone. You will once again have all the rights that you had in your Tribe or Clan."

Swift Arrow looked around. "Are there any questions?"

An older man stepped away from the front edge of the crowd, a young girl clinging to his arm. Zephyr turned her attention to him just as he began to speak. He looked weary and his words came slowly. "My name is Mushi. I have two small children. It has been a struggle to protect my family, since my wife and I were exiled. How do you plan to protect so many?" He motioned to the large gathering.

"We will have warriors, just as any other Tribe or Clan. Anyone who chooses may carry weapons without fear of repercussion if a Tribeswarrior were to see you. We will track down and punish any raiding parties."

"What will the village look like?" Someone shouted.

"We will enlarge this clearing," Bark said. "Quite a lot by the looks of it. There will be plenty of space for rackleens and family gardens. We plan to leave some trees standing to provide more privacy, since most of us are well accustomed to living alone.

A middle-aged woman raised her hand. When Swift Arrow acknowledged her, she said, "Will work assignments be like the Tribe?"

Zephyr smiled. She had asked the same thing of Swift Arrow just that morning. Now, after a discussion with Zephyr, Sunblossom, and Cornflower, he had an answer. "Not quite. All the women will take turns working in the fields, helping the healers, and working in the kitchen. You will always have the afternoons to do your own work, and one day out of four will be yours to work in your rackleen."

"Will not the Day of Rest interfere with such a schedule?" The woman demanded.

Zephyr had to hide a smile behind her hand when Swift Arrow looked helplessly at his wife.

A ripple of laughter spread through the crowd. "You will have to ask my wife. I do not, and probably have no chance of understanding it, but I am sure that you will have no such problems.

"Are there any more questions?" Swift Arrow asked. When no one else pushed forward, the large assembly voted, and every person still present, the hermits having already left, voted with a resounding *aye*.

Swift Arrow addressed the people one more time. "Tomorrow, we will begin the work of building our village. For now, let us feast for the very first time as the Wind Tribe!"

Zephyr joined Sunblossom behind the tables on which giant pots of steaming panther stew were set. She had finally detached herself from the loud-mouthed woman curious about work assignments. The woman, named Soft Clouds, had been under the impression that the new Chieftess needed to know everything that had happened in the forest for the last twenty-five years.

What made Soft Clouds' information so impressive, though, was that she had only been an exile for two years.

A young girl walked hesitantly up, holding an empty bowl. She looked behind her and got an encouraging smile from her mother. Zephyr recognized her as Mushi's daughter.

"Peace, birdie, can I get you something?" Zephyr asked cheerfully.

"May I have some more stew, please?" The girl asked shyly.

"Of course!" Zephyr leaned around the pot to take the bowl. "What is your name?"

"Azal," The girl cocked her head. "Are you our Chieftess? I saw you in the tree beside the Chief."

"Well, now, that depends," Zephyr said. "Are you part of the Wind Tribe?" She hooked the ladle onto the side of the pot.

Azal's brow furrowed. "Father and Mammy are. Does that mean I am too?"

Zephyr grinned and handed over the bowl. "Most definitely."

"Oh, goodie! I have never been part of a Tribe before. Wait 'til I tell Ekro. He's my brother," she added confidentially. Azal turned to go, then came back. "Thank you for the stew, Chieftess."

Zephyr smiled, not bothering to correct Azal's improper word choice as she watched the little girl walk back to her family, carefully balancing the stew. She laid her hand on her stomach. *How long before You bless Swift Arrow and I with a child, Protector?* She prayed.

Swift Arrow's words from earlier that day echoed in her head. She whispered to herself. "This is my Tribe, and they need me now."

CHAPTER TEN

One Year later

wift Arrow stood beneath the shade of a large yna tree, hands clasped behind his back, eyes darting around the clearing. It certainly was a far cry from the small clearing of a year ago.

Trees and underbrush had been cleared for yonkas[13] around. Rackleens circled the clearing in ever-widening circles, with the Gathering Rackleen in the center. A few rackleens remained to be built, but the carpenters were working quickly.

A pack of wolfurnuts fought over some bones behind the smokerackleen,[14] and a tabby of flowercats[15] curled together in the sun beside another rackleen.

Swift Arrow tilted his head upwards and studied the sky, remembering the day some weeks back when a dragon had landed in their clearing to the shock and consternation of the Wind Tribe.

---

13 A Continental unit of measure equal to three miká's or two miles.

14 The equivalent of a smokehouse.

15 A group of flowercats.

Screams filled the air as mothers dragged their children out of the way. Warriors grabbed their weapons and formed a line three deep as the dragon folded its wings and landed on the practice field.

Zephyr ran up beside Swift Arrow, both worry and curiosity etched on her face. "What is happening?" She asked.

"I do not know," Swift Arrow replied, accepting his bow and quiver from Fast Rain. "Stay here."

Swift Arrow pushed his way through the warriors. A man slid off the dragon's back, arms in the air. "I come in peace!" He said.

"What do you want?" Swift Arrow demanded. He didn't know if messenger dragons could breathe fire, but he certainly was not going to discount the massive animal as a threat.

"I am a messenger from King David of Eulgaria."

"I thought the King of Eulgaria was named Francis."

"He died earlier this year, and his distant cousin, David, became King."

"Interesting." Swift Arrow said. "But I do not think you came to tell us that."

The messenger smiled and let his hands fall to his sides. "No, I did not. King David wants to hold a meeting for the Chiefs of some of the Clans and Tribes of The Continent. To allow them to meet each other and form alliances.

"King David understands that The Continent does not wish to form alliances with outside countries, and he and his wife, Queen Abihail, wish only to provide a meeting place."

Swift Arrow thought a moment. "Must I give my answer now?"

"Not at all. I can return in a week, or simply tell the King and Queen that you might be coming."

"One moment." Swift Arrow turned and motioned to his head warriors. Strong Oak and Bark strode forward. After conferring with them for a moment, he said, "You may return in one week."

The messenger bowed his head. "May peace follow you all your days." He turned and climbed up the dragon's foreleg, swung his leg over the dragon's back and settled himself in the saddle. "Let us go!" He called in Eulgarian, and the dragon unfolded his wings, growled deep in his throats,[16] and jumped up, beating his wings.

A moment later, rider and dragon were gone.

"Are you alright?" Zephyr asked, coming up beside her husband and resting her hands on his shoulders.

"I was just thinking about the dragon." Swift Arrow said, turning and putting his arms around Zephyr. "Fast Rain and I leave tomorrow, you know."

---

16 Dragons have, of course, two throats and two stomachs, one for liquid, and one for solid food.

"Trust me, I know," Zephyr cuddled deeper into his arms. "I pray that the Protector will make it a profitable time."

"Perhaps I will bring you something from Eulgaria." Swift Arrow suggested.

"Oh, Arrow," she leaned her head back. "You do not have to do that. Just bring me yourself, and that will be more than enough."

Swift Arrow kissed the top of her head. "I love you, Zephyr."

She sighed contentedly. "I love you too."

Swift Arrow looked around the Forest wharf. Elvish sailors and officials moved around the docks. A group of young ladies giggled as they were escorted onto a pleasure yacht by a group of young gentlemen, while forty or so Continental warriors milled about in various groups.

If Swift Arrow understood correctly, that meant that twenty Tribes and Clans had responded to King David of Eulgaria's invitation to attend the Confederation of the Tribes and Clans of The Continent.

Fast Rain suddenly appeared at his elbow. "Chief Mark-hai sent La-kaodai."

Swift Arrow glanced skyward. "Lovely." He looked around again and saw La-kaodai sauntering in their direction. "Here he comes."

"Well, well, Exile. What are you doing here?" La-kaodai drawled, obviously feeling that he was in a position of power.

"I am not an exile." Swift Arrow said evenly but firmly. "I am the Chief of the Wind Tribe."

La-kaodai scoffed. "Right, and there are lands beyond the sea. I hardly think—"

An Elvish official suddenly stepped in, his flowing garments seeming to move by themselves. "Excuse me warriors, but if you, Warrior La-kaodai, will please board that boat," he said. "The Eulgarian boat will be here any moment and we want to be as expedient and efficient as possible."

La-kaodai bowed his head stiffly to the official and walked away.

"Thank you," Swift Arrow said to the Elf. He held out his hand, having learned that this was an Elvish custom when greeting someone.

The other man shook his hand. "Think nothing of it. One of the ambassadors to The Continent came down yesterday and made us aware of the situation."

The official simply walked away. Swift Arrow followed him with his eyes. "Handshaking and avoiding thanks whenever possible. I wonder if the Eulgarian have strange customs, too."

Fast Rain shrugged. "I do not know, but praise the Protector for that official stepping in when he did."

Swift Arrow nodded his agreement.

Fast Rain looked over Swift Arrow's shoulders. "Look, Chief. That boat is flying the Eulgarian colors. Perhaps we will get underway now."

Swift Arrow turned and studied the boat as it tied up at the ancient but well-preserved dock. "I hope so."

Thanks to the Elves' efficiency, the remaining delegates were soon on the ferryboats. They pushed off from the dock, the wind caught the sails, and they were off across the deep River Avon that separated The Forest and Eulgaria.

Swift Arrow leaned against the railing and stared into the water. A colony of mermaids frolicked alongside the ships. Each mermaid had a long pleat of braided hair down her back and wore a shimmering shirt that ended just above her tail. With flicks of their hands, they sent jets of water into the air, entertaining the warriors who had never seen such a large body of water, let alone mermaids.

Swift Arrow wondered if La-kaodai would try to cause trouble for the Wind Tribe. Although it was likely, he hoped fervently that it would not be true. Fast Rain and Swift Arrow planned to use this trip to gain much-needed allies.

Swift Arrow and Fast Rain entered the Great Hall of Emerald Pointe, the Eulgarian castle, and stopped in the center of the room. The other Continental warriors wandered around, examining the tapestries, but Swift Arrow was content to observe from afar, and Fast Rain was content to stand by his Chief's side.

"Zephyr would love this," Swift Arrow said wistfully.

"Cheer up, Chief. You can take her a gift, and she will forgive you for leaving." Fast Rain grinned.

Swift Arrow laughed. "I wonder how she is doing."

"I am sure she is fine. You *did* leave Bark to help her."

"Excuse me," a soft voice spoke in Eulgarian from behind them. They turned to see a young man and woman standing before them.

"King David?" Swift Arrow guessed, also in Eulgarian, seeing the crowns.

"'Tis I," King David smiled. "This is my wife, Queen Abihail."

Swift Arrow and Fast Rain bowed. "I am Chief Swift Arrow of the Wind Tribe, and this is my newest head warrior, Fast Rain." Fast Rain's eyes widened slightly at *that* introduction.

Queen Abihail smiled. "Welcome to Eulgaria. I pray you will enjoy your stay."

Swift Arrow smiled back. "I am sure we will."

The Queen cocked her head. "I have not heard of the Wind Tribe before. I would love to invite you and Fast Rain to sup with the King and I one day."

King David hid a smile. "I am afraid the Queen is a better scholar than I. In truth, when I saw *Wind Tribe* on the list of Tribes and Clans, it did not occur to me to be curious."

Swift Arrow smiled back, instantly liking this man. "We are alike in that. My wife, Chieftess Zephyr, is much like the Queen."

The King and Queen smiled at each other. "We will not keep you any longer."

"They are nice. Will we eat with them?" Fast Rain asked once the King and Queen had walked away.

"Perhaps," Swift Arrow said, watching as the royals walked to a group of which La-kaodai was part.

"And Chief?" Fast Rain asked.

"Yes?"

"When were you planning to tell me that I was a head warrior?"

"I was waiting for an opportune time. This felt like such a time."

Fast Rain grinned. "Well, thanks for warning me."

"I do not know." Zephyr bit the inside of her lip. "Did you ask Bark?"

"I did." Mahli looked frustrated. "How is it that no one knows where the Holding rackleen is supposed to be built? Mushi and the other carpenters are ready to begin work on it now."

Zephyr stood taller in sudden decision. "Follow me." The two women headed towards the Chief's rackleen. Zephyr pulled out a large scroll of paper from one of the cubbies built into the wall and laid it out on the floor. The twosome knelt over it.

"This is the Gathering Rackleen." Zephyr pointed to a large circle in the center of the sheet.

"Is that Core Speech?"[17] Mahli asked, pointing at the characters besides the circle.

"Yes, the Chief has been practicing lately." Zephyr smiled fondly.

Mahli traced the concentric circles of the village on the scroll with one finger. "We have to think like a man, I suppose."

Zephyr giggled. "You make it sound as though men are from a different planet. Really, though, this is simple. Chief Swift Arrow had two scrolls, one for the plan of the village and one to which he added rackleens as they were built. Since the Holding rackleen is the last one to be built, all we have to do is find the empty space."

Mahli ran her hand over the map. "So it should go—there."

Zephyr peered closer. "Yes, you are right. It goes in-between two storage rackleens on the north edge."

---

17 The original language of The Continent from which all dialects come.

Mahli stood. "Thank you, Chieftess. My husband and the other carpenters will be quite pleased."

Zephyr smiled as Mahli disappeared out the door. *One more problem solved. How does Swift Arrow do this all day?* She wondered.

Bark knocked on the door frame and stuck his head into the rackleen. "Chieftess? Sunblossom is looking for you."

Zephyr sighed and rolled up the map scroll. "Coming."

Swift Arrow looked around the large parlor. The Confederation events had been carefully planned to allow Chiefs and warriors to meet men they would otherwise not. Tonight's event was meant to introduce the delegates to ambassadors from all the nations with which Eulgaria was currently aligned. That meant ambassadors from all the known countries but one.

King David and Queen Abihail stood in the center of the room, holding court with a large group of delegates, including, Swift Arrow noted, La-kaodai.

The Queen broke away from the group, leading a couple dressed in sumptuous clothes and dripping with jewels. "Chief Swift Arrow," Queen Abihail began. If La-kaodai had told her his view of the Wind Tribe, it did not show on the Queen's face. "May I introduce you to the Caldonian ambassador and his wife, General Izhar, and Princess Chionia."

Swift Arrow bowed. "General. Princess."

Queen Abihail nodded as though pleased. "If you will please excuse me," and moved gracefully away.

"I have been told that you come from The Continent. It must be dreadful living so far away from civilization." Princess Chionia spoke with just the right amount of languid disinterestedness.

Swift Arrow smiled charmingly. "While we hardly have all the comforts of Caldonia, we do not quite consider ourselves barbarians. We are quite content."

"Of course, of course, one never *thinks* one is a barbarian." The General was doing a remarkable job of holding himself aloof from the conversation while still participating in it.

"That is undoubtedly true." Swift Arrow bowed his head. "I am told that Caldonia is a large exporter of fine cloth?"

The General and Princess seemed taken aback that he would know such a fact about their country. General Izhar deigned to answer. "We are the best maker of fine cloth. The most fashionable dresses are made from it. Perhaps you are seeking a gift for your wife?"

"Do not be silly, General." The Princess scolded. "The backwoods are no place for our fabrics."

"Chief?" Fast Rain touched Swift Arrow on the elbow. "The Prokaryotan ambassador wishes to meet you."

"Oh, of course. Please, excuse me, General Izhar, Princess Chionia."

The ambassador and his wife gave the Chief permission to leave by their stately nods.

Fast Rain led Swift Arrow to the Prokaryotan ambassador, a cheery man dressed in a white toga with a wide strip of blue along the edge.

"Chief Swift Arrow, this is Senator Dumah of Prokaryota."

"It looked like ye could use an escape," Dumah smiled jovially and continued, "and I did want to meet ye. I am quite curious about governments and banishments on The Continent."

A butler tapped the senator on the shoulder. "Tiffin[18] is served, gentlemen. Will you please follow me to the dining room?"

The three men nodded. "We can discuss this over tiffin, then," Dumah said as they moved off.

Zephyr found Sunblossom in the center of the village. "What seems to be the trouble now?" Zephyr asked, brushing a strand of hair from her face.

"You had better just come look." Sunblossom led the way to one of the two springs that serviced the Wind

---

18 Eulgarian term for the noon meal.

Tribe. Dirt, leaves, and broken twigs swirled around in the pool of water. It was muddied, entirely unfit for drinking, or even washing.

"What happened?" Zephyr exclaimed.

"I do not know," Sunblossom said helplessly.

Zephyr knelt and examined the trampled ground around the spring. She touched some tracks gently. "It looks like a herd of wild pigs came through here. We need to get some warriors on this right away. If it is wild pigs, we need to thin the herd out enough that they will not come so close to us for a long time."

Sunblossom looked down at her friend admiringly. "You are doing a wonderful job, Ze."

Zephyr stood and smiled at her friend. "We should be able to use this spring again in a few days, once the flowing water washes the dirt and muck away."

"How much longer 'til Swift Arrow returns?" Sunblossom asked, falling into step beside the Chieftess.

"Two days. Unless something happens to detain him."

"Who do you think the Tribe sent?" Sunblossom asked.

Zephyr sighed. "It would not surprise me one bit if Father sent La-kaodai. I have been praying that La-kaodai will leave Swift Arrow alone since they are not in The Continent."

"Do you think he might try something once they return?"

"I doubt Swift Arrow will give him a chance," Zephyr said. "Swift Arrow will make sure that he and Fast Rain travel with allies as much as possible."

"Do you think La-kaodai will ever convince Chief Mark-hai to move against us?"

A worried frown creased Zephyr's face for a moment, telling Sunblossom that she had already thought about it. The only thing she said, however, was, *"Do not waste time counting unseen trouble,"* quoting an old Continental proverb.

"Wise words," Sunblossom nodded. "Hard to live by, it is true."

"Worry is an easy snare to fall into." Zephyr agreed. "Ah, Bark," she added when she spied her cousin up ahead. "I believe a herd of wild pigs muddied the lower spring. We need to track them down before they can do more damage or find the upper spring."

Bark nodded smartly. "Right away, Chieftess."

"Chieftess! Chieftess!" Soft Clouds called as she came running up. "I just heard the most distressing news! You must come immediately."

Zephyr exhaled and murmured, "Here we go again."

Sunblossom leaned closer to her friend and whispered, "Tell Soft Clouds about the spring. The whole Tribe will know to use the upper spring by supper."

Swift Arrow and Fast Rain wandered down the street in company with Jamain, one of the royal knights they had befriended.

"This is the best weaponry in the whole country." Jamain was saying, motioning to an unassuming shop on a street filled with eclectic shops. It was three stories high, with a thatched roof and white shutters.

The three warriors entered. Jamain went straight to the back wall and removed a bow from its pegs.

"This was the Queen's idea. It is for those who control a kamina.[19] It allows us to create bolts of our kamina and shoot them. Come, see."

Jamain led them out the back to an open area for testing weapons. Two knights were trying out a pair of swords while a Weapons Master looked on.

Jamain drew back on the bow. A shimmering shaft of water appeared in the place where the arrow should have been. He released, and the bolt went slamming into a target, knocking the hefty wooden object backward.

Swift Arrow raised his eyebrows. "Impressive."

Fast Rain spoke eagerly. "That is amazing!"

"In truth, 'tis the most wonderful weapon I have ever possessed." Jamain agreed. He led the way back inside.

"Do they have one for every Gift, or — what did you call it?" Swift Arrow asked.

---

19 A Eulgarian word meaning "an aspect of nature" the same as the Continental term "Gift" — pronounced as spelled.

"*Kamina*," Jamain supplied. "Yes, there is. This is one for those who control sound." He picked up a bow from the wall.

Swift Arrow took the bow and examined it. "Or those who control wind?"

"I have been told that they are one and the same," Jamain said, waving his hand in the air. Swift Arrow had noticed no Eulgarians shrugged, and sensed that the gesture stood in for a shrug.

Swift Arrow bounced the bow lightly in his hands. "Will one of the Weapons Masters engrave this for me?"

Zephyr moved around her rackleen, straightening up after another long day. She pulled back the curtain that hid the bed during the day and fluffed the pillows that sat on three benches on the other side of the room. Swift Arrow and Mushi planned to make two chairs for the rackleen once Harvest and the subsequent hunt were over.

There was a knock on the doorframe, and she smiled as she walked over to answer it. It was probably Bark again, checking on her last thing.

She removed the door tacks and pulled aside the flap. "Yes, Bark?" She asked good-naturedly, looking at the door flap and not the man beyond it.

"Wrong warrior," an amused voice responded.

"Arrow!" Zephyr dropped the door flap and flung herself into his arms.

Swift Arrow dropped his knapsack, laughing, and pulled her close. Fast Rain smiled to himself on the path behind them and then kept walking.

"What are you doing back already?" Zephyr exclaimed.

"It does not take as long as we thought to cross the River Avon. Ferryboats make the trip several times a day."

They walked inside. Betsy bounded forward, sniffing Swift Arrow's legs, and the Chief bent down to pet her head. "So you got up to come to greet me, huh?"

"Oh, I want to hear everything and tell you everything, but you are probably tired," Zephyr said.

"You tell me the most important things, what I would be expected to know, and we will talk more tomorrow." Swift Arrow said, sitting on the bed and pulling her down beside him.

"Alright," she cuddled close and thought for a moment. "The carpenters almost have all the rackleens built. They think another two days will finish the last one. A herd of wild pigs muddied the lower spring, but some warriors thinned out the herd, so they should not be a problem now. There was a young woman who was pregnant, named Summer Breeze. Her baby came early and did not live to see the sunset."

Sorrow filled Zephyr's voice. "Summer Breeze is recovering, and Cornflower thinks she will be alright in time."

Swift Arrow pressed a kiss to her head. "The loss of a life is a terrible thing, no matter how young the child is."

"He was so tiny," Zephyr marveled, "but there was no mistaking that this was a baby human. It was amazing."

Swift Arrow smiled and hugged her closer. "I have a gift for you."

"For me, really?" She asked, looking up and pulling back slightly. "You did not have to."

"I know." He walked over to his knapsack, untied a leather-wrapped object from it, and then brought it to his wife.

"Open it," he said, placing it in her lap.

Zephyr quickly unwrapped it. "Oh, Swift Arrow, it is beautiful."

CHAPTER ELEVEN

Zephyr straightened up and deftly pulled her hair back into a bun. Working all day in the fields with the rest of the Wind Tribe harvesting the grain and corn had left her sweaty and tired.

It was the last day of Harvest, however, so her fatigue was mixed with the anticipation of a well-earned rest. She looked at Sunblossom.

"One would think that banishment would get one *out* of helping with Harvest." Sunblossom groaned, hoisting a large basket.

"One would think," Zephyr said with a laugh. "Let us put the last of these baskets into a storage rackleen and go for a stroll before dinner."

Sunblossom frowned at a piece of hair which had fallen from her bun into her face and then fell in step beside Zephyr. They passed other groups of two's and three's as the Wind Tribe gladly finished their Harvest tasks for another year.

As the women ambled toward the perimeter of the clearing, Sunblossom begged, "Will you show me how your bow works now?"

Zephyr smiled. "Let me get it." After stopping at the Chief's rackleen to get Zephyr's bow, the ladies headed to a spot on the outskirts of the Wind Tribe.

"Do you see that large flower there in that yna tree?" Zephyr asked, pulling her bow off her back.

Sunblossom nodded and turned to watch her friend. Zephyr drew back on the string. In place of an arrow, the air began to shimmer. "Do not watch me; look at the flower," Zephyr instructed.

Zephyr released, and the flower went flying off the branch. Sunblossom gasped. "You did that?" She exclaimed. "Absolutely incredible."

The Chieftess smiled self-consciously. "It has taken a lot of practice, but I do believe that I am starting to get the hang of it."

"May I?" Sunblossom asked. Zephyr willingly handed the bow over. The wood was stained a deep purple, and images of the wind were carved on one side, and on the other, a woman stood with her hair blowing behind her.

"It is beautiful. Do you think—" Sunblossom began, but Zephyr quickly motioned her to be silent.

Sunblossom watched her friend closely as Zephyr took her bow back and drew it. She tilted her head into the wind, listening intently.

"Someone is coming," Zephyr stepped backward. "I do not like this."

Sunblossom bit her lip, growing more nervous by the second.

Footsteps in the trees came closer and closer to the two women. Sunblossom took another step back and gulped.

A furry head poked around a tree. "Ella," Zephyr sighed in relief. She slung her bow onto her back and walked over to her llama. "How did you get way out here?" She asked, rubbing Ella under her chin.

"Um, Zephyr," Sunblossom said, fear coloring her voice. Ella flattened her ears against her head.

Zephyr looked over the llama's neck and narrowed her eyes. "La-kaodai." Her voice was cold. She leaned into Ella and murmured, "Ella, tock."[20]

The llama trotted away, and Zephyr faced down her unwanted visitor. "What are you doing on my land, La-kaodai?" Zephyr demanded. Sunblossom hovered in the background, torn between wanting to go and find five or six warriors and not wanting to leave Zephyr alone.

"Your land?" La-kaodai chuckled. It was not a pleasant sound.

"I am Chieftess Zephyr of the Wind Tribe. You are standing on land claimed by the Wind Tribe, therefore I order you to remove yourself from our land."

---

20 Means "find it," "find him," "find my sandwich," etc. Considered a Eulgarian word by most, it was probably picked up by those Tribes that came in contact with the Settlers.

"I hate to be the one to tell you this, but you are all exiles," La-kaodai said mockingly, arms spread wide.

Her eyes flashed. "You will leave our land at once or be arrested for trespassing."

He wagged a finger at her. "You should be more polite, young lady."

She darted backward as he lunged forward, but he was faster than her and caught her around the waist. Sunblossom screamed, but Zephyr ignored her. "Release me this instant." *Help me, Protector.*

La-kaodai disregarded her demand, instead leaning forward slightly to pluck the bow off her back and toss it aside. "A little lady like you has no need of such a big bow, does she?" There was a hint of amusement in his eyes.

She huffed, annoyed at herself for forgetting about the weapon that could have put an end to the confrontation before it began. "Release me." She repeated.

"Why?" La-kaodai's grin turned to shock and then anger when she slapped him, the slap carrying the full force of a bitter, stinging winter wind.

He forcefully grabbed her hand. "How dare you strike me? You little—"

"How dare you touch me?" Zephyr interrupted him. She wrenched her hand from his grasp and put both hands on his chest to push herself away; but, once again, he was too fast for her. La-kaodai grabbed both her hands with one of his beefy ones, keeping her pinned against him with the other.

Zephyr threw her head back and yelled with all her strength, "Swift Arrow!"

Sunblossom finally found her bravery and, with a deep breath, scurried forward to pick up the discarded bow and crack La-kaodai over the head with it.

La-kaodai snarled and turned around, letting go of Zephyr. She jumped back and held her hand in the air. Her bow leapt out of Sunblossom's hand and into her own, cracking La-kaodai on the head again.

Zephyr drew back on her bow and sent a bolt of air slamming into La-kaodai's shoulder. Sunblossom hurried to stand behind Zephyr.

La-kaodai snarled and took a step towards the women. Zephyr reacted much more calmly than she felt, drawing her bow again.

"You don't want to do that."

Swift Arrow was standing in front of the Gathering Rackleen with several other warriors, discussing the upcoming hunt when he heard a humming sound and looked up.

"Ella?" Confusion filled his face. "Wait a minute, Fast Rain." Swift Arrow looked around, then back at the llama.

Ella turned, trotted a few feet, then turned and grunted. Swift Arrow frowned. "I think she wants us to follow her."

Fast Rain raised his eyebrows. "Really? Should we not just put her in a pen?"

"No, we should follow her," Bark said. "Zephyr is not here."

Swift Arrow nodded. "All of you come with me."

Fast Rain was the last warrior to take off after the llama. "And now we are following llamas." He murmured to himself.

They were halfway to the edge of the village when Zephyr's scream pierced the still air. Swift Arrow and the warriors with him broke into a run, as did several other warriors standing nearby.

They arrived at the edge of the clearing just in time to see Zephyr shoot La-kaodai. Even as the warriors drew their weapons, La-kaodai took a threatening step towards Zephyr and Sunblossom.

"You don't want to do that," Zephyr said calmly, but Swift Arrow heard a slight tremor in her voice.

"She is right." Swift Arrow said, coming up behind his wife. Fast Rain and Strong Oak hurried forward and grabbed La-kaodai's arms. He tried to shrug them off, but, upon realizing that he was surrounded, he gave up.

"Take him to the Holding Rackleen." Swift Arrow ordered.

"Come on, Sunblossom," Bark said, one arm around his wife as he hurried her away from the scene.

Swift Arrow turned Zephyr around and took her bow. Deliberately, he set it on the ground, looking into her eyes the whole time. "Are you alright?" He asked, his voice low and quiet.

In answer, Zephyr clung to him.

"It is alright now," he murmured, pulling her close. "I have you now." Zephyr trembled against him. "Did he hurt you?"

"No, not physically. I just — I was scared, Swift Arrow." He pulled her closer.

A warrior came running up. "I am sorry to interrupt, Chief, Chieftess, but La-kaodai is claiming to be a messenger."

Sounds of laughter and light conversation floated into the Chief's rackleen as the prisoner was led inside. Zephyr and Swift Arrow sat side by side on a bench in front of the fireplace, her hand locked in his.

La-kaodai stood in the middle of the room, eyes darting, taking in every detail of the unconventional rackleen. Fast Rain and Bark stood flanking the door, eyes trained on La-kaodai.

"What message do you bring us?" Swift Arrow's tone demanded that La-kaodai's curiosity leave the rackleen alone and focus on the matter at hand.

La-kaodai answered with his eyes fixed on the cubby holes. "Chief Mark-hai sends me to inform the exile, Zephyr, that he will still welcome her back if she will only wed the man he chooses."

"There are no exiles here." Swift Arrow said immediately, dismissively. That was enough to bring La-kaodai's eyes to the Chief and Chieftess.

"Then your answer is *no*, Zephyr?" La-kaodai asked.

"You will not address the Chieftess of the Wind Tribe in such a manner." Swift Arrow interjected coldly. "You came onto *our* land, attacked *our* Chieftess, brought a worthless message, and now you have the audacity to speak so flippantly to a Chieftess?"

La-kaodai simply stood there and silently seethed.

"You have come to us as a messenger; therefore, two of my warriors will escort you to the edge of Wind Tribe land. Your weapons will be returned to you there."

"This is the hospitality you give messengers?" La-kaodai asked angrily.

"We do not show hospitality to those who attack us, so you will leave immediately. And know this, La-kaodai. Should you ever return, you will face punishment for attacking Chieftess Zephyr."

La-kaodai's fury was evident on his face, but he was wise enough to not allow it to rule him. Fast Rain spoke impassively. "We will *escort* you now."

La-kaodai's head snapped around in surprise. There was no pity in his brother's voice, not that he expected any. No, it was the lack of anger that surprised him.

Fast Rain stood still under his scrutiny for a moment before motioning to the door.

"'Well?" Chief Mark-hai leaned forward eagerly.

"Her husband refused your terms." La-kaodai gave his carefully crafted response. "He also stole your llama."

"Husband? Whom did she marry?" The Chief raised his eyebrows."

"Swift Arrow. He calls himself 'Chief of the Wind Tribe.'"

Chief Mark-hai leaned back. "She married Swift Arrow." He scoffed. "What did I expect to happen? We should let them come home now."

La-kaodai winced. "Perhaps you should listen to the rest of my account first?"

The Chief nodded his consent, and La-kaodai gave his convoluted account, so strange that no one who had participated in the attack would have recognized it.

He described the Wind Tribeswarriors as thieves who took his weapons as soon as he hailed them. He spoke of men and women who jeered at him and mocked the Tribe, and of being kept overnight in a small rackleen with no food. He added a detailed account of his own efforts to be polite and reconcile to Swift Arrow. "And they stole your llama." He ended.

Disbelief filled Chief Mark-hai's face. "Is this who they have become?"

La-kaodai nodded sorrowfully. "It seems so."

"Swift Arrow never seemed a cruel sort."

"Or a thief," La-kaodai said quickly. "He stole your llama."

Chief mark-hai went on as if he hadn't heard. "I have to save her. I cannot leave my daughter alone with a cruel man."

"He is also a thief. He stole your llama." La-kaodai reminded him.

"Oh, La-kaodai, leave the llama alone!" The Chief exclaimed. "Let them have it! I have bigger things to worry about. Now leave me alone, let me think."

La-kaodai bowed, but before he could leave, Running Eagle broke into the rackleen. "Three messengers from the Clan requesting to see you, Chief." Worry was etched on his face.

La-kaodai and the Chief exchanged looks. The number of messengers sent between Tribes and Clans mattered a great deal. One messenger was good news, two meant help was needed, three meant war.

All thoughts about Zephyr and Swift Arrow would have to be set aside for the time being. War was coming.

CHAPTER TWELVE

The warriors of the Wind Tribe had become the best warriors in The Continent. Already well trained before their exiles, under the tutelage of Swift Arrow and Bark they had blossomed into true warriors. No one else in the entirety of the Southern Continent could take down a gazelle from the distance of one yonka away while balancing on a high tree branch.

Zephyr and Sunblossom were standing in the shade of a large yna tree, watching the men run through a practice battle. One group was posted in the treetops, armed with "arrows" that were nothing more than shafts of wood padded with leather. A second group attempted to storm and take the trees, also armed with the "arrows" and long wooden poles, and all the warriors wore thick padded leather armor to help stave off the blows.

The watching women heard footsteps running up behind them, and Azal called out, "Chieftess!"

Zephyr and Sunblossom turned and smiled at the young girl who was often found hanging around the Healer's rackleen. "Peace be on you, Azal," Zephyr said.

"Peace be on you, Chieftess." The ten-year-old dropped a breathless curtsy. "Healer Cornflower sent me. She needs you right away."

Zephyr looked at Sunblossom and frowned. "I wonder what could be wrong?"

"Go on ahead with Azal. I will go find Swift Arrow and tell him where you are." Ever since La-kaodai's attack, Swift Arrow had increased the number of scouts and had been keeping his wife closer.

Zephyr nodded. "Thank you. Let us be going, Azal."

Azal led the way to the Healer's rackleen, but Cornflower blocked the way inside when they reached it.

"I think you should go help your mother now, Azal," Cornflower said firmly. Azal's eyebrows met in a frown, but she turned and retraced her steps. "Come in, Chieftess."

Zephyr entered the dim rackleen. Cornflower had covered most of the windows, leaving one uncovered over the workbench so that she could see. Strong Oak stood beside the worktable, arms crossed, looking at the form lying on a bed on the other side of the room.

A second healer crouched beside the prone form, and, as Zephyr approached, she recognized the warrior as her former guard from the Tribe. "Running Eagle?" She turned. "What happened?"

Cornflower sighed and moved to the workbench. "It seems that the Clan has attacked the Tribe again."

Zephyr raised her eyebrows. Such news was hardly surprising. The Clan was the largest Clan in the Southern Continent, and larger than any Tribe, and it and the Tribe had been rivals for years. The Clan had often attacked Zephyr's people in the years now past.

"But this time is different. It seems that the Clan had decided that it really wants the Tribe this time, and Clanswarriors outnumber Tribeswarriors two to one."

Now Zephyr frowned. Yes, the Tribe and Clan had been enemies for years, but the Clan had never bothered to attack with more warriors than the Tribe had. It was almost as if fighting the Tribe was a rite of passage for young Clanswarriors.

"What does this have to do with Running Eagle?" Zephyr asked.

"Chief Mark-hai realized that the Clan means business this time, so he sent two warriors to request help from the River Clans. On the way, however, Running Eagle and his companion were attacked by a group of Clanswarriors. Our scouts happened upon the fray and stopped it before Running Eagle was killed."

Cornflower's eyes dropped to the bed. "The other warrior did not make it."

Zephyr sucked in a breath. "Will he be alright?" She asked, motioning to the injured warrior.

"Yes, but it will be some weeks before he is able to return home."

"Praise the Protector that his wounds are not life-threatening," Zephyr said reverently.

"Yet," Cornflower said. "We shall have to watch him carefully and make sure that infection does not set in."

Zephyr laid her hand on her friend's shoulder. "I trust you, Cornflower," she said in a low tone, "and I trust the healers that you have trained."

Cornflower smiled back wanly. Zephyr rested her hand on Cornflower's shoulder a moment longer before turning to speak to the others. Running Eagle was asleep, so after talking to Strong Oak and the other healer, she slipped out of the rackleen.

Strong Oak followed her out into the bright sunlight, where Zephyr stood for several seconds, taking deep breaths and thinking.

"Is everything alright, Zephyr?" Swift Arrow asked, coming up the path, Bark on his heels.

"No," She slipped her arms around her husband's waist and stood there for a moment.

"What has happened now?" There was a touch of something in his voice that Zephyr couldn't identify. Fear? Concern?

"I need to speak to youand the head warriors," Zephyr said. "It is a longer tale, and I would much prefer to only tell it once."

It was not long before all the head warriors were gathered in the Chief's rackleen, especially as they had only needed to find Fast Rain.

Zephyr quietly explained what had transpired and then sat silently, her hand intertwined in Swift Arrow's. "It is a breach of Continental law to attack messengers." Swift Arrow said decisively.

"Can we allow such an attack to go unpunished?" Zephyr asked fervently, her passion leaving no room to doubt where she stood on the issue.

"What a horrible time for such an attack." Fast Rain said. "If the Tribe is busy fending off the Clan's attacks, how can they go on their Great Hunt and lay in enough food stores for the winter months?"

"They cannot," Bark agreed, "but the Clan has enough warriors to keep two or three small Tribes busy and still hunt plenty of food."

"Perhaps that is their plan." Fast Rain said. "Perhaps they want to force the Tribe to rely on them for food."

"That would explain why they brought more warriors than the Tribe could defeat, but not enough to overwhelm the village." Swift Arrow said. "Are the warriors trained to be able to go into battle for another Tribe, Bark?"

Bark shrugged. "I believe so, but such a thing is never certain. The question we need to be asking is, I think, can we let the Clan destroy the Tribe?"

Fast Rain nodded. "Even though they banished us, I do not think that we can, in good conscience, allow them to be destroyed. It would not be right."

"I do agree with you, Fast Rain, but do we have other options that will not endanger our people?" Swift Arrow asked.

The warriors were silent, each considering this Chief's request. "No, I do not think so." Bark finally said slowly. "The only other option I can think of would be to send messengers of our own to the River Clans."

"And that would be useless since the River Clans do not recognize us." Fast Rain said. "We could, I suppose, send messengers to the Clan, but they ignored us during the Confederation, so I do not know where we stand with them."

"I find that I agree with you." Swift Arrow sent a smile in Zephyr's direction. "What say you, Strong Oak?"

Strong Oak looked directly at Chieftess Zephyr while he spoke. "This is right."

Chief Mark-hai was in conference with his warriors, and it was not going smoothly. Unlike the meeting of head warriors at the Wind Tribe, opinions flew around the room like sparrowbats, and often they were shared in loud voices.

The Chief ran his hand wearily over his face and tried to pick out just one voice from the cacophony. Some favored retreating and abandoning the village. Others said that was folly, with winter approaching. Some favored suing for peace, and others for holding out until the River Clans arrived.

Privately, Chief Mark-hai wondered why the Clan had not sent the warriors needed to defeat his men entirely, but he had no hope of making his voice heard.

While attempting to not repeat his father's mistakes and listen to all voices of council, Chief Mark-hai had somehow ended up with an over-large group of head warriors who spoke whatever they wished, whenever they wished; so the Chief but rarely consulted all of them.

La-kaodai's voice was the loudest, and the only one that could be clearly heard by those who were not speaking. "We must hold our ground here." He proclaimed. "To abandon our homes is to declare that the warriors of the Tribe are cowards."

Chief Mark-hai suddenly rose and peered over the heads of his warriors. One by one, voices quieted as heads swiveled around to look at the boy who had burst into the rackleen.

La-kaodai was the last to stop speaking and the only one to react when he finally saw the boy. "This is a closed meeting!" He spat.

The boy ignored him. "You've gotta come see this, Chief." He said excitedly.

"'You must,'" someone corrected automatically as Chief Mark-hai began leading the way out of the rack-leen. What they saw in the middle of the village stopped them in their tracks. A compact body of men stood there, fully armed with bow and arrow, spear and kameiz.

The Tribe's most notorious exiles brazenly led the group: Swift Arrow, Zephyr, and Bark. They looked utterly unafraid, even though they were breaking Tribal law, and deserved to die in the eyes of those they came to save.

When they saw Chief Mark-hai, both Zephyr and Swift Arrow stepped forward and bowed their heads. "Your messengers were attacked by the Clan, and my scouts found them." Swift Arrow said. "We believe that the Clan intends to force you to rely on it for food this winter, and so we have brought you both provisions and our best warriors to help you fight off the attackers."

Several mouths gaped open at Swift Arrow's speech. Chief Mark-hai blinked. "Why?"

"As the first Tribe to learn that messengers were attacked, it is our duty to punish that offense. If you will not allow us to assist you, then we will attack the Clan from a different position." Swift Arrow said calmly.

The Chief's eyes swung to Zephyr. She sent a glance towards Swift Arrow with something like admiration filling her eyes.

La-kaodai was the first to regain his composure. "They cannot be trusted. They are exiles and should be killed where they stand." He hissed in Chief Mark-hai's ear, loud enough for all to hear.

A bolt of air whizzed between the two men. They turned to see Zephyr holding her bow. "Now that we have your attention again, esteemed warrior," she said calmly, without a trace of sarcasm. "We did not come to be killed. If you do not want our help, then we will leave and trouble you no more."

Chief Mark-hai studied the Wind Tribeswarriors coolly for a moment. "I am willing to set our differences aside for a short time, if you can, indeed, help us."

"I firmly believe that each of these men is more than a match for any Clan warrior." Swift Arrow said. "We will take a defensive position in the trees to the north while you cut them off from behind or perhaps attack from the side."

Chief Mark-hai nodded. "I will send a boy to inform you when we leave."

Zephyr, Swift Arrow, and Bark bowed their heads once more and led the Wind Tribeswarriors off towards the trees. As the warriors walked past, La-kaodai grumbled loudly, "I still do not think we can trust them."

"What choice do we have?" Chief Mark-hai asked. "Sometimes, to survive, one must do unpleasant things. Besides," he added in a much lower tone. "Perhaps this is how we save Zephyr."

The afternoon came quietly to a golden close with no movement on the part of the Clan forces. The Wind Tribe took full advantage of the time, creating solid, defensible positions in the trees, adding to the underbrush, and retrieving more arrows from their village.

Cornflower arrived late in the afternoon with a few helpers and plenty of medical supplies.

"How is Running Eagle?" Zephyr asked as she helped her friend organize and lay out her supplies.

"'Better. I left Azal's mother in charge of him. Methinks that by the time I return, he will have fattened up on Mahli's good gazelle stew!"

A shout from below interrupted their conversation. Zephyr peeped cautiously over the edge of the large branch upon which the girls were working on. "Who is it?" She called.

"Chief Mark-hai," came the return shout.

"I am going down," Zephyr said to Cornflower before swinging down on a vine. When Chief Mark-hai came into view, Zephyr was waiting for him.

He tilted his head back and surveyed the treetops. "When Swift Arrow said 'in the trees,' he really meant *in* the trees, did he not?"

"Yes, the Chief always means what he says." There was a double-edged, gentle rebuke in her words.

"May I come up?" He asked, motioning upwards.

Zephyr regarded her father for a moment. "Follow me." She turned and led the way around a few trees to the spot where a rope ladder had been hung. "You first."

She waited for Chief Mark-hai to start up the ladder before shimmying up after him. Chief Mark-hai navigated the ladder with minimal problems, but once aloft, he promptly discarded the notion of walking around as easily as his daughter did and leaned against a tree trunk.

"It looks as though you are preparing for a siege." He noted, looking around.

"Chief Swift Arrow and Bark wished to use the time to prepare thoroughly."

Before Chief Mark-hai could reply, a warrior handed Zephyr her bow. "I finished restringing it, Chieftess."

Zephyr turned slightly and reached out to take the bow, one hand resting lightly on an overhead branch to balance herself. "Thank you, Strong Oak." She smiled.

Strong Oak turned to face Zephyr and put his hands on the branch to pull himself up. Just before he hoisted himself up, he whispered, "The Chief sent me."

Zephyr smiled back at the head warrior.

"Are you happy, Zephyr?" Chief Mark-hai asked earnestly.

Zephyr fingered her bow as she thought about her answer. "Happiness is so fleeting. That is the trouble with it. Life is harder at the Wind Tribe village than it is here. Everything that I took for granted here, we are building from the ground up. That is not to say that we go without food or shelter; I am speaking of things like ovens that don't smoke or Prokaryotan washers." She laughed a little.

"I am content, and I am joyful. I have everything I need and more." A peaceful smile filled her face.

"More?" Chief Mark-hai asked softly.

"I am married to the man I love, I am surrounded by my friends, and I have more freedom than I ever had here."

Her bluntness surprised him a little. "Were you unhappy before your exile?"

"No, no, please do not misunderstand me." She reached over and laid her hand on his arm. "I was content here, too. Now I have things that I did not have before, but I also do not have things that I used to have."

Chief Mark-hai was silent, thinking over all she had said. After La-kaodai returned from the Wind Tribe, Chief Mark-hai had been ready to storm the forest and save his daughter, now he was not so sure.

He was opening his mouth to ask about La-kaodai's account, which no longer made much sense, when a wordless shout came from above them, and Strong Oak pulled Zephyr out of the way of a hail of arrows that suddenly filled the air.

"It is La-kaodai," Strong Oak grunted, pulling an arrow from his hand and working to stem the flow of blood. "I saw him."

Zephyr took one look at Strong Oak and acted. Swinging her bow onto her back, she grabbed a vine and zipped to the ground in front of La-kaodai before the Tribeswarriors could reload their bows.

Snatching the arrow that La-kaodai was trying to fit to his bow, she snapped it in half across her knee. "This is how the Tribe treats her allies?" Zephyr cried. Her courage stunned most of the Tribeswarriors into inaction, but La-kaodai ground his jaw in anger.

"Where is Chief Mark-hai, Exile?" La-kaodai demanded. "When he came out to your camp, I followed, and saw you forcing him up a tree." He said angrily.

Sparks flashed from the Chieftess's eyes. "The Tribe has changed much from when I was last here, if its warriors cannot be respectful to their allies, nor allow their Chief to have a conversation with his daughter!"

"My apologies, Zephyr." Chief Mark-hai spoke from behind her. "We are all nervous from the attacks." Bark and Swift Arrow were by his side as he climbed from the trees.

Several replies to his comment sprang to Zephyr's mind, comments about respect for fellow Chieftains, or how nervousness was not La-kaodai's problem, but she held her tongue and stepped aside.

As soon as they reached the ground, Mark-hai walked over to La-kaodai and spoke in low tones to him. Swift Arrow stood next to Zephyr and put his arm around her.

"Are you alright?" He whispered in her ear.

"Mostly," Zephyr suddenly felt all the cares of the day weighing on her shoulders.

"Let us go back up to the trees." Swift Arrow spoke a few words to Bark before guiding Zephyr to a large and shady branch where some hammocks had been hung. They sat in one, facing the sunset.

"That was quite brave." Swift Arrow pulled Zephyr a little bit closer.

"I just did what needed to be done."

"That is just what a hero is. Someone who is in the right place, faithfully doing what she is supposed to do, at the right time."

Zephyr smiled sleepily. "I am glad you think I am brave." She murmured. It was not much longer before she fell asleep, cuddled beside her husband; but Swift Arrow stayed awake for a long time, watching as the stars came out and praising the Protector for the wife he'd been given.

CHAPTER THIRTEEN

The day dawned bright and fair, promising to be the soft sort of late autumn day that invited one to go for a long, quiet walk in the woods, with a picnic by a waterfall afterward.

Zephyr sat on a tree branch, nursing a cup of sparking tea[21] and thinking about the day's grim work.

"What are you thinking about in that pretty head of yours, Ze?" Swift Arrow asked, lowering himself to the branch and holding his own cup of tea.

"I wish that we did not have to go to war," Zephyr said regretfully.

"Me, too." Swift Arrow sighed. "Not a single warrior here wants to fight today — or any day for that matter." He rubbed her back with his free hand. "It is not too late for you to go back to the village."

Zephyr shook her head. "I want to be here. Silly as it sounds, I feel that I *must* be here. Besides, I do not wish to pull any of the warriors away from their duties."

---

21 Sparkling tea is a lemongrass tea allowed to brew overnight or for several days and made with sparkling water from the Golden Springs.

"Alright." Swift Arrow smiled. "Have I told you lately that you are wonderful?"

"Maybe." Zephyr drew out the word thoughtfully. "I cannot quite recall." She tilted her head as though thinking harder. "Perhaps you told me last night, or maybe you only said I was beautiful."

Swift Arrow pulled his hand back, looking offended. "Only beautiful? My exact wording was 'gorgeous.'"

"No, no," Zephyr said seriously, shaking her head. "I would have remembered that."

"Your memory is faulty," Swift Arrow said, setting his tea down.

Zephyr knew she was in trouble and started to rise but was saved from being tickled by the sudden appearance of Bark. "The Clan is on the move, Chief."

Swift Arrow stood and bent to help Zephyr to her feet. "This is not over." He whispered in her ear.

A smile flitted over her face. "I will win."

Swift Arrow snorted and handed her his cup. "Not likely."

When the first Clanswarriors carelessly entered the area defended by the Wind Tribeswarriors, not expecting resistance this far from the Tribe's village, the Wind Tribe was ready.

"Their scouts had no idea that we had arrived," Bark said grimly, watching the Clanswarriors hack their way through the thick underbrush. Most of the invaders had discarded their shields for the time being, the better to carve a path through the forest.

"No one can find Wind Tribeswarriors if they do not want to be found." Strong Oak replied. It was a statement of fact, not one of pride. "Shall I give the order to shoot now?"

Bark's answer was a terse nod.

"Chose your targets!" Strong Oak called. "Just like we practiced, warriors!"

The leading Clanswarriors looked up and around, searching for the source of the command, since it certainly had not come from their ranks.

"Ready, fire!" A carefully aimed volley of arrows spread chaos through the Clan racks. Clanswarriors rushed to find cover, tripping through the thick underbrush and on logs that the Wind Tribe had hidden the day before.

More and more Clanswarriors poured into the forest, whilst some climbed up trees trying to grapple with the defenders on equal ground.

The Wind Tribeswarriors were like squirrels, leaping from branch to branch, shooting arrows mid-stride, even drawing kameizs and engaging in sword fights high in the boughs.

Never had the Clanswarriors encountered such foes, defenders who had the advantage in every way.

Soon after the battle began, a Tribe boy clambered up the tree from which Swift Arrow was directing his warriors.

"Our warriors just left the village. They will attack the Clan from behind." The boy reported, eyes wide as he scanned the treetops.

Zephyr was sitting on a high branch, safely ensconced behind a triple screen of branches. She listened with only half an ear, knowing that Swift Arrow would handle it.

Her eyes narrowed. Something was wrong.

Before she could put her finger on what it was, or even begin to dissect *why* she knew instinctively that something was wrong, a warrior came running along the branches, shouting, "Chief! Chief! The wind is blowing our arrows off course!"

A strong wind, almost a gale, had begun blowing straight across the field of battle. The wind reached from above the treetops all the way to the ground, roaring with a seemingly unstoppable force, throwing men off balance, and tossing the Wind Tribe's arrows off mark.

The battle had become a shooting match between the Wind Tribe and Clan for the most part. The Clanswarriors were not as precise, but they had modern crossbows that were more powerful than the Wind Tribe's accurate, but older, bows. All the accuracy in the world would do them no good if their arrows could not even penetrate the West Wind.

Zephyr, Swift Arrow, and Fast Rain all came to this conclusion in a matter of seconds, "We will handle it." Swift Arrow said tightly, as Zephyr moved from her perch, and Fast Rain picked up a bow and quiver.

"Do you know where you are going?" Swift Arrow asked as the threesome moved off.

"Yes," Zephyr replied, leading the way.

Before long, they had reached a broad, west-facing branch. Swift Arrow and Fast Rain leaned against two tree trunks and drew their bows. Zephyr turned into the wind and stood, unprotected and seemingly unbothered by the gale. She took a deep breath and threw up her hands.

Instantly, silence replaced the roar of the wind.

Zephyr, Chieftess of the Wind Tribe, was holding back the West Wind. It was an event that would go down in history. A shout went up from the Wind Tribe all along the battle line, and they began beating back the enemy once again.

Zephyr's arms quickly began to tremble. Swift Arrow glanced over his shoulder at her and came to a quick decision. "Go find Bark and Strong Oak." He ordered Fast Rain, but then Zephyr gasped and dropped her arms.

The West Wind came howling back in full force. Swift Arrow dropped his bow and hurried over to her.

"Never mind Bark and Strong Oak!" He shouted. "Come here, quickly."

Zephyr raised her hands again and stumbled backward. Swift Arrow and Fast Rain reached her, each supporting her from opposite sides. Even with their help, though, Zephyr's whole body was trembling with the effort. Every fiber of her being strained towards the task.

The knowledge of the many men and families depending on her beat a rhythm in her skull. The West Wind pushed against her, testing her limits and endurance. Every breath she drew was only drawn so that she could keep going for another few seconds.

Her whole world had shrunk down to this branch, to this moment in time, to this task of keeping the West Wind in line. It took two hours for the Tribe to move into position, and it felt like years. Zephyr could only focus on the very act of focusing to make it through to the end.

Slowly, she became aware that Swift Arrow was speaking to her. "You did it, Zephyr. We won. You can stop now."

Zephyr lowered her hands, and the wind came bounding back through the trees with an angry growl. Swift Arrow caught her as she sagged against him, nearly toppling over, himself, with the force of the West Wind.

Swift Arrow moved to the lee side of the trunk and lowered her down. "A hero again, Ze. You saved both Tribes." He said gently.

Zephyr smiled, her exhaustion apparent in every move she made. "I will appreciate that comment more when I am not so tired."

"Go ahead and take a nap then. I am taking you home as soon as I can manage it." Swift Arrow smiled tenderly when Zephyr went limp before he could even finish speaking.

Swift Arrow gently gathered up his wife and turned back to Fast Rain. Strong Oak had joined the two warriors, going in search of his Chief and Chieftess as soon as the fighting ceased. "Let us head back to headquarters and find Bark."

"Zephyr!" Cornflower exclaimed in a hushed whisper when Swift Arrow carried Zephyr onto the healery branch.

"She is fine, just worn-out." Swift Arrow laid her in a hammock. "I am going to take her home as soon as possible, but I have a few things to do first. Will you keep an eye on her?"

"Of course, Chief. I will make sure no one panics." Cornflower said, reading between the lines of his request.

"Thank you." Swift Arrow said gratefully. He moved off the branch to speak to his head warriors.

"Wounded?"

"Twenty-five, mostly caused by the West Wind," Bark said.

"Casualties?"

"Two," Strong Oak said soberly.

"Who?" Swift Arrow asked quietly.

"Running Bear and Brilliant Comet."

Swift Arrow sighed. "It is a high price to pay for victory. I will let their families know once I return to the village."

"It would have been higher if not for Chieftess Zephyr." Fast Rain said quietly.

"Zephyr?" Bark asked, confusion filling in his face.

"She stopped the West Wind." Swift Arrow explained.

Understanding dawned on Bark's face. "Is she alright?"

"Exhausted. I am going to take her home as soon as possible."

"Go on ahead," Bark sighed. "There is nothing here that Strong Oak, Fast Rain, and I cannot handle."

"Take the healers and injured warriors with you." Fast Rain added.

Swift Arrow nodded gratefully. "Thank you, I will do just as you suggest."

CHAPTER FOURTEEN

"How did she look?" La-kaodai's voice caused Crab Apple to turn from the small pot of cocoa oatmeal that she was stirring and look at her husband.

"How did who seem?" She asked in her gentle, lilting voice.

La-kaodai rolled his eyes. "Do not play games with me, wife. Think!"

Crab Apple mentally recoiled from his harsh tone. Swiftly, she ran over everyone she had spoken to the day before. She could think of no one her husband would be asking about. *Unless...*

"Do you mean Chieftess Zephyr?" She asked carefully.

"Of course, I mean Zephyr!" He snapped. "I know that you talked to the *Chieftess* yesterday."

Crab Apple took a deep breath and turned back to the pot before it burned. It was easier to speak to La-kaodai when she wasn't looking at him. She also wished that her mother-in-law was home. *Everything* was better then.

"I spoke to Swift Arrow. Zephyr was asleep." She forwent the titles this time. If Last Spring had been there, she would not have bothered.

La-kaodai narrowed his eyes as he watched his wife's movements. This was not what had been reported to him. "What was she doing asleep in the middle of a battle? And why did you come out to the trees after I expressly forbade you from doing so?" He was baiting her, mocking her, and demanding that she defend herself.

Patience and gentleness, she reminded herself silently. "Swift Arrow and Zephyr were here, in the village, along with the healers and wounded. It was after the battle. I had gone out to get more water and saw them. I believe Swift Arrow said he was taking Zephyr home because she was exhausted from keeping back the West Wind."

She was stirring the oatmeal vigorously, trying to keep back her emotions. In their short days of marriage, Crab Apple had already learned that with La-kaodai, mocking could quickly turn to anger, and his anger was not to be trifled with. Also, without Last Spring to serve as a barrier between her son and his wife, Crab Apple had to watch her words a bit more carefully.

"This will not do at all," La-kaodai spoke to himself, and Crab Apple wisely remained silent, even as she wondered how he planned to resolve this bump in the road. She knew that he schemed to become Chief one day.

She carried the pot to the table and dished two bowls. Sitting down, she silently thanked the Protector for His provision.

"You are to speak of our conversation to no one," La-kaodai said suddenly, sharply, "and do not tell anyone else what Swift Arrow said. Do you understand?"

Crab Apple nodded, but she bit the inside of her lip. Her heart cried out that there had been other women present. *I shall simply have to beg them not to spread the tale and pray that it has not gone far.* She decided.

A small smile curved her lips upwards. Last Spring would have come right out and informed La-kaodai that his request was impossible since other women knew of Swift Arrow's visit.

"It is a bit early in the season for the West Wind to be blowing, do you not think so?" La-kaodai said conversationally after a space of quiet.

Crab Apple smiled, grateful that this was the direction his mood had gone, albeit surprised at the same time. "Indeed. I was quite surprised."

"I wonder if we could use that to our advantage." La-kaodai mused. Crab Apple groaned inwardly. "Since our warriors were not in the area when the gale began, perhaps we can convince others that it never happened. Yes, this could work."

Crab Apple swallowed and scrambled for a diplomatic answer. Last Spring was good at this. "I am sure you know the best means to your ends." She settled for, though she had a nagging feeling that she could have done better.

La-kaodai accepted it. He was silent until Crab Apple began gathering the dishes into a basin so that she could take them down to the river and wash them.

"Where is my mother?" He demanded.

Crab Apple's heart sank. Her mother-in-law had left three days past. "Mammy is visiting her sister."

"She should have at least informed me." He said, affronted.

"She asked your permission." Crab Apple said quietly.

"Oh," it was not often that she saw her husband groping for words, and a small part of her enjoyed it; but she quickly quashed such uncharitable feelings.

"I will be out most of the day. Do not expect me for supper. I will be invited to eat with the Chief."

"Only you?" Crab Apple asked, both cautious and hopeful. She'd been hoping for a glimpse of the rackleen where Zephyr had lived for so long. Zephyr was famed throughout the Tribe as having been an excellent homekeeper.

"Yes, just me," La-kaodai said evenly, rising from the table. "You have not earned that privilege yet."

Crab Apple bowed her head in submission. La-kaodai's word was law.

Zephyr stretched, enjoying the sunshine coming in through the rackleen window. Swift Arrow's head poked through the curtains that hung in front of the sleeping area.

"You awake?"

Zephyr smiled in answer and pulled herself up to a sitting position, the blanket pooling around her. "Come in." She invited.

"How did you sleep?" Swift Arrow sat on the edge of the bed.

"Wonderfully." Zephyr smiled again. "Is it horribly late?"

"Not at all. We only finished breakfast an hour ago."

"An hour ago!" Zephyr tossed the covers back and bolted out of bed. Swift Arrow laughed at her haste.

"Sunblossom and Cornflower are taking over your duties for the day."

Zephyr stopped with her shirt halfway over her head. "Why?"

"You did more than a full day's work yesterday, and you work hard every other day. The whole Wind Tribe agrees that you deserve a day off."

"Did you take a vote?" Zephyr asked, amused, pulling her shirt on.

"Yes, I did, over breakfast." Swift Arrow said, hiding his smile.

"A day off would be nice," Zephyr admitted. She continued dressing, but without her earlier haste. "Who is leading the kitchen staff[22] today?"

"Sunblossom. She made Crown of Throns porridge[23] for breakfast."

"With candied citrus?" Zephyr asked hopefully, pulling her hair up.

"Of course." Swift Arrow smiled.

Zephyr settled a cluster of maple leaves in her bun and then turned to her husband. "How do I look?"

"Gorgeous."

Zephyr sat down on the bed next to him and pressed a kiss to his cheek. "I know that you did not actually vote." She whispered in his ear.

"Do you now?" Swift Arrow looked down at her, amusement filling his face. He kissed her.

Zephyr smiled into her husband's eyes. "I love you." She murmured.

"I love you more." He whispered, bending to kiss her again.

"I believe it." She said just before his lips touched hers.

---

22 Translated from a very complicated word *(Kgbjrkeoowkay)* that is impossible to pronounce for all but the extremely annoying. Most likely means *staff*, could mean *nose*.

23 Cooking experts say that this dish is yummier than it sounds. All thorns and soggy petals are removed after cooking.

Zephyr and Swift Arrow walked hand in hand to the large, central Gathering Rackleen where, unlike the Tribe, *all* meals were eaten in common.

"Have you seen Running Eagle this morning?" Zephyr asked.

"Yes, he joined us for breakfast. If I understood him correctly, the healers told him that he could return home, but warned him to be careful for a few days, so he left shortly thereafter." He nodded to a group of warriors who passed them. "I believe Cornflower was sad to bid him safe journeys."

"Sometimes," Zephyr remarked quietly. "You are entirely too perceptive."

Swift Arrow stopped. "What does that mean?"

"Cornflower knows that she has no business falling in love with a man she hardly knows and from the Tribe no less. Since it seems that it is not the Protector's will that they marry, she is working hard to master her feelings. The poor girl hardly wants her struggle known all over the Tribe!"

"She told you that?" Swift Arrow blinked in surprise.

A smile tugged at the corners of Zephyr's mouth, and she shook her head. "She did not have to. I am a woman, too, and her friend. But you, of course, being a man, did not think of such things."

"No, I had not." He shook his head ruefully. "So, I should not say anything to her?"

Zephyr's eyes widened in horror. "No, do not do that! Perhaps tell her you are praying for her in a general way. She will figure it out."

"Very well, I shall be the very model of discretion." Zephyr breathed out a sigh of relief as they headed toward the Gathering Rackleen. Crisis averted.

"Chief Mark-hai? May I have a private audience with you?" The humble face that La-kaodai presented to his Chief was a world away from the one he had shown his wife and warriors in the past few hours.

"Of course," Chief Mark-hai smiled at his favorite warrior and heir and led the way into the rackleen. La-kaodai lingered a moment to ensure that the young man whom Mark-hai had been talking to didn't hang around to eavesdrop.

"I am afraid that we have a traitor in our midst," La-kaodai said solemnly.

"Do you have proof?" Mark-hai asked.

La-kaodai went on as if he had not heard. "Well, I suppose 'in our midst' is not entirely accurate since Running Eagle still has not returned."

"Running Eagle?" Mark-hai was surprised. "This is indeed a serious matter. How do you know that he is a traitor?"

"The facts speak for themselves. Running Eagle has betrayed us."

Mark-hai cocked an eyebrow, but La-kaodai went on smoothly before the Chief could realize what was wrong with that statement.

"Zephyr sent messengers to the Clan airing her grievances and begging them to attack us. The Clan, always eager to add more land to their holdings, complied. Zephyr had already paid Running Eagle off to inform her once we were in dire straits. I am not exactly sure what happened next, whether Running Eagle killed his compatriot or if they were indeed attacked.

"Either way, one messenger dies, conveniently leaving Running Eagle alive to tell Zephyr how we will be annihilated without help. The 'Wind Tribe' races to our rescue, and now we will accept them back with open arms, allowing Zephyr and Swift Arrow to seize control of the Tribe."

Mark-hai hesitated. He had indeed entertained ideas of undoing the banishment of Zephyr and her friends after the conversation that they had, had the day before. Was she really capable of such deceit?

"I did not get that sense when I spoke to Zephyr."

La-kaodai sighed. "My brother came to me yesterday morn. He said that exile has changed Zephyr for the worst, now that she can no longer be Chieftess of the Tribe."

More hesitation.

Chieftess Lasha had trusted La-kaodai. Why else would she have said his name right before she died? *I can trust La-kaodai also…right?*

"What about the West Wind?" He finally asked.

"It could have come early, I suppose, but I would not be surprised to learn that the whole thing was staged in order to make her seem better in your eyes. It *is* rather early in the season for the West Wind." La-kaodai could hardly contain his smirk. This was going better than he had hoped.

It never once occurred to the Chief to question the first of La-kaodai's "facts." His trust was too great. "Could she really have changed so much?" He murmured.

"I have heard stories of people who have gone completely mad after being exiled," La-kaodai said regretfully. "If you would like, Sire," he spoke slowly now, as if the thought had just occurred to him. "I can deal with Running Eagle."

Mark-hai nodded slowly. "Yes, yes, bless you, La-kaodai. What would I ever have done without you?"

La-kaodai smiled. "You will never have to find out, Chief." He stopped just short of rubbing his hands together as he left the rackleen to put the next phase of his plan into action. This was rather fun.

CHAPTER FIFTEEN

Through breakfast was over, and dinner some hours away, the Gathering Rackleen was a hive of activity when the Chief and Chieftess walked in.

The children were finishing the first part of their school day, during which they studied reading, writing, counting, and history in one corner of the vast building. Cornflower and the other healers were sorting dried herbs at one long table. Other groups were busy making and mending birch bark paper, soap, clothing, fur rugs, and weaponry.

As Zephyr and Swift Arrow walked to the kitchen entrance at the very back of the rackleen, greetings were called to them from across the hall like the cheerful chirping of quail-doves.

The kitchen, attached to the main rackleen by a short, covered walkway, was already in the throes of dinner preparations. Sunblossom was bent over a table skinning a trout and stopped for a moment to wave a fishy hand at her friends.

Mahli, Azal's mother, also on kitchen duty that day, stepped away from chopping root vegetables to show

Zephyr where the porridge was. Stepping gracefully around a large table where bakers shaped large loaves of bread every day, Mahli led Zephyr to a fireplace and reached around a large pot of rice to pluck a small, lidded pot from the back spit. Handing it to Zephyr, she yelled, "I will get the citrus and meet you by the door."

Zephyr nodded, not having much hope of being heard above the din and glad to get out of the way. It was a relief to her ears when she and Swift Arrow finally emerged into the quiet outdoors.

"It is rather loud in there if you walk into the middle of meal preparations. I never noticed it before." Zephyr said, running a hand over her ear.

Swift Arrow laughed and led her to a bench outside the Gathering Rackleen. "What are your plans for the day?" He asked after Zephyr had, had a chance to eat some food.

"Since I have been relieved of all official duties, I think I will sit in the sun and do some sewing and then practice with my bow later. You?" Zephyr took another bite.

"I am going to help the carpenters with repair work this morning. One of the rackleens is starting to sag. I need to plan the Great Hunt too."

The children marched by, laughing and singing an old song, as they headed to their tree-walking classes. As though they reminded her of something, Zephyr set the pot down and said, "Darling?"

"Hmm?" Swift Arrow had tipped his head back and was lazily watching a few clouds drift across the sky.

"Do you remember when you told me that you want lots of children?"

"Yes."

"Well, one is a start, at least."

Swift Arrow slowly looked down at his wife. He blinked. "Well, yes, one is generally considered—wait, Ze, are you—?"

Zephyr nodded happily. "I am with child, Arrow!"

He crushed her to his chest, then froze. "Yesterday—"

"I told Cornflower last night when she came to check on me. She thinks the baby is fine."

Swift Arrow let out a slow sigh of relief. "When?"

"Late summer." She grinned cheekily up at her husband.

Swift Arrow smiled down at her. "We are parents." He said in wonder. He jumped away from the bench suddenly. "I am going to tell Bark." He started away at a fast jog and called over his shoulder, "and Fast Rain!"

"Do not forget Strong Oak!" Zephyr called after him, laughing.

Swift Arrow turned around and ran backward. "Do not worry," he called. "I will make sure the whole country knows!"

She laughed long and hard over that one.

Zephyr grunted and shook her head. Her wind bolt had gone wide of the mark. After telling Swift Arrow her news, she had decided to skip sewing in favor of practice with her bow.

She released another bolt and smiled in satisfaction when she hit her target. She heard someone call her name and turned her head slightly. It was Swift Arrow, accompanied by Bark and Fast Rain, and they all looked much more sober than the last time she'd seen her husband.

"Do not tell me," she said lightly, releasing another bolt and hitting her target. "Sunblossom is pregnant also, and in your excitement, Swift Arrow and Bark talked over each other so that neither got to share his news properly."

She turned, expecting to see the warriors trying not to laugh, and seeing their somber faces, a feeling of dread settled over her heart. "What is it?"

"Running Eagle just returned. He met La-kaodai in the forest. La-kaodai said all sorts of things about traitors and the good of the Tribe that Running Eagle did not understand before La-kaodai told him that he was banished."

"Why would he do such a thing?" Zephyr exclaimed. "What had Running Eagle done wrong? I am convinced that La-kaodai just enjoys making people suffer."

"La-kaodai always has a reason for the suffering he inflicts." Fast Rain said darkly.

"It is worse than simply another banishment." Swift Arrow moved closer to Zephyr. "La-kaodai seemed to imply that war would come 'because of our treachery.' Running Eagle has not the faintest clue what he meant." He was observing his wife carefully and saw the exact moment she figured it out.

"Father has now seen what we have become," Zephyr said quietly. "He knows that I am married, and that he has no chance of getting me to marry La-kaodai. All that would make him ready to undo our banishment. La-kaodai knows this, so he must have found some way to convince my father that we were behind it all."

"The Clan's attack, you mean?" Bark asked.

Zephyr looked up at him. "Yes." She shook her head. "La-kaodai is quite persuasive, and Father trusts him."

"He wants to be Chief," Swift Arrow said, one arm around Zephyr, "so he has to keep us out of the picture."

"Hmm," Zephyr agreed.

"Well," Bark said briskly. "We cannot do anything about La-kaodai's deSires. All we can do is be prepared for war if it comes."

"It will come." Fast Rain spoke with conviction, and his eyes were filled with pain. "La-kaodai always gets his way, one way or another."

The Gathering Rackleen was full of people. Loud, talking, worried people. Swift Arrow, Zephyr, Bark, Strong Oak, and Fast Rain stood at the front of the room. Swift Arrow attempted to speak twice, but both times could not be heard above the tumult.

Zephyr bent down beside Betsy. "Speak, girl," she said. A resounding bark, amplified by Zephyr, cut through the clamor. Everyone quieted and turned towards the front.

"Thank you, Chieftess Zephyr and Betsy." Zephyr, now standing quietly with her hand on the wolfurnut's head, nodded at her husband. "I am sure that you have all heard the rumors by now, and knowing the truth will be of benefit to us all. The Tribe intends to wage war on us."

A fresh wave of murmuring broke out, but Zephyr waved her hand, causing Swift Arrow's voice to grow louder above the noise, requesting quiet and at least a semblance of calm.

With a grateful look at Zephyr, he continued. "This is the only thing that is certain; La-kaodai banished Running Eagle, and he will try to wage war on us. Chief Mark-hai may have put a stop to this, but we must prepare for war."

The room was quiet enough to hear a door-tack drop. "Our first order of business will be to go on the Great Hunt as planned. We know that the Tribe is not immediately ready to fight, and we must have food for the coming winter. Once we return, we will have only a short time to prepare the village for winter and the coming of war."

It is incredible how quickly the world can go from light and joy to darkness and war. The whole Wind Tribe rallied together just as their Chief had asked. Once the warriors returned from the hunt, everyone was acutely aware that time was running out. The blacksmiths turned out large quantities of arrowheads and spearheads, while the carpenters made shafts for arrows and spears.

The women assembled the weapons and sewed armor and shields. The few remaining weeks until winter arrived passed in feverish activity, for everyone knew that all of this work would be nigh impossible once the snows came. When the first snow came, the Wind Tribe was ready.

The Tribe, on the other hand, was not faring so well. La-kaodai had managed to hold the whole Tribe in limbo while he convinced Mark-hai that an active attack on the Wind Tribe was the only right thing to do. When the Great Hunt finally happened, far too late in the season, only half of the warriors were allowed to go, the rest staying behind to make weapons.

The women of the Tribe were not allowed to help as much as they were in the Wind Tribe, instead being relegated to cooking and cleaning. As if all these setbacks were not enough, the fields had not yielded crops as expected, due in part to the attacks of the Clan. It would be a hard winter for the entire Tribe.

"Gather close, children. I have a tale to tell." Zephyr smiled at the children sitting excitedly around the fire in the Gathering Rackleen, eyes riveted on the Chieftess's face.

"It all begins in Acaidia," Zephyr began, "so the histories say. Acaidia is an ancient city, the first center of Continental learning and arts, although now it is lost. It is said that the Protector Himself founded Acaidia, and that it sprung from the earth like a splendid garden, and that afterward He created men and women and placed them into Acaidia to work and keep it.

"Many years later, humankind founded a second city, called the First City, and many left Acaidia, believing that their work and way were better than the Protector's. The First City had many tall buildings, and it was indeed an achievement for mankind; but some remembered the shining city with regret, wishing that they had never left it.

"After the Great Rebellion, many returned to Acaidia as though seeking to regain what they had lost; however, a place alone is not holy unless made so by the Protector, and they could not find what they sought."

"What happened next?" Azal breathed.

"They left," Zephyr said simply. "At first in ones and twos, and then in huge groups. They founded Tribes and

Clans and often fought one another. At times, they would all band together; but then, invariably, they would splinter and be enemies again.

"There was one Chief, named Cibola, who united many of the Clans and Tribes together. Chief Cibola believed the old tales that there were still people living in Acadia, and he wanted to find it; so he gathered a group of warriors and went exploring."

"Did he find it?" A wide-eyed little boy asked.

Zephyr smiled. "No one knows. Cibola never returned, and the rescue parties sent after him could not find a single trace of him or his warriors. Some people believe that Cibola found Acaidia and still lives there today."

"Which, of course, cannot be true," Swift Arrow said, walking up and placing a hand on Zephyr's shoulder, "because no one can live for hundreds of years. But that is why Acaidia and its villages are now known as the lost cities of Cibola."

"No one has ever found the cities?" Azal asked, brow wrinkled.

"No," Zephyr shook her head. "Mayhap, they do not exist anymore."

"Now, run along and play, children." The Chief instructed. "I need to speak to the Chieftess."

"Is everything alright?" Zephyr asked once the children had run away, already pretending to be Cibola and his warriors.

"I do not know," Swift Arrow knelt by Zephyr's side. "Do you know why a dragon landed on the practice field or why his Rider is asking for you?"

Zephyr's eyes widened. "I have not the faintest clue."

"Well then, I suppose we should go ask." Swift Arrow stood and pulled Zephyr to her feet. Bundling up against the cold, the Chief and Chieftess made their way out to the practice field.

A sleek black dragon stood on the field, grooming itself, his breath coming out in puffs. The Dragon Rider leaned against a tree, closely watched by several warriors.

"This is Chieftess Zephyr." Swift Arrow said. The Rider reached into his messenger bag and pulled out a scroll.

"My lady," he said, offering the scroll.

Curious, Zephyr split the seal. She read it and burst out in laughter.

"Zephyr?" Swift Arrow asked, giving her a sidelong look.

"Everything is fine." She wiped tears from her eyes and addressed the Rider. "Come into the Gathering Rackleen and get warm while I write a reply to the Queen."

Zephyr started walking towards the Chief's rackleen, and Swift Arrow hurried to follow her. "The Queen of Eulgaria wrote you?"

"Yes," Zephyr said, trying not to laugh again. "She wished to offer her sympathies at the death of my husband and assure me that she and King will do anything in their power to assist me." She burst out in laughter again.

Swift Arrow raised his eyebrows. "Yes, it appears condolences are in order. When were you planning to tell me that I had died?"

That set Zephyr off on a fresh wave of merriment that lasted until they were almost at the rackleen. "It seems La-kaodai told the Elvish ambassador that he had personally killed you, right before La-kaodai punched the ambassador in the nose."

"It would have been more polite if La-kaodai had informed me *before* he went around telling ambassadors." Swift Arrow frowned.

Zephyr giggled. "Stop that. I need to write a reply to Queen Abihail."

"Well, seeing as I am dead, I am of no help around here, so I can go with the Rider and deliver your message by mouth if you prefer." He offered helpfully.

"Swift Arrow!" Zephyr said through her laughter. "If you are not going to behave, you can just go wait outside."

Swift Arrow held his hands up in surrender. "Fine, fine. I will behave now."

"This is the worst winter I have ever seen. The storms are still leaving behind deep snows."[24] Zephyr tossed another log into the fireplace and watched the flames momentarily climb higher.

"The elders agree with you. Soft Clouds told me the other day that her mother will not even leave the rackleen anymore. She claims the snow depresses her." Sunblossom said.

"The cold is what I hate." Cornflower shivered. "You have your own personal furnace." She added with a grin in Zephyr's direction.

Zephyr rolled her eyes, but she was smiling. "Baby is hardly big enough to keep me warm." She was only three months pregnant.

The twang of bowstrings rang out through the sharp air from the direction of the woods. "There they go again." Zephyr shook her head.

"I cannot understand why the Tribe persists. They have not won a single battle. Why do not the warriors simply refuse to fight anymore?" Cornflower sounded frustrated.

---

24 In modern meteorologic terms, this sentence might be translated to "the average daily snowfall is three feet, but the weather is expected to turn warmer later this week."

"It is La-kaodai," Sunblossom said, simply, yet wisely. "He wants revenge. He has tried to start a war,[25] and he will not give up until he has beaten us or Chief Markhai finally decides that La-kaodai is finished."

"When it comes to *why* Father listens to La-kaodai, your guess is as good as mine." Zephyr sighed.

"I still do not understand why the warriors do not simply refuse to fight." Cornflower's brow furrowed.

"Fear is a powerful force," Zephyr said quietly. "They do not know what we truly are. Do you remember that family our scouts stumbled upon last week?"

Cornflower nodded. "The husband was a warrior who had been banished, and he said that if he had known what we were, his whole family would have joined us much sooner."

Swift Arrow and Bark walked into the rackleen. Sunblossom arched her eyebrows. "Finished already?"

"It started to snow." Swift Arrow said by way of answer, planting a kiss on Zephyr's head.

"I do not think La-kaodai was pleased," Bark said wryly. "There was a lot of yelling."

Zephyr shook her head. "He is never going to give up. You were right, Sunblossom." She snuggled close to

---

25 "A war is a series of at least three pitched battles that were not accidents. Therefore, when one group of warriors are shooting at another group of warriors who are rather clumsily trying to find the first group, this is not a war." —from the 0098 *Debster's Dictionary, abridged version.*

Swift Arrow. "Warmer now?" She asked, tilting her head up.

"Much," he whispered, pressing a kiss to her lips. Swift Arrow glanced over at Sunblossom and Bark, who had their heads close together. "What are you two whispering about?"

Sunblossom blushed and glanced at Bark. He nodded. "My oldest child is just three months younger than yours, Zephyr." She said.

"Oh, Sunblossom!" Zephyr exclaimed. She and Cornflower jumped up to hug their friend.

"Congratulations," Swift Arrow smiled at Bark.

"Cornflower, will Running Eagle be joining us for supper again?" Zephyr asked once they were all seated again, her face a picture of innocence.

"Where Running Eagle chooses to sit at meals is his own business. I have nothing to do with that." Cornflower said primly.

"Oh, really?" Bark asked, raising his eyebrows.

Cornflower leaned over and poked him in the shoulder.

"I heard something most interesting this morning." Sunblossom smiled. "He said that he needed to talk to Swift Arrow about an important matter."

"Yes," Cornflower agreed demurely. "He wants to build a rackleen." Her statement had the opposite effect that she had deSired.

"Cornflower!" Sunblossom exclaimed. A warrior did not build his own rackleen until he was ready to marry.

"He has not offered me a contract." Cornflower blushed. "We wish to take it slowly."

"I knew it!" Swift Arrow all but shouted. Everyone else stared at him. "Sorry," he mumbled.

Zephyr laughed at him. "Swift Arrow was just saying last night that he thought you and Running Eagle would end up together," Zephyr explained. "I am just glad he waited this long to say something to you."

That brought a round of laughter from all.

The snow lay several feet deep in the village of the Tribe. A few lone cooking fires burned outside, but most Tribesfolk chose to stay inside on such a bitterly cold day.

La-kaodai rode his llama into the Tribe, head held high, a small band of handpicked, ruthless men riding behind him.

Each of the men had been an exile before La-kaodai found him, and not a single one was from the Tribe. Neither of those facts bothered La-kaodai in the least. He was perfectly comfortable working with what he had.

As La-kaodai's men headed towards the Gathering Rackleen for a hot meal, La-kaodai reined up his llama and watched them go. As future Chief, Mark-hai had given La-kaodai a large amount of responsibility and a good deal of trust.

Mark-hai had not had a word to say when La-kaodai expressed his deSire to give these poor warriors a home. In fact, La-kaodai had been surprised at the ease with which his request had been granted—so surprised that it had shown on his face, and Mark-hai had shared Chieftess Lasha's dying words with him.

La-kaodai could never allow himself to show his Emotions so easily again, nor had he let on that he knew of Lasha's last words,, but he was pleased to know that he held Mark-hai's trust quite firmly.

La-kaodai turned his llama towards the Chief's rack-leen. He needed to report to Mark-hai on the day's successes, or lack of them, before heading to his own rack-leen for some hot stew. Hopefully, Crab Apple would have managed to procure better ingredients this time. *Last night's supper was unacceptable.* He thought.

"Peace be on you, Chief Mark-hai!" La-kaodai did not bother to tack the door flap behind him.

"Peace, La-kaodai." Mark-hai sounded weary.

"We are so close to our objective. If it had not begun snowing, I am confident that our warriors—"

"Your warriors, you mean." Mark-hai interrupted. "When did you become Chief?"

La-kaodai was shocked by the turn this conversation had taken. "Sire," he bowed. "You have always been ruler of this Tribe. I have only—"

"Stop," Mark-hai said testily. "I know about the whipping that you gave Strong Pine."

La-kaodai mentally gulped. "Was that not pleasing to you?"

"Pleasing?" Mark-hai scoffed. "You are my heir, La-kaodai, but the right of giving punishment rests with me alone. Do you understand?"

"Yes, Sire. Please, accept my sincerest apologies." La-kaodai bowed his head, his face a picture of repentance.

Mark-hai softened. "Yes, yes, I forgive you, but we are done fighting. Zephyr is smart enough. She knows why we attacked, and they will not try it again."

"But we can win, destroy the exiles, and then they will never be a problem again!"

"No. We. Will. Not." Mark-hai ground out the words. "Enough is enough. They must be suffering as much as we are."

"Surely you do not mean to make *peace* with them?"

"No! We are leaving them alone, not becoming allies."

"As you wish, *Sire*." There was a mocking tone just beneath the surface of the last word. Almost as if he meant to imply the unfitness of his Chief.

Mark-hai chose to ignore it.

La-kaodai stormed straight to his rackleen. As he entered, Crab Apple and Last Spring looked up. "Can I get you anything, dear?" Crab Apple asked, anxiously trying to read her husband's mood.

"I came in here to be left alone." La-kaodai snapped, dropping onto a low trunk. He started mumbling to himself about unfit Chiefs and impertinent princesses.

Crab Apple and Last Spring exchanged looks but wisely went about their chores in silence. They were careful to avoid the corner where La-kaodai sat, and the arrangement worked well, until Crab Apple accidentally dropped the kettle lid while checking on the stew.

La-kaodai jumped up, clearly startled. "I asked for peace and quiet!" He roared.

Crab Apple silenced Last Spring's retort with hand on her mother-in-law's arm and quickly said, "I am so sorry, La-kaodai. 'Twas an accident. It will not happen again. Please, forgive me."

Satisfied with his wife's cowering, La-kaodai turned and left the rackleen without a word.

"Now where is that son of mine going?" Last Spring muttered. "He did not even stop to eat the stew on which you worked so hard."

"Mammy, please," Crab Apple admonished gently. "Respect."

Last Spring raised her eyebrows at Crab Apple. "And why should you defend him when all he does is yell at you?"

"I do not," Crab Apple dropped her voice to a whisper. "You do so much to protect me. I thought perhaps I could return the favor."

Last Spring touched her arm gently. "Thank you, dear, but it is only yelling. I am used to it. He is just like his father."

Crab Apple smiled wanly. "Yet somehow, two of Running Panthers's children turned out nothing like him, while La-kaodai is his mirror image."

"And Mahli and Fast Rain are both exiled now." Last Spring said with a pointed glare at the door. "I never did understand why such a sweet girl like you would choose a man like *him* as a husband."

"You did it." Crab Apple pointed out.

Last Spring waved her hand as if the point were of no consequence. "I did it for Mahli. She is one of sweetest girls that ever lived, just like you. You, however," she jabbed a finger in Crab Apple's direction, "are dodging the question."

"It was what my father wished."

Something in Crab Apple's voice made Last Spring turn towards her curiously. "What did you want?"

"It does not matter anymore." And Crab Apple turned away with a sad sigh.

CHAPTER SIXTEEN

Five Years later

hief Mark-hai led the small group of young men, boys really, who were embarking on their first overnight hunting trip, deeper into the sun-dappled forest. This was an important milestone on the path to becoming a warrior, but there was a conspicuous lack of warriors.

Mark-hai was the only one.

Over the last five years, Mark-hai had been turning more and more authority over to La-kaodai in preparation for that warrior becoming Chief. In fact, this hunt was La-kaodai's idea.

Mark-hai was tired of the responsibilities of ruling a Tribe and was only too ready for the day when Crab Apple would have a child, and La-kaodai could become Chief.

Did Zephyr have a child yet? Mark-hai wished he knew. When his wife had died, the passing years slowly brought a fading of sorrow, but the years had done nothing to ease the pain of losing his only child. Perhaps it was because she lived so near and yet oh so far away.

Mark-hai was not paying attention to where they were going, automatically guiding his llama around trees and branches. The boys, full of youthful excitement, were not paying attention either.

But even if they had been, they were not experienced enough to realize how far they had gone. Or to notice the eyes that had been watching them for the last half yonka.

Mark-hai was jolted back to the present moment when his llama hummed and stopped. He found himself face to face with a warrior, who was holding the bridle, a hint of amusement dancing in his eyes.

"May I help you, young man?" Mark-hai asked as imperiously as he could manage. *How did I miss him?*

"Yes, actually, you can. You are trespassing on Wind Tribe land, and since you are quite obviously not messengers, you will have to come with me." He spoke in a quiet, commanding tone, with an air of confidence.

The Tribe's name sounded familiar. "I do believe that we will continue with our hunt, if it is all the same to you," Mark-hai said, resting a hand on his kameiz.

The amusement in the other warrior's eyes grew, and a bell rang in Mark-hai's mind, although he could not quite place the warrior.

"It is not the same to me." The warrior whistled, and more than a dozen warriors dropped from the trees, weapons at the ready.

Mark-hai let his hand drop from the kameiz hilt. "It seems that we will be paying a visit to the Wind Tribe then."

"Good choice." The warrior finally let himself smile then. "Chieftess Zephyr would be disappointed to learn that her father passed through our lands without stopping to see her."

All of the pieces clicked into place. "Fast Rain, it is you!" He exclaimed.

Fast Rain did his level best to hide his smile, but he didn't entirely succeed. "I most certainly hope it is me."

"Is Zephyr well?" Mark-hai asked eagerly, not at all minding as his weapons were taken from him.

"That is a question for the Chieftess herself, yes? Come, let us be going."

Fast Rain and his warriors guided Chief Mark-hai and the boys through the woods to the village. When they arrived, Fast Rain ordered his prisoners to dismount and then a few warriors to take the llamas to the corral.

"I am sure that you will be going home soon." He remarked conversationally. "We will keep your llamas safe until then. I am afraid that you will have to spend the night in a holding rackleen, though. The Chief will insist upon that."

As they were led through the village, Mark-hai craned his head, trying to see everything. The village was empty, except for a young mother with her baby on her hip, who gave the group a curious look as she hurried past towards the largest rackleen, which was lit up.

Mark-hai and the boys were marched all the way across the village and ushered into a sturdy rackleen.

The door flap was tacked securely behind them from the outside. They could hear Fast Rain giving orders to his warriors.

"Running Eagle, I know that you are eager to get back to Cornflower, but I need you to stay here with Rolling Stone. I will ask the Chief to send two warriors out here to relieve you." The prisoners could find only kindness in his tone.

"Yes, sir!" Came the ready reply. The boys looked at each in wonder.

"He must be the nicest warrior ever." One of the boys said.

"That, or La-kaodai is the meanest."

Mark-hai raised his eyebrows, but he was much too interested to interject.

"Do not say that!" The first boy exclaimed. "He is married to my sister."

"Then you should know exactly what he is like." Another boy retorted.

The first boy didn't reply.

"Peace be on you, Chieftess."

"Fast Rain, peace! How was patrol?" Zephyr smiled when Fast Rain appeared at the table where she was eating supper.

"I have some news, but I would rather tell you and Chief Swift Arrow together."

"Is anyone hurt?" Zephyr asked anxiously. On the opposite side of the table, Cornflower leaned forward to catch his reply.

"No, but we took some prisoners." Fast Rain said. "That is where Running Eagle is." He added, with a nod in Cornflower's direction. She smiled gratefully and sat back, leaning against the wall.

Zephyr sighed comfortably. "Then I can wait." She glanced at her oldest child. "Ziph! If you put your food on your sister's plate one more time, we shall have to go have a talk with a willow switch."

"Yes, Mammy," the five-year-old ducked his head.

"Chief Swift Arrow is getting Maon more food," Zephyr added to Fast Rain. She did not bother asking him to sit. She knew full well that not a single Wind Tribe head warrior would sit and relax while some of his warriors were still on duty.

Swift Arrow and Maon walked up then. Swift Arrow swung his son up onto the bench and set his bowl of root vegetable and salmon stew down on the table. "Peace be on you, Fast Rain."

That warrior took a deep breath and spoke quickly. "Chief Mark-hai is one of my prisoners."

"What?" Zephyr dropped her spoon. "*My* father?" Everyone at the table had grown quiet.

"How did this come about?" Swift Arrow asked calmly, sliding his son over so that he could sit next to Zephyr and put his arm around her.

"We spotted him about mid-afternoon, leading a hunting party of boys through Meadowlark Clearing. An hour later, they entered our land. It looked like Chief Mark-hai was letting his llama wander where it willed. We followed them for half a yonka, and when they still did not turn back, I felt that we had to bring them in. I did not think it wise to let an armed party of Tribesmen wander our land, even if they are young."

"Of course, I completely agree with you." Swift Arrow assured him. "I will order two warriors to watch them for now." He added without being asked.

"I can take them some stew." Cornflower offered quickly before Swift Arrow could stand again.

Zephyr glanced at her friend before taking hold of Swift Arrow's hand. "Let her go, please, Swift Arrow." She murmured. Swift Arrow nodded his assent, and both he and Cornflower walked away.

When Swift Arrow returned, he leaned down and whispered in Zephyr's ear. "Why?"

She smiled. "Trust me. I have a feeling that she has some good news to share."

Swift Arrow smiled back before sitting down next to his son. "Here, Maon," he said. "Eat your vegetables."

Cornflower carried a pot of stew across the village. She was accompanied by Black Bear and Angry Duck, Bear carrying a basket with bread and bowls. When they reached the holding rackleen, Running Eagle greeted her with surprise and pleasure. "I brought supper for the prisoners." She said, lifting the pot a little.

Running Eagle dropped his voice. "Did you hear who they are?"

Cornflower nodded. "Everyone knows. You know how Swift Arrow feels about preventing rumors."

Running Eagle took the cast iron pot from her and nodded to Rolling Stone. "You go ahead. We will see you later." The other warrior gave a curt nod and walked away.

"Poor man, he has not been the same since his sister died." Running Eagle said under his breath.

Cornflower took the basket with the other supper things from Bear, waited for Duck to open the door, and glanced sympathetically in the direction of the retreating warrior. "Dancing Waves was a sweet girl and such a beautiful singer."

Running Eagle and Cornflower entered the rackleen. Bear and Duck tacked the door back behind them. "Here is supper." She chirped, setting the pot down. "There are bowls and bread in the basket." She said as Running Eagle set the basket down.

"Thank you, Cornflower," Mark-hai said.

She smiled, pleased. "You recognized me."

"I should hope that I can recognize my daughter's friend, even if I do not remember the warrior that she is with."

"Running Eagle." Cornflower supplied. "My husband." She added, slipping her hand through Running Eagle's.

Mark-hai's lips compressed into a thin line. He obviously recalled the name.

As she and Running Eagle waited for the door to be opened, they heard one of the boys whisper to another. "My brother was right. The Chief does know everything, even the exiles!"

They exited the rackleen, giggling. Running Eagle took Cornflower's hand again when they had gone a few yards. "I am glad you came out here. I have spent the last three days missing you."

"Me too," Cornflower said fervently. "I have something to tell you." She added somewhat breathlessly.

Running Eagle pulled up short. "What is it?" He asked, searching her face.

"I am pregnant." Her face glowed. "I am finally pregnant, Running Eagle."

He picked her up and spun her around before crushing her to his chest. "Oh, darling, you have been so patient this last year, and the Protector has finally blessed us!"

"Four years," Cornflower whispered against his shoulder. "Four long years of waiting while the Protector has blessed all my friends, but now, *finally,* it is our turn."

Running Eagle smiled and leaned back to see her face. "Have you told anyone else?"

Cornflower shook her head. "Of course not! Zephyr suspects, though."

"Do you want to tell them tonight?"

"Well, yes," she answered slowly, "but, with Chief Mark-hai here, perhaps we should wait?" She looked up at his face.

He nodded. "Let us see what the evening brings. It may be best to wait."

Cornflower nodded back. "Alright," she smiled playfully. "Let us get you fed before you keel over from hunger."

CHAPTER SEVENTEEN

The sun had begun its slow descent over the western trees when Chief Mark-hai was led from the holding rackleen. This time his walk was much shorter to the Chief's rackleen. Wind Tribesfolk were everywhere, enjoying the warm summer evening before the sun set entirely and sent them to their rackleens.

Mark-hai swatted away a skeeterfly, and Running Eagle noted, "If you stay around long, we will have to get you some of Healer Cornflower's bug spray."

"Cornflower is one of the healers?" Mark-hai asked, although it should not have surprised him.

"The best we have." Running Eagle said proudly.

A group of children cut across the path, laughing. "Any of them yours?" Mark-hai asked conversationally, feeling a strange deSire to be friendly with these warriors.

Running Eagle smiled. "Not yet."

Fast Rain was also escorting Mark-hai. He opened his mouth to speak, then shut it again.

They reached the Chief's rackleen. Bark was standing outside, as was another warrior that Mark-hai could not place. Chief Mark-hai's heart began to pound as Bark opened the door flap and followed his unlac and escort into the rackleen.

Swift Arrow and Zephyr were seated in wooden chairs facing the door. When Mark-hai entered, they rose and bowed their heads. The Tribe's Chief did likewise.

"Peace be on you and your Tribe, Chief Mark-hai," Zephyr said, fulfilling the traditional role of hostess.

"And peace be on the whole Wind Tribe." Her father responded automatically.

"Chief Mark-hai, these are my head warriors, Strong Oak, Running Eagle, Fast Rain, and Bark. I believe you have met them all." Swift Arrow said, motioning to each warrior in turn.

Mark-hai winced internally to the veiled reference to the fact that he had banished all of the Wind Tribe's head warriors.

"And now, for business." Swift Arrow and Zephyr sat and motioned for Chief Mark-hai to do the same on a bench. "What was your business on my land?"

"I was leading a hunting party."

"Of young boys, without any other warriors?"

Mark-hai hesitated. "La-kaodai suggested it."

Zephyr made an impatient sound, and Swift Arrow raised his eyebrows. "And he thought it wise for you to travel into enemy land guarded only by boys?"

"That was an accident. We were making for the west fork."

Swift Arrow met Fast Rain's eyes for the briefest of moments. "Yet you ended up on my land." Was that concern Mark-hai heard in Swift Arrow's voice? He couldn't be sure.

"I was deep in thought and not paying attention. Matters at home captured my attention more than the hunt."

Swift Arrow nodded. "That is exactly what my warriors reported."

Curious, Mark-hai asked, "And if my account was different?"

"I would have had to assume that you were lying for some reason." Swift Arrow said evenly. "I trust my warriors completely.

Mark-hai could not blame the other Chief. He trusted his warriors the same way.

Swift Arrow glanced at his wife before handing down judgment. Zephyr had remained silent throughout, her eyes focused on her father. "Since you did not come onto our land bearing weapons with malicious intent, *this time,* you will be escorted to the edge of Wind Tribe land tomorrow morning. Your llamas will be returned to you at that time; however, your weapons will not be returned until you are off my land."

Mark-hai bowed his head in acknowledgment. "A gracious decision, Sire." When he raised his head, Zephyr was smiling at him, and tears were gathering in her eyes.

"Will you be missed tonight?"

"We were not expected back until late tomorrow."

Swift Arrow nodded. "Good, good. That makes matters quite simple. Now, we have one more piece of business to take care of." He looked over at Zephyr. "You need to talk to your daughter."

"Yes, yes, I would like nothing better," Mark-hai said eagerly.

Zephyr smiled and rose gracefully. She moved to a bench placed beneath one of the windows. "Come, join me, Father."

Strong Oak, Bark, and Running Eagle discreetly left. Fast Rain and Swift Arrow moved to the opposite side of the rackleen to talk.

"This is a beautiful rackleen." Mark-hai let his gaze roam the rackleen. "Are they all like this?"

Zephyr smiled again, just as readily as she had six years ago. "Some, but not all. This was my idea, and Swift Arrow indulged me. Over the years, many others have visited our rackleen and decided to rebuild their own homes. Swift Arrow and I had to rebuild ours a few years ago, when we started having children."

"You have children?"

"Yes, you have grandchildren," Zephyr said gently. "I have three children, ages five, four, and three. The oldest is Ziph, then Jattir, and finally Maon. Bark is married to Sunblossom now, and they have twins, brother and sister, aged five, named Keilah and Keilan; and Sunblossom is pregnant again.

"Cornflower married Running Eagle. He was exiled after the—" Zephyr trailed off, remembering and wondering what she had been thinking to say such a thing.

"I remember," Mark-hai murmured. "How could you do it, Zephyr? How could you betray us?"

Zephyr's eyes flew upward to her father's face. "You still believe that?"

"How can I not?" Mark-hai asked bitterly. "I love you, Zephyr, but I cannot forgive you for what you have done."

"I did nothing," Zephyr said calmly. "The first time I learned that the Clan was attacking the Tribe again was when Cornflower sent for me because our scouts had just found Running Eagle in the forest."

Mark-hai's only response was to raise his eyebrows, much as he had when Zephyr was a little girl.

"What proof did La-kaodai ever give you of my treachery?"

Mark-hai was keenly aware of the way Fast Rain and Swift Arrow turned to watch father and daughter at that question. "Zephyr," he murmured.

"No," she said. "Answer me. I deserve to know what charges are brought against me."

Her repose floored her. What were the accusations that La-kaodai had made? "You and Swift Arrow wish to rule the Tribe," he began.

Zephyr cocked her head. "What need have we to rule the Tribe when the Wind Tribe is just as big as the Tribe? Look around, Father, and you will see that La-kaodai's accusation has no weight. What else?"

Mark-hai searched his memory. "There was…there was…nothing else." He finally admitted.

"Do you mean that La-kaodai's entire argument was based on the premise that I wish to be Chieftess of the Tribe?"

Mark-hai had no words left to answer. It had all seemed so logical and reasonable five years ago.

"How is Crab Apple?" Zephyr asked suddenly.

Mark-hai was immeasurably grateful for the change in topic. "I do not see her much, but I know that she married La-kaodai and that they have no children."

Mark-hai completely missed the way Zephyr's eyes sought Fast Rain's face and the way Fast Rain started.

"La-kaodai has been taking over more and more responsibility as future Chief. He seems quite capable."

Zephyr's eyes closed as if in pain. "May I tell you a tale?"

Mark-hai nodded.

"Many years ago, a harsh Chief banished a young warrior for falling behind during a battle. This warrior's wife followed him. In the course of time, they had two children. Their daughter is now seven. All she and her older brother have ever known is banishment.

"For almost her entire life, she only had three friends; her brother and two little girls whose parents were banished before they were born. These precious children are suffering for things that their parents did, so-called crimes that have long been paid for.

"This is the sad story that I have been told over and over again, and they all start with Grandfather. That is why I refused to marry La-kaodai, even before I met these people. La-kaodai is just like his father. La-kaodai used to boast to me of the people his father had banished, including his step-sister's husband, and I hated it.

"Back then, La-kaodai had not banished anyone. I was determined to keep it that way. Now that I am exiled, I can do nothing to stop it, but I can minister to those banished by La-kaodai, his father, and my family. I can help ease the misery that La-kaodai and Chief Lodebar caused.

"Please, Father, do not let him continue this sin!" A sob caught in Zephyr's throat.

Wonder grew in Mark-hai. "You beg me to stop, yet, when you refused to marry La-kaodai, the Tribesfolk turned against you. How can you care for them so?"

Zephyr smiled sadly. "The Protector calls us to love all people, and I cannot forget that I was born Princess of the Tribe." She sighed. "I was taught that a ruler does not care about her people only when the people care about her. A wise Chief told me that."

Mark-hai shook his head. "That 'wise Chief' does not know if he has done right anymore. Your words plant seeds of doubt in my heart."

"It is never too late to mend your mistakes." Zephyr laid a hand on her father's knee. "It is the wise man who admits his mistakes and fixes them. Please, Father, for the good of our people, think about it."

Mark-hai looked into his daughter's deep, earnest eyes. He remembered a day long ago when a girl stood before him and impressed him with the depth of her conviction. Now, that young girl sat before him once again, but she had matured into a woman.

Back then, he had wondered, almost every day, what the Protector had planned for this daughter of his. Now, he could not help but ask himself if it was for such a time as this. If the reason she had been placed on Hereth was for this moment, to plead for her people.

He nodded slowly. "I will think on these things."

She removed her hand and smiled, like a ray of sunshine coming through the clouds. "Thank you, Father. That is all I ask."

"Zephyr, the sun is almost down." Swift Arrow said from the other side of the rackleen.

"Oh," she glanced out the window and stood. "I had better go and find the children. You can meet them tomorrow at breakfast."

"I shall look forward to it."

Zephyr and Swift Arrow exited the rackleen. Bark appeared at the door. "I will escort you back to the holding rackleen."

Mark-hai stood and moved outside, Bark following. "I am glad that you came."

"Really?" Mark-hai turned to look at his nephew.

"Of course. Zephyr and I missed you." Bark said simply. "Have you been leading many hunts lately?"

"La-kaodai and I often lead them together, yes."

Bark felt slightly jealous at that, remembering the days when he had been the one to lead hunts with his unlac, but he quickly quashed it. "It is a good thing La-kaodai did not come on this hunt."

"Why?" Mark-hai asked, confusion evident in his voice.

"Should he ever return, he will face punishment for his actions the last time he was here."

Mark-hai stopped short, brow creased in bewilderment. "What actions?"

"Why, when he attacked Zephyr. What else?" Bark asked, equally confused.

Mark-hai's brows shot up. "Attacked Zephyr? When was this? I was never told of such an attack."

Bark looked heavenward and shook his head. "Why am I surprised? Of course, La-kaodai would not have told you." Bark related the events of five years past.

Mark-hai shook his head. "How is it that he has never told me of this?"

Bark shrugged and gently prodded the older Chief to continue walking. "It sounds perfectly in line with his character to me. I would also imagine that it was a rather humiliating episode for him, especially since he still considers us exiles."

They walked in silence for a few minutes. "Do you still think of us as exiles?" Bark asked quietly.

"You do not *act* like exiles," Mark-hai said, his eyes roving the clearing. "Everyone here was banished, however, either by Chief Lo-debar or me. Does that not make you exiles?"

Bark sighed.

"You do not agree with me?"

"Of course not," Bark grinned. "I do not want to be an exile." His grin faded. "But the banishments were unjust."

Mark-hai looked back at Bark for a long time. "Were they?"

CHAPTER EIGHTEEN

hief Mark-hai lay on his pallet in the holding rackleen, hands behind his head. It was late at night, that much he knew, although he could not see the stars.

Mark-hai had tossed and turned for hours before coming to a simple conclusion. Puzzling over La-kaodai's supposed attack on Zephyr had kept him awake, but, at last, he had the answer he sought.

It had been five years since the attack, and of course, with time and retelling, the tale had grown until it and the original event had become two separate stories. La-kaodai could not have attacked Zephyr.

Whatever *had* happened, there was a simple explanation. Perhaps Zephyr had fallen, and La-kaodai had caught her, and the Wind Tribe had misconstrued the event because it was La-kaodai, and so everyone assumed the worst.

Why hadn't La-kaodai told Mark-hai what had happened? Well, that was simple. La-kaodai had been embarrassed and, perhaps, worried what Crab Apple would think, so he had kept silent on the matter.

Yes, that was what had happened, plain and simple.

The following morning, Chief Mark-hai was pleasantly surprised to discover that Chief Swift Arrow had given orders that the Wind Tribe's "guests be escorted to breakfast in the Gathering Rackleen."

When they reached the Gathering Rackleen, the boys were told to sit where they pleased and gravitated towards the tables where the Wind Tribe youth were seated.

Mark-hai was led by a stoic Rolling Stone to a table cozily tucked away in a corner. It was evident that breakfast was well underway as he approached, at least among the younger members of the table.

"Peace be on you, Father!" Zephyr exclaimed merrily when she saw him. An awkward silence descended on the other adults. Even the children stopped eating, giggling, and chatting long enough to gravely survey the stranger.

"Come sit by me," Zephyr said, patting the bench beside her.

Mark-hai slid into his spot, watching with what could only be called professional curiosity as Rolling Stone waited to be dismissed by his Chief. Zephyr was talking again, and Mark-hai forced himself to focus.

She introduced her three children and Sunblossom's two, then, with a smile, told him that Cornflower was now expecting as well. She dished him a bowl of plum oatmeal from a pot in the center of the table while relating a story about being pregnant at the same time as Sunblossom.

Suddenly her voice dropped. "There," she said, sounding satisfied. "Now they have all decided that I am fine, and they will stop staring at us." She smiled. "Sleep well?"

"Actually, I did more thinking than sleeping." Mark-hai began thoughtfully.

"Was your bed uncomfortable?" Zephyr asked worriedly, setting her spoon down.

"No, no," Mark-hai hastened to reassure his favorite daughter. "It was more comfortable than my bed at home. No, I needed to do some thinking, so my wakefulness was by choice. I think perhaps it is time for some things to change.

"You have a wrong perception, however. I do not allow La-kaodai to banish whomever he pleases whenever he pleases. *I* am still the Chief of the Tribe, and when I say that it is time for you," he waved his hand around the rackleen, "to come home, then he will simply be alright with it."

Zephyr's face turned serious. "Be careful, Father," she warned him. "La-kaodai is crafty and revenge-seeking. If he discovers that you want reconciliation, then who knows what he will do."

Mark-hai laid a hand on her shoulder. "Thank you, dear, but I can handle him."

Something in his tone told her that he was not taking La-kaodai as seriously as he needed to. "Father, did you know that La-kaodai attacked me five years ago?"

"Bark told me last night," Mark-hai said calmly, taking a bite.

"La-kaodai has lied to you for years. How can you trust him?"

"He lied about one incident that would have ruined his reputation. I have no reason to believe that he is not trustworthy."

Zephyr held his gaze for several minutes before accepting that no matter how many facts she presented, Mark-hai's faith in La-kaodai was strong, and he would not be swayed.

La-kaodai was crafty. It was in his very blood. To sit someplace quietly and figure out how to arrange everything to accomplish his goals was his idea of an afternoon well spent. Sending the Chief on that hunting trip was an idea born of one such quiet time and was only part of his grander scheme.

He knew many things could happen to a warrior who was getting up in years when on a hunting party attended only by boys. Such a warrior might never return. If

Mark-hai wandered into Wind Tribe territory, he would most likely have a change of heart, which would give La-kaodai the excuse he needed to move on certain favorite plans of his.

Last Spring still held enough influence over La-kaodai that he felt he needed an excuse to get rid of Mark-hai. His mother could be a rather effective conscience at times. At the very least, if the improbable happened and the old man had an uneventful trip, La-kaodai would have gotten him out of his hair for a while.

For the first time in over five years, Mark-hai hugged first his daughter, then his nephew goodbye.

"I am going to change and bring the whole Tribe with me." He said with a smile.

Zephyr searched his face for a moment. "Show me," was all that she said.

Mark-hai mounted his llama and led the boys off at a trot, following Bark, their guide. Mark-hai spent most of the ride quizzing his nephew about the Wind Tribeswarriors. Bark answered patiently, expertly dodging questions that would have given too much away.

After Bark turned his llama around to go back to the Wind Tribe, Mark-hai and his hunting party rode in silence for a yonka before the Chief decided to engage the boys in conversation.

"What did you think of the Wind Tribe?" Mark-hai asked.

"I wish I could bring my sister to live there." Crab Apple's brother said honestly.

"What is your name?" Mark-hai half-turned in the saddle to look at the boy who had spoken.

"High Mark, Sire." The boy said, slightly awed that his Chief would bother to ask.

"And your sister is Crab Apple?" Mark-hai asked thoughtfully, turning back to the front.

"Yes, Sire."

"Do you live with La-kaodai?"

"No, Sire. I live with my father."

"I heard that if La-kaodai is really mad at a person, he can make the Chief banish him or her." Another boy said conspiratorially.

Mark-hai chuckled quietly. "That is a bit of an exaggeration. We did not banish that young girl, Sour Plum." He glanced over his shoulder and saw High Mark's brows furrow. A feeling of dread settled over the Tribe's Chief. "What is it?"

"When I went to tell my sister farewell yesterday, I heard La-kaodai tell Crab Apple that he was going to banish Sour Plum this morning while you were still away." The boy said slowly. "He said it was time they learned who is really in charge."

Mark-hai could not believe his ears for half a moment. The girl in question was only thirteen or fourteen.

He did not even understand La-kaodai's reason for wanting her banished. "Which one of you has the fastest llama?" He asked, reigning his llama in quickly.

"I do, Sire. Obadiah, that's my llama, beat all the other llamas, *badly,* in a race last week." Another boy spoke up without hesitation.

"Ride back to the Wind Tribe as fast as you can. Tell whichever warrior you find first that Chief Mark-hai just learned that a young girl may be banished this morning."

"You can count on me, Sire." The boy said earnestly. "Sour Plum is my sister." He wheeled Obadiah around and galloped off in the direction they had come.

"Come on, boys," Mark-hai urged his own llama forward. "Let us see if we can crash a banishment."

Mark-hai arrived too late to stop the banishment. He first headed to the rackleen where Sour Plum had lived, reassuring her grieving parents about their daughter's fate. When his boy-messenger returned, Mark-hai learned that Swift Arrow, Zephyr, and several other warriors had found Sour Plum and taken her back to the village.

The next order of business was to speak to La-kaodai.

"Peace be on you, La-kaodai."

"Peace be on you also, Chief Mark-hai. I trust you had a good hunt?" La-kaodai actually looked pleased that his Chief had returned.

"It was—intriguing."

"Oh?" *Has something happened after all?*

"We were arrested by your brother."

Perfect, now he will let me move against them again!
"That is it! Those exiles have gone too far this time. I do
not want to, but perhaps it is time to teach them another
lesson."

"Not exiles." Mark-hai corrected him, leaning back
in his seat.

What? "Excuse me, Sire?"

"I was not captured by a ragged group of exiles. I
was arrested by a Tribe for trespassing."

*Fantastic, Swift Arrow put on a show. That is just
what I need.* "But, Sire, they are, in fact, exiles."

"I do not know anymore," Mark-hai said quietly.
"I banished them all, but they ignored that and act as a
Tribe would."

Zephyr must have gotten to him. "What are you saying, Sire?"

Mark-hai shifted in his seat. "Nothing. I must think
on this for some time. In the meanwhile, we shall not
exile anyone anymore. There is no point."

Oh really? I am not *going to sit idly by while you give
away my chance to rule.* "Of course, Sire, I understand
you perfectly." La-kaodai rose from the bench where he
had been sitting. "Oh, there is something that I need to
talk to you about."

"Yes?"

"The Clan sent a message while you were away.
They want a trade treaty."

"The Clan, truly?" Mark-hai raised his eyebrows in surprise.

"Well, we are at peace with them, for the moment. Perhaps they want to ensure that we will not attack them?"

"They have always been the aggressors in the past." Mark-hai pointed out.

"Be that as it may, they want a treaty." La-kaodai shrugged.

"Very well. I shall speak to the messenger."

"There is one slight problem."

"Which is?" Mark-hai's voice rose a notch.

"They will only talk in their village, and I do not think it would be wise for you to travel to the Clan."

Mark-hai was silent, thinking through the possibilities. The Clan was very wealthy, and, as he had told Zephyr, he genuinely believed that La-kaodai was trustworthy.

"Very well, you may go."

La-kaodai bowed. "Thank you very much, Sire."

Perfect...

CHAPTER NINETEEN

With some difficulty, La-kaodai finally managed to obtain an audience with the Grand Council of the Clan. After all, there had been no messenger, no deSire for further peace. That was what La-kaodai was counting on.

La-kaodai and his five thugs had ridden northwest together and halted a yonka away from the Clan's village. La-kaodai had left his men waiting in the forest while he rode onward. It had taken some fancy talking, but now he was standing before the Grand Council.

"What do you want?" Soaring Hawk, the Clan's Chief demanded.

La-kaodai bowed low before the assembled elders. "It has come to my attention that the Clan has long deSired to conquer and acquire the rich lands to the south before the Tribe grows in size to become a more prominent foe. I can give it to you."

Soaring Hawk cocked an eyebrow. "Oh? And why would you do that? I can see that you are a Tribeswarrior."

La-kaodai nodded. "Very astute, Sire. They cast me out, exiled me." There was an audible gasp and a slight recoil from the Council members. "It was unjust, I assure you." They relaxed somewhat. The Clan was more forgiving of exiles than the Tribe.

"Tell us what happened." One of the Council members ordered.

"There was a slight disagreement between myself and the Princess's husband. One night it came to blows. I escaped with only a black eye, whereas the Prince received a broken arm. The Princess and Chief were furious and banished me without hesitation.

"My humiliation was not ended, however. There is a group in the forest that *claims* to take in exiles. It was rumored to be founded by the Princess herself, but I did not believe that until I went to them for aid. They, too, cast me out."

The Grand Council appeared to accept his lies tip, shaft, and feather. "And what do you wish for in return?" Soaring Hawk asked.

"Not much, just a token really, a trifle. What I want from you is to be regent of the Tribe's former village in your absence. You see, I have a wife, aged mother, and young son. I wish to see them and provide for them properly." *I shall have to make sure that my brother-in-law, High Mark, is at my rackleen when the Clan attacks.*

"Hmm," Soaring Hawk leaned back. "We must think." He waved for a warrior to escort La-kaodai out. "We will call you in once we have reached a decision."

Soaring Hawk waited 'til the footsteps of their unexpected guest and his guard had faded before leaning forward and speaking. "He is lying. The question is, why? Does he truly seek revenge, or does he seek to lure us into a trap?"

"He is only a pesky spiderfly."[26] One of the younger, hot-tempered members of the Council said. "If we want the Tribe's land, let us just take it!"

"Calm yourself, Saidi," Soaring Hawk said. "Do we want their land? They are, after all, a small Tribe."

"The craftspeople of the Tribe are second to none." One of the other Council members pointed out. "We could increase our riches greatly if they worked for us."

"We have such a long tradition of animosity, though." A third Council member said sadly.

"Traditions are made to be broken," Saidi said fiercely. "Perhaps it is time for a new tradition."

"The Tribe has crafty warriors and many allies. That is what makes them strong. If we are to take their land, we must strike swift and sure."

"Could La-kaodai be the means for such a strike?" mused another member of the Council.

Soaring Hawk tapped his fingers impatiently on the arm of his chair. "Perhaps we test him? Tell La-kaodai

---

26 "They have red and black stripes and are very pesky." — from *Hosie's Notes on Continental and Eulgarian Insects* by Hosie Vine-ager, published by Vine-ager Vintage Design Studios.

that he must bring us some piece of information which we already know or can easily gather?"

"But what could we know that he would not?"

"The strength of the Wind Tribe." The oldest member of the Grand Council spoke, who had served under three Chiefs and gained much wisdom with the passing of time.

Soaring Hawk considered the old one's words for a moment. "If we send an emissary, we can gain the knowledge independently of La-kaodai."

Saidi took a minute to catch up. "Would that not be overly difficult for him?"

The old one nodded his sage head slowly. "Yes, it will force him to prove his loyalty to us. It is as you said, young one, some traditions are made to be broken."

Soaring Hawk nodded his head sharply. "So we have spoken. So we shall do." With those traditional words, the decision of the Council became law which would never be revoked.

The scribe sitting in the corner hastily copied down the decision. A sly smile blossomed on Saidi's face. "Perhaps we should move on to other matters and let the traitor sit for a while?"

"Your best suggestion all week, Saidi."

La-kaodai sat on a bench, his impatience climbing higher just as steadily as the sun did. *How long can it possibly take those imbeciles in there to reach a decision?* He fumed. The hulking warriors on either side of him were the only thing that kept him from pacing.

Finally, one of the younger members of the Council came out to get him. "We are ready for you now."

La-kaodai rose quickly. *Too quickly,* he chastised himself. He stretched lazily. "I am glad the Council took so long to decide my case. I know great wisdom has been put into the decision, and it has been ages since I had an opportunity to laze in the sun."

The other man rolled his eyes. "Right. We finished your decision ages ago. There were other, *more pressing* matters to attend to before we could speak to you again."

La-kaodai hid his fury at being thus dismissed under a tight smile that only left one wondering if it was sincere or forced.

"Ah, Saidi, you brought our guest." Soaring Hawk said magnanimously as the two warriors entered the rackleen. Saidi took his seat before the Chief continued.

"We have decided to accept your offer. You must, however, prove that we can trust you first. We require a certain—*piece of information.* It should be fairly simple for you to gather." Soaring Hawk was watching La-kaodai closely. "We deSire to know the strength of the Wind Tribe."

218

La-kaodai was, without a doubt, smooth. "Wind—Tribe? I am afraid that I do not understand."

Soaring Hawk smiled and clicked his tongue. "Come now, La-kaodai. I know that the exiles you spoke of are the Wind Tribe just as assuredly as I know that you brought five warriors with you in case of trouble, who even now wait in the woods."

La-kaodai matched Soaring Hawk's smile and waited five seconds before answering. "I must confess, the reports which said that you find out about everything that happens in your domain were far from wrong, Chief Soaring Hawk."

There was a collective gasp from the Grand Council. The secret which was most closely guarded from outsiders by the Clan was the name of their Chief. That was, the name that he chose upon becoming Chief.

Saidi half rose. "How did you—"

La-kaodai kept the smile pasted on his face as he bowed. "The same way this Council learned of my men, excellency."

Soaring Hawk hid the very real smile that threatened. "Very well, fair is fair. Tell us the strength of the Wind Tribe, and we will trust you."

"I am glad that we can be perfectly honest with each other at last." La-kaodai left then.

Saidi grinned slyly. "Perfectly honest? That is a bit of an exaggeration."

Soaring Hawk shook his head. "This is simply good politics. You have much to learn, my son. That is why the Council commands you to be our emissary to the Wind Tribe."

Saidi sat up straighter. "Thank you, my Chief."

Zephyr sat on a bench outside her rackleen. She had been mending a hole in one of Swift Arrow's pants; now, however, the mending lay forgotten in her lap, and she stared unseeingly into the distance.

Swift Arrow came and sat beside her. "What is wrong?" He asked gently.

"I am worried." She confessed. "Father did not seem overly concerned with La-kaodai's actions, and a hunting party reported that they saw La-kaodai ride off to the north. He had his men with him."

"Why should that worry you? He could be hunting or going to visit another Tribe or Clan on Tribal business. More likely than not, Chief Mark-hai knows exactly where La-kaodai is going."

"Perhaps," Zephyr did not sound convinced.

Swift Arrow put his arm around her and pulled her close. "Listen to me, Ze. We cannot protect the Tribe from La-kaodai. It is not our job, and I have a feeling that more interference on our part would not be welcome."

Zephyr sighed. "I know that you are right, but I still feel as though we should be doing more."

"Our job is to protect the Wind Tribe," Swift Arrow continued as though he had not heard her, "you must not worry, but we do know that La-kaodai wants revenge on us. Therefore, I think that, in the interest of protecting our people, we should keep an eye on La-kaodai's doings."

Zephyr kissed his cheek. "Oh, thank you, Swift Arrow!"

"You are most welcome." Swift Arrow grinned and leaned in to claim another kiss.

"Chief Soaring Hawk, Chief Soaring Hawk!"

The Clan's Chief turned in the direction of the voice. "Yes?"

"I just heard a terrible rumor." The warrior said nervously. "Strong Beech told me that the Tribeswarrior who came to see you earlier knew your name."

Soaring Hawk sighed. "It is no rumor. It is true."

The warrior's eyes widened in horror. "No, no, no. He has brought bad luck on our Clan!"

"Fear not. I clipped a hawk feather to my belt immediately afterward."

The warrior relaxed slightly. "Should I do the same?"

Soaring Hawk fought the urge to roll his eyes. The Clan was extremely superstitious, but as Chief, he knew that every single belief was made up. "It cannot hurt," Soaring Hawk managed to say kindly, laying a hand on the other warrior's shoulder.

"I shall do it right away."

"Spread the word," Soaring Hawk called after him. The Chief really did not want to spend his day having the same question a hundred times.

"Did the treaty meeting go well?" Mark-hai asked La-kaodai over dinner the next day.

"It is hard to tell." La-kaodai pushed his spoon around his bowl of stew, sounding quite unsure. "They said that they need more time to discuss it among themselves. I pushed for very generous terms on our side, which will, of course, have to come down."

"Of course," Mark-hai agreed, lifting his piece of sourdough bread. "I trust you, La-kaodai, in this matter."

"Thank you, Sire." La-kaodai bowed his head respectfully. Inside, however, his heart swirled with dark deSires.

And he listened to them.

CHAPTER TWENTY

unblossom, Zephyr, and their daughters, Keilan and Jattir, along with Sour Plum, sat in the shade of a large maple tree. They were all sewing, which for the younger ones meant jabbing a needle through a square of gazelle hide.

Sour Plum was staying with Sunblossom and Bark during her banishment, which everyone prayed would soon be revoked. "Who is that?" Sour Plum suddenly asked.

Sunblossom and Zephyr looked up as a young man emerged from the trees. "Peace be on you, Saidi," Zephyr said evenly. There was a slight, almost imperceptible rustle in the tree above the ladies.

"Peace be on you, Chieftess Zephyr." Saidi bowed his head.

"What is your business here, Saidi?" Zephyr bundled her sewing into Sunblossom's lap and stood.

"I am here as an emissary from the Clan."

Behind Zephyr, Sunblossom pulled the girls closer to her. The two women were painfully aware that this sudden appearance of Saidi could mean the beginning of a Clan attack.

Zephyr raised her eyebrows. "The Clan has but rarely sought peace with our people."

"The Clan has sought neither war nor peace with the Wind Tribe."

"The Wind Tribe considers itself all but a part of the Tribe." Zephyr returned.

"Currently an unwanted part." Saidi half-smiled. "Please, I beg of you, allow me to speak to Chief Swift Arrow."

Zephyr tilted her head, listening, and then smiled. "There is no need to beg. The Chief and his head warriors will be here shortly."

Saidi's head whipped around in surprise as the sound of galloping hoofbeats reached them *after* Zephyr finished speaking. Swift Arrow, Bark, Fast Rain, Running Eagle, and Strong Oak came bounding up the path on their llamas. Swift Arrow pulled Ella to a halt and swung off beside Zephyr.

He leaned down and whispered in her ear. She nodded, and he turned to their unexpected visitor. "Peace be on you, Saidi. To what do we owe this visit?"

Saidi bowed his head. "My father, the Chief of the Clan, wished to know this new Tribe. I have been sent as an emissary."

"This is indeed a surprise," Swift Arrow said, "especially as six years have passed since our founding."

"The Chieftess made it quite clear that you still consider yourself part of the Tribe. In the eyes of my Chief, however, you are quite a separate people. Does that satisfy your curiosity?"

"Not quite, but it will do for now. Fetch your llama, and then my head warrior, Fast Rain, will escort you to a rackleen. I will see you at supper."

Fast Rain dismounted and tossed his reins to Strong Oak. Saidi returned momentarily, and the two warriors headed for the center of the village on foot. Swift Arrow turned to the ladies. "What do you think of our visitor, girls?"

Jattir cocked her head. "He seems nice?"

"Kelian?" Sunblossom gently prompted.

The five-year-old shrugged. "He's fine."

"I have seen him before." Sour Plum said thoughtfully.

"His unlac served as emissary to the Tribe six years ago," Zephyr replied. "Saidi came with him."

Sunblossom separated her sewing from Zephyr's and handed Zephyr's back. "Come along, girls." She said. "Let us head back to the rackleens and find the boys."

As Sunblossom led the girls down the path, a warrior dropped from the tree and landed on the trail in front of Zephyr and Swift Arrow. "Thank you for watching over us, Deep Waters." Zephyr smiled.

"Any time I can be of service, Chieftess." Deep Waters smiled, brushing leaves off his shirt.

"Who was with you?" Zephyr asked.

Deep Waters looked up and frowned. "How did you know someone was with me?"

"I heard a noise in the tree after Saidi appeared. I know full well that a Wind Tribeswarrior does not make noise unless he chooses to, so I assumed that whoever else was up there was letting me know that he was going to get Chief Swift Arrow."

Deep Waters smiled. "Strong Oak was with me. I wondered why he brushed that branch as he left."

Strong Oak unslung his bow. "Chief, I think we will make sure that no Clanswarriors are lurking nearby."

Swift Arrow nodded. "Very well."

Running Eagle's llama pawed the ground and snorted, eager to be going. Deep Waters took the reins from Strong Oak, mounted Fast Rain's llama, and the four men rode off.

Zephyr slipped her sewing into Ella's saddlebag and pulled herself up onto the llama. Swift Arrow swung into the saddle behind her and took the reins.

"What do you think?" Swift Arrow asked.

"About Saidi?"

"Yes."

Zephyr sighed. "I do not know. He seemed sincere, but so can La-kaodai." She stiffened. "Do you think that Saidi's visit has anything to do with La-kaodai's visit to the Clan?"

"First, we do not know if La-kaodai actually visited the Clan. Second, why do we not ask him? We can see if Saidi seems surprised that we think La-kaodai visited the Clan."

Zephyr leaned back against her husband. "Good idea."

La-kaodai knelt high in a tree. It was dangerous what he was doing, and he knew it. Wind Tribeswarriors practically lived in the trees, yet here was La-kaodai in a tree on Wind Tribe land.

He had been there for hours, arriving while everyone was eating breakfast, and painstakingly counted and recorded the number of women he saw exiting the Gathering Rackleen. At dinner, he had counted the men and children. Now, as the Tribesfolk streamed into the Gathering Rackleen for supper, he was recounting the warriors.

A llama rode right beneath him, and La-kaodai stiffened. Swift Arrow and Zephyr sat on the llama as it paused just past the tree where La-kaodai hid.

A dozen calculations ran through his head. What was to be gained by killing Swift Arrow then and there. Whether or not he could escape the fury of the Wind Tribeswarriors. How long it would take them to realize what had happened.

With a silent growl of frustration, La-kaodai forced the hand that held his bow to relax. There was simply too much to be lost if he tried to kill his enemy. Zephyr and Swift Arrow dismounted the llama and walked out of arrow range unscathed.

They had no idea of the danger that had threatened them, La-kaodai thought, *but they will. They will know and fear it.*

It was clear that Saidi was bemused by the fact that Chief Swift Arrow sat with all his children and the children of his head warriors.

Saidi rose quickly when Chief Swift Arrow and Chieftess Zephyr approached the table. Swift Arrow waved him back down and sat beside the emissary.

"Supper will be ready soon." Swift Arrow informed Saidi. "There is something I wanted to ask you. Does your visit to us have anything to do with La-kaodai's visit to the Clan?"

Saidi's fist clenched, the only reaction that they got. "La-kaodai's visit? Is La-kaodai a Wind Tribeswarrior?"

"La-kaodai is a head warrior of the Tribe," Zephyr said.

Saidi shrugged. "We have not had any visits from the Tribe that I know of."

"Have you ever met La-kaodai?" Swift Arrow pressed.

"Perhaps. My unlac was an emissary to the Tribe years ago, and I might have met him then, or, perhaps I did not."

Zephyr narrowed her eyes. "I remember that visit. You spent the whole visit standing in a corner of my rackleen and looking as if you wanted to be anywhere else. La-kaodai was not at that celebration."

"Then I have not met him before," Saidi said calmly.

Swift Arrow studied the other warrior for several long seconds. Sunblossom and Cornflower, seated on the opposite bench with the children in between them, looked back and forth between the two men.

The sound of a gong filled the room, and all eyes turned to Swift Arrow. He stood. "We have an emissary from the Clan with us tonight, Warrior Saidi." His eyes swept the room. "Deep Waters has not returned yet from scouting duties, but he is to be commended for his diligence in guarding the Chieftess and Princess today. Let us thank the Protector for His provision."

All across the room, heads bowed, and one warrior from each table quietly praised the Protector aloud. Saidi squirmed slightly as Swift Arrow gave thanks and sat up quickly in noticeable relief when he finished.

"Come, Saidi." Swift Arrow said. "It is our custom that guests are served first." The two men moved toward the food tables at the front of the room.

"Where are the other warriors?" Cornflower asked.

"Scouting around the village, checking for Clanswarriors," Zephyr replied, glancing around. "Where is Fast Rain?"

"Is he not with the other head warriors?" Sunblossom asked.

"No, Swift Arrow asked him to take Saidi to a rackleen. Do you remember?"

"Oh, yes, I do remember now. I wonder where Fast Rain went." Sunblossom frowned.

"Perhaps he joined the other head warriors." Cornflower shrugged and stood. "Here come Saidi and Swift Arrow. It is time to serve the children."

La-kaodai rolled his neck, trying to stretch a kink out. The head warriors of the Wind Tribe had finally returned and entered the Gathering Rackleen. La-kaodai should leave now, while it was safe. He had seen something, however, that made him curious.

Fast Rain had led Saidi past La-kaodai's tree some time ago and had not reappeared. Cautiously, La-kaodai dropped to the ground and crept through the village in search of Saidi's rackleen.

He peeked into a few rackleens before finding it. It was a travel rackleen, obviously set up specially for Saidi's use. Looking around him, La-kaodai stepped inside. In the center of the rackleen, tied to the central pole that all travel rackleens had, Saidi had added a touch of his own. La-kaodai was going to enjoy this.

"How was your journey, Saidi?" Zephyr asked.

"Longer than it should have been. I had to take a detour to avoid the Tribe."

"The Clan and the Tribe are hostile again?"

"It would be more accurate to say that we have an uneasy peace. Ever since the Tribe defeated us five years ago, there have been no open hostilities, and my Chief has been reluctant to begin another war. A group of our warriors attacked the Tribe's messengers during the last war, and, although they were punished, my Chief is worried about retaliation."

Zephyr and Swift Arrow exchanged secret smiles. Saidi continued. "During that last battle, we entirely underestimated the number of Tribeswarriors. We thought we were fighting them all, and then some warriors attacked us from the rear. Did you know that the Tribe has warriors who fight from the trees? We had no idea. It was incredible."

Zephyr smothered a giggle, and Saidi sent an annoyed look her way. Swift Arrow intervened before Saidi could speak. "We aided the Tribe in that battle."

Saidi's eyes grew wide. "Those were Wind Tribeswarriors in the trees? Most impressive."

Swift Arrow inclined his head modestly. "It began as a matter of necessity for us and has become our greatest strength."

Strong Oak, Running Eagle, Bark, and Deep Waters approached the table. "The forest is clear, Chief," Bark reported.

"Thank you, Bark." Swift Arrow nodded. "You four may go eat now." Bark paused to press a kiss to Sunblossom's head. Saidi frowned but wisely held his tongue.

"May I speak to you, Chief?" Bark asked in a low tone.

"Of course," Swift Arrow immediately stood and followed Bark to the door. They stood in one of the entrances to the Gathering Rackleen.

"Someone is out there."

"I thought you said the forest was clear." Swift Arrow's brow creased.

"It is. But we found trails through the underbrush that were not there before."

"Could they be from Saidi's llama?"

Bark shook his head. "Too small. They were made by one person."

Swift Arrow frowned. "I want the scouts to keep a close eye out, and I want a few groups of warriors to patrol the woods tomorrow. I will warn everyone to stay close to home tonight."

Bark nodded. "Yes, Sire."

When all the warriors had returned to the Chief's table, Strong Oak took Sunblossom's place next to Keliah.

Cornflower frowned and looked around. "Where is Fast Rain?"

"He was not with us." Running Eagle said, helping his wife up and taking her place next to Maon.

Cornflower's eyes met Zephyr, concern filling her gaze. "I wonder where he could be."

"Perhaps he went to join the other warriors and got lost." Saidi said carelessly.

Zephyr straightened. "Wind Tribeswarriors do not get lost," she said stiffly.

Swift Arrow laid his hand on hers. "Fast Rain said he had a headache earlier. Perhaps he went to his rackleen early."

Cornflower's gaze cleared, and she picked up her spoon. "Yes, that is most likely. Running Eagle and I will take him some tea after dinner."

Saidi, Swift Arrow, and the other warriors spent the rest of the meal talking about both the Wind Tribe and the Clan. After the meal, Swift Arrow, Zephyr, Saidi went outside in the gathering twilight to sit on a bench.

The quiet of the evening was suddenly broken by Cornflower and Running Eagle who came running up, yelling, "Chief, Chief!"

"What is wrong?" Swift Arrow asked.

"Fast Rain is not in his rackleen, and we cannot find him anywhere." Cornflower said breathlessly.

Swift Arrow jumped to his feet. "What?"

"He is gone, Chief," Running Eagle said. "Fast Rain is missing."

CHAPTER TWENTY-ONE

earch parties combed the forest from top to bottom, and Saidi willingly joined in. Finally, Swift Arrow was forced to call a halt when it became too dark to continue the hunt.

Slowly, the warriors made their way back, still pausing every now and again to shout Fast Rain's name. Swift Arrow laid plans for the next day's search before everyone dispersed to their rackleens with heavy hearts.

After an early and hasty breakfast the following day, the warriors headed off into the forest. Saidi rode off on his llama after expressing his regret for not being able to help anymore.

The women watched the men move away and turned back to the village. There was much work waiting to be done, and Swift Arrow didn't want them wandering the forest when they did not know who was lurking out there. Besides all this, there was still the hope that Fast Rain might return to the village on his own.

Zephyr stopped outside the Gathering Rackleen to confer with some of the other women. "I have teaching duties today," Mahli said.

"I am to work in the kitchen." Soft Clouds said. Fast Rain's disappearance had stilled even her active tongue.

"We need to clean and take down the rackleen Saidi staying in," Zephyr added.

"I will help you." Sunblossom offered.

"I have some work to do in the healing rackleens." Cornflower rolled her shoulders.

The five women dispersed. Zephyr and Sunblossom made their way toward Saidi's rackleen, carrying a bucket of water and some rags. Zephyr tugged at the door flap and frowned.

"What is it?" Sunblossom asked.

"It is tacked from the inside," Zephyr said.

"I can open it." Sunblossom offered. It was possible to put door tacks in backward from the outside of the rackleen, but it required both slender hands and made it impossible to completely close the door flap.

"No," Zephyr shook her head. "I can get it." She waved her hand, and they heard the sound of tacks falling to the floor. Pushing aside the door flap, the two women halted just inside the door.

They would not have been surprised to find one or more children hiding in the rackleen, trying to get out of school. What they did find, however, shocked them to no end.

Tied to the central pole and gagged was the missing warrior. "Fast Rain!" The two women exclaimed. Relief filled the captive warrior's eyes. Sunblossom hurried to untie him, and Zephyr quickly hunted up a drinking gourd and filled it with water from her basket.

Fast Rain gulped it down. "Thank you, Chieftess." He said through dry lips. "Saidi would not give me any water this morning."

Sunblossom finished untying his ropes, and Fast Rain rubbed his sore wrists. "Did he leave already?"

"Saidi?" Zephyr asked. "Yes, he did, and the other warriors—" She trailed off and ran out the door as fast as she could.

Sunblossom gigged nervously and hastily stepped out the door. Fast Rain followed, making sure to keep space between them. "Where is she going?" He took another long drink of water.

"We discovered that you were missing last night. All the warriors are out searching for you."

"Oh," Fast Rain said quietly.

"Are you hungry?" Sunblossom asked inanely. She immediately shook her head. "That is silly. Of course, you are hungry. Come with me."

Zephyr practically flew through the village, ignoring the shouts of curious women from all around here. That morning, Swift Arrow and Bark had carried the meal gong outside and told Zephyr that she was to ring it if anything happened.

The gong was loud enough by itself, and, of course, Zephyr could amplify sound. She picked up the mallet, took a deep breath, and struck the gong.

Deep in the woods, warriors heard the echoing sound and headed for home as quickly as possible. Swift Arrow was the first to reach the village. "Are you alright?" He asked, holding Zephyr's arms. "What happened?"

"I am fine," Zephyr spoke hastily. "We found Fast Rain. He was bound and gagged in Saidi's rackleen."

"What? Why?" Swift Arrow shook his head. "I am asking the wrong person, am I not?" Zephyr smiled. The Chief turned and saw Strong Oak standing behind him. "Did you hear what the Chieftess said?"

"I did," Strong Oak affirmed.

"Will you stay here and pass the word along as the warriors return?" Strong Oak nodded by way of reply. "Thank you. The Chieftess and I will be in the Gathering Rackleen. I will see you and all the other head warriors there as soon as the last warriors have arrived."

Zephyr and Swift Arrow made their way through the swiftly convening crowd and into the Gathering Rackleen. Mahli was trying without success to corral the children and prevent them from swarming Fast Rain. Sunblossom was nowhere to be seen.

"Children," Swift Arrow put a warning edge into his voice. "Sit down, and leave Warrior Fast Rain alone. You can talk to him later, *after* supper."

There were a few groans, but for the most part, the children obeyed cheerfully and filed back to the corner to resume their interrupted school day. Mahli smiled gratefully in Swift Arrow's direction. "Thank you, Chief." Swift Arrow nodded as Zephyr tapped his arm.

"Fast Rain is sitting at our table," she said once she had his attention.

The couple made their way over and sat down opposite Fast Rain. "Are you alright, Fast Rain?" Swift Arrow asked.

"As fine as I can be, I suppose." The warrior shrugged.

"What happened?"

"Mushi and I set the rackleen up, and then Saidi went inside. I stopped to talk to Mushi before I went into the rackleen to check that Saidi had everything he needed, but, when I walked inside, I did not see him. Saidi was standing beside the door, and he jumped on me and tied me up before I realized what had happened."

"Do you think he was planning it the whole time?" Zephyr asked with a shudder.

"He must have," Fast Rain said. "Mushi and I did not talk overly long, but there was no hesitation on Saidi's part."

"But, why?" Swift Arrow asked.

Fast Rain leaned forward. "He was here to spy us out. He needed me out of the way so that he could look around, and I am sure that the search was an excellent way to count warriors. At first, I thought the Clan was planning to attack us, but I do not believe that is the case anymore."

"Why not?" Zephyr asked.

"La-kaodai."

Swift Arrow's brow creased in confusion. "La-kaodai?" He repeated.

Fast Rain nodded. "La-kaodai was here, in the village, last night. He showed up in Saidi's rackleen and told me that he was here to count warriors for the Clan so that they could attack us. I do not understand, though, why the Clan would send two spies, especially one who is not a Clanswarrior."

"So, why did La-kaodai lie?" Zephyr asked slowly.

"If he was spying on us, then he must have known that Saidi was here. Perhaps he wanted to scare us." Swift Arrow suggested.

"It all seems suspicious to me," Zephyr said, at the same time that Sunblossom arrived with Fast Rain's food, and the head warriors walked up. Running Eagle, Strong Oak, and Bark sat down. Swift Arrow filled them in while Fast Rain began eating.

Running Eagle frowned. "Why would La-kaodai help the Clan? Or lie about helping the Clan?"

"Perhaps he was trying to cause the very confusion that we now seem to be experiencing," Bark said.

"Let us ignore La-kaodai for a moment." Zephyr began. "Why would Saidi come spy on us?"

"The Clan wants to attack us." Strong Oak stated the obvious.

"Or they want to make sure that we will not interfere if they attack the Tribe again." Running Eagle motioned with his spoon.

"There is no 'if they attack.'" Running Eagle said. "It is *when* they attack."

"And now the Clan knows that we helped the Tribe." Swift Arrow sighed.

"At least we know who was in our woods now." Zephyr said gently. "It was La-kaodai."

Swift Arrow nodded slowly. "Let us increase scouts on the borders and keep a close watch to make sure none of the Tribesfolk wander off until we know what the Clan and La-kaodai are planning; and, Bark, the sooner we can get eyes on La-kaodai, the better."

Bark nodded and stood. "Yes, my Chief."

THREE DAYS LATER

Zephyr stood on a branch, enjoying the late summer breeze. "Mammy, where are you?" She heard a little boy's voice call out.

"Up here," Zephyr called back. She heard the scramble of little feet and hands on rough bark. Hooking her legs around the branch, she flipped upside down. Maon was sitting on a limb three feet off the ground, watching his older siblings deftly climb higher.

"Maon," Zephyr called.

He looked up, saw his mother, stood, held out his hands, and said, "Fly me, Mammy, fly me!"

Zephyr laughed. "Fly you? Alright." She stretched out her hands, and Moan slowly floated within her grasp. Zephyr grabbed him and flipped upright with ease.

"Peace, birdies. What brings you to my nest?"

Ziph and Jattir giggled. "Father sent us to find you," Ziph said.

"It's breakfast," Jattir chimed in.

"Jat! I was supposed to tell." Ziph frowned.

"Ziph." Zephyr raised her eyebrows and put a rebuke into her voice. "Jattir."

"Yes, Mammy?" They chorused.

"Do you have something you need to say to each other?"

"Jat, I'm sorry I got annoyed." Ziph said.

"Will you forgive me?" Zephyr prompted quietly. Ziph repeated after her.

"Yes, will you forgive me for—" Jattir's brow creased. "Mammy, what do I do wrong?"

Zephyr bit back a smile. "You were rude."

"Oh, yes, Ziph, will you forgive me for being rude?"

"I forgive you," Ziph said promptly.

"Well done, my little birdies. Now come along, a little bird told me that breakfast is ready." Ziph and Jattir giggled as they climbed down the tree while Maon watched his siblings with serious eyes.

Swift Arrow met them halfway to the Gathering Rackleen. "I need to talk to your Mammy," he said, taking Maon from his mother's arms and setting him down. "Go sit with your cousins."

"Is everything alright?" Zephyr asked as the children scampered away.

Swift Arrow shook his head. "A cousin of Crab Apple's was just escorted in by one of the scouts."

"Another banishment?" Zephyr asked sadly. "I had hoped those were over."

Swift Arrow shook his head again. "No, worse. Crab Apple sent her cousin because there is trouble at the Tribe. La-kaodai made a deal with the Clan and traded the Tribe for a position as regent. Clanswarriors surrounded the Tribe and attacked. The warriors who survived are scattered in the forest."

Zephyr inhaled sharply. "My father?"

"Chief Mark-hai is being escorted to the Clan for a probable execution tomorrow. They will leave late this afternoon, camp in the woods tonight, and arrive at the Clan's main village tomorrow morning. La-kaodai is mobilizing his warriors for war against the Wind Tribe."

"Again?" Zephyr asked wearily, pain showing in her eyes. "Have we not already played this game?"

"Revenge is a powerful force. He will not stop until he has what he wants." He pulled her close.

"We have to save them," she said against his chest, deep conviction filling her voice.

"We will," Swift Arrow said with certainty.

"How?" She pulled back.

"We will send everyone but the warriors and Cornflower to The Fortress.[27] Fast Rain and Strong Oak will defend the village while I lead a group of warriors to save Chief Mark-hai. We will send messengers to our closest allies, the Forest Tribe.

"Once I return, we can liberate the Tribe. Should Lakaodai gain our village, all he will have gained is a ghost town."

"May I go with you?"

"We will need to discuss that."

Zephyr blushed slightly. "I would just hate to not know what is happening."

"Like I said," Swift Arrow cradled her face in his hand. "We will talk about it. Now come, we have a lot of work to do today."

---

27 *The Legend of the Hill* speaks of The Fortress as a hidden home within a hill. It has been the subject of hundreds of ballads and is found in almost every book of legend. According to Swift Arrow, it is quite real, or at least it was in Year 99.

CHAPTER TWENTY-TWO

The Chief and Chieftess calmly ate their breakfast before requesting that the head warriors meet them in the Chief's rackleen. Sunblossom offered to watch Zephyr's children until school started, and Zephyr gratefully accepted.

"It seems to be a sound plan, but we must move quickly," Bark said, rubbing his chin. "Wasted time means lives lost."

"What must we accomplish before supper tonight?" Swift Arrow asked his warriors.

"We need to send scouts to learn where Chief Mark-hai is and post scouts on the borders." Bark began.

"Send messengers to the Forest Tribe." Running Eagle added.

"Divide the warriors. One group to defend the village, one group to free Chief Mark-hai, and one to escort the women and children." Strong Oak said.

"Strengthen and organize the village defenses." Fast Rain finished.

"The sooner the women and children are gone, the better," Zephyr said.

Swift Arrow nodded his head decisively. "Very good. Fast Rain, you are in charge of the defenses. Bark, get the scouts sent out, then assist Fast Rain. Running Eagle, I want you to send the messengers before you help Strong Oak. Strong Oak, you are in command of the warriors."

Chief Swift Arrow turned to his wife. "Chieftess Zephyr, will you take charge of the women and children?"

"Of course."

"If you do not mind my asking, Sire." Bark began, glancing at his cousin. "Is Chieftess Zephyr going to The Fortress as well?"

Swift Arrow looked at his wife before turning his attention back to Bark. "She will stay in the village to help me. The elders will be in charge at The Fortress."

Zephyr smiled gratefully, knowing how many anxious wives would be waiting at The Fortress.

Swift Arrow rose, signaling the end of the meeting. The head warriors moved toward the practice field, where the warriors would be gathered. Zephyr moved toward the Gathering Rackleen, where she hoped the women would be waiting after the mysterious disappearance of the Chief and Chieftess.

The women were all waiting outside the Gathering Rackleen. "Ladies," Zephyr called. Slowly, the chatter died down. "The Chief and I learned this morning that La-kaodai has betrayed the Tribe into the hands of the Clan." Gasps and murmurers broke out.

"Chief Mark-hai is awaiting execution, and La-kaodai intends to attack us. We will save Chief Mark-hai and rescue the whole Tribe. You all need to go to your rackleens and pack for a week's stay at The Fortress. We expect you to return before then, but it is best to be prepared.

"Do not take anything extra, but if your family owns something valuable, such as an ancestral sword, or precious metal, then take it with you."

The women dispersed. Zephyr turned and saw Swift Arrow standing behind her. "Was that alright?"

"Wonderful. I thought perhaps I could speak to the children while you talk to Sunblossom."

"Thank you," Zephyr said quietly, an edge of worry in her voice.

"What is it?" Swift Arrow asked. "What are you worrying about?"

"Everything," she said even more quietly. "This whole situation."

He stepped closer and hugged her. "Why?" He asked. "Will your worrying defeat La-kaodai or save your father? Pray instead, because prayer can actually change the situation."

Zephyr tilted her head back. "Thank you for the reminder, darling."

"You are welcome." He smiled. "Now, come along. We have much to do today."

Zephyr stepped back and led the way into the Gathering Rackleen, walking over to the table where Sunblossom was teaching. Zephyr gently touched her friend's elbow and waited for her to stop talking.

"Children, I need to borrow Teacher Sunblossom for a moment. Listen to Chief Swift Arrow." Zephyr motioned for Sunblossom to follow her.

Swift Arrow took Sunblossom's place at the head of the table, and he and the children gravely regarded each other for a long moment. "Do you like going on trips?" He asked suddenly.

The kids looked at each other. What kind of a question was that? "Of course, we like going on trips." One of the older boys said.

"Well, that is good." Swift Arrow said.

"Why, Father?" Ziph asked.

"Because you are going on an adventure!" Swift Arrow's voice filled with excitement, and voices rose all around the table in delighted whispers. Swift Arrow let them have their fun until he saw the ladies approaching again. "Teacher Sunblossom will tell you all about it, I am sure."

"That is a wonderful idea." Sunblossom smiled brightly. She selected a map from a large basket and spread it out on the table. "Who has heard of The Fortress?"

"You can put your pack on that white llama with the red bridle. No, the one to the left."

"All warriors need to report to Strong Oak and Running Eagle."

"The kitchen staff will be bringing plenty of food. Do not worry about that."

"The village defense should extend at least three yonkas out, but I would prefer it to be five."

"Yes, all of the llamas are going to The Fortress; however, you should still only take what you need."

"I exempted the blacksmith and his assistants from warrior duty. We need all the weapons we can get."

"All women and children are leaving in fifteen minutes."

"You men need to get moving. You are escorting the women and children, and they are leaving in less than ten minutes."

"Goodbye, Maon. I love you. Listen to your anlac[28] Sunblossom now."

"No, Bark cannot come help the blacksmiths. I need my head warriors to be head warriors."

The Chief and Chieftess were finally able to sit down to a late dinner after being on the move all morning. It was with heartfelt relief that they sat down to relax, if only for a little while.

---

28 Means *aunt,* This common term of respect was used to refer to family friends as well.

"The women and children should be at The Fortress within an hour," Zephyr commented, taking a bite of bread and cheese.

"The defenses were set up five yonkas away. I think that should be more than enough to hold La-kaodai off." Swift Arrow said, stirring his bowl of panther stew.

"Who was assigned to free Father?" Zephyr asked.

"Myself, Running Eagle, Strong Oak, Rolling Stone, and Deep Waters. I do not know how I feel about you coming with us."

Somehow, Zephyr refrained from speaking. Then she had a thought. "Ask the head warriors." She urged. "They are all like family, and why has the Protector appointed head warriors if not to give a Chief wisdom?"

Swift Arrow nodded thoughtfully. "I think I will do that."

Zephyr giggled. "Our head warriors have become quite popular in the village."

Swift Arrow raised his eyebrows. "Why do you say that?"

"Soft Clouds started telling me, among other things, that she is not at all worried because 'The Four' are protecting the Wind Tribe. When I, in my ignorance, asked to whom she was referring, she explained that she meant Bark, Fast Rain, Running Eagle, and Strong Oak. Apparently, The Four is what the women call our head warriors."

"The Four?'" Swift Arrow grinned. "I had not heard that one yet."

"Yes, according to Soft Clouds, so you know it must be true, 'The Four' surpass all the other warriors in wisdom, bravery, and deeds."

A smile tugged at the corners of Swift Arrow's mouth. "That explains how they became head warriors."

An ample smile alighted on Zephyr's mouth. Swift Arrow looked up and grinned. "Oh, look, Chieftess, it is The Mighty Four."

The head warriors joined the Chief and Chieftess at the table. "Oh, no, Sire," Bark said seriously. "It is just 'The Four.'"

Running Eagle made no attempt to hide his grin. "I kind of liked 'The Mighty Four' better."

"Is everything ready out there?" Swift Arrow quickly came back to the matter at hand.

Strong Oak nodded. "Yes, Chief. We are just waiting 'til dark to move out."

"Good, I want to ask your advice about something." Swift Arrow said.

Zephyr stood, brushing crumbs off her hands. "I am going to see if Cornflower needs help." Swift Arrow watched her walk away without speaking.

"What is it, Chief?" Bark asked.

"I allowed Zephyr to stay, because things always run better with her by my side, but she wants to come with me to free her father, and I know not where she will be safest."

"With you." Strong Oak said decisively.

Swift Arrow raised his eyebrows. "Would you care to elaborate?"

"If La-kaodai makes it to the village, there will be a lot of warriors running around, and when you have that many people, it is easy to lose track of someone. Cornflower will be here already, but La-kaodai is not angry at her.

"Besides, Chieftess Zephyr will be with you. Will you be able to focus if she is not with you or safely at The Fortress? Not to mention, she is very astute. She might notice something that the rest of us would miss."

"I agree," Bark said.

"As do I." Fast Rain said. "I do not think she would be safe here."

"What say you, Running Eagle?" Swift Arrow asked.

"I disagree. I think the safest place for Chieftess Zephyr will be here, where there will be more warriors to protect her. I have no qualms about leaving my wife here, nor about leaving Chieftess Zephyr here."

"Hmm," Swift Arrow leaned back against the wall.

"I may disagree with them, Chief, but I respect their judgment. It is probably safest to do as they suggest." Running Eagle rose.

"In many counselors, there is safety," Swift Arrow agreed. He rose and picked up his bowl. "Thank you for your advice."

"Of course," Bark said readily as he and the other head warriors stood, "and remember, Swift Arrow, should you choose to allow her to go, every warrior on that mission is completely loyal to her and you."

The afternoon was drawing to a close. A tabby of flowercats trotted out into the woods to hunt for their supper, and a few sparrowbats were already flitting from one tree to another in search of the insects they ate.

Running Eagle, Strong Oak, Rolling Stone, and Deep Waters met in front of the Gathering Rackleen. Each warrior was clad in tough leather armor, covered in valuable chainmail vests,[29] and fully armed with spear, bow, and kameiz.

Swift Arrow and Zephyr joined the warriors. "Are you ready?" He asked.

"Yes, Sire." Running Eagle answered for the group while sending a glance at Zephyr. Her bow and quiver were slung across her back.

---

29 Chainmail vests were extremely labor intensive, being composed of thousands of tiny metal rings, so they were generally reserved for Chiefs and head warriors.

"Let us be off then." Swift Arrow took Zephyr's hand and led the way into the trees. They walked several yards in before Swift Arrow ordered, "To the trees," and they all disappeared into the boughs.

Rolling Stone, who had acted as one of the scouts that morning, took the lead. A few hours would bring them to the place where Chief Mark-hai was imprisoned by the Clan.

CHAPTER TWENTY-THREE

Quiet reigned throughout the whole forest. Clouds drifted lazily across the midnight blue sky, and the full moon watched the world like a benevolent grandmother. The entire world was peaceful and still, giving not a hint of the storm that lurked just beyond the horizon, but many eyes watched and waited in the darkness.

The moon was high in the sky before Fast Rain received word from the advance scouts that the La-kaodai was on his way. Quietly, silently, warriors were roused from their berths in the boughs. Fast Rain and Bark led a small force to reconnoiter.

"They are oblivious." One of the Wind Tribeswarriors chuckled quietly.

"Only so long as they do not hear us." Fast Rain whispered sternly. All movement ceased among the watching warriors.

"We have seen enough," Bark whispered a short time later. The warriors made their way back to the line of trees where the other warriors waited.

Bark surveyed the tents and hammocks that the warriors had put up in the trees. "You move our camp back half a yonka." He ordered the right half of the warriors. "The rest of you draw your bows and prepare to ambush La-kaodai's warriors."

An hour later, when La-kaodai led the Clanswarriors within sight, they were greeted with a hail of arrows. "Shields up!" La-kaodai snapped almost before the first arrow hit its mark.

Each Clanswarrior raised his shield and fitted the rounded groove on its underside onto his head. The warriors on the outside of the column wore large shields on their backs and now turned smartly around so that the Clanswarriors were wholly protected.

La-kaodai raised his voice over the twang of arrows and battle cries. "They are scared of us! That is the only reason they ambushed us instead of fighting us like warriors!"

The Clanswarriors cheered and began slinging taunts at their attackers since that was the only weapon they could safely use. The Wind Tribeswarriors did not deign to respond.

Above in the trees, Bark cocked his head. "Do you think that they will come out anytime soon?" He asked Fast Rain.

Fast Rain shook his head. "Not a chance, at least, not as long as they think we are shooting at them." He grinned slyly.

Bark raised his voice. "Switch to rocks, men! No sense in wasting arrows that cannot penetrate their shields."

Fast Rain tipped his head back and studied the sky. "It looks like rain. It will be quite the downpour, if I am reading those clouds correctly."

Bark followed his gaze. "No one can read the weather like you, Fast Rain. Perhaps we should head back once it starts raining so we will not get wet?"

Fast Rain grinned. "Let us pass the word along."

Two complete hours passed before La-kaodai realized that something wasn't quite right. He had assumed that the Wind Tribeswarriors would run out of arrows, and then his men could break ranks and attack.

However, that had not happened yet, and though the Clanswarriors had long since ceased to taunt the unseen enemy, they were too well-trained to betray their restlessness by any shifting of position.

It struck La-kaodai that there was something wrong with the outside sounds. No longer was there the sound of battle cries and arrows leaving bows, only the sound of arrows *hitting* shields. In fact, even that sound had become very rhythmic—

"Break ranks, break ranks, you fools!" La-kaodai bellowed. "You have been hiding from a *storm* for the last two hours. Break ranks!"

As the warriors dispersed and began hurriedly setting up a makeshift camp, La-kaodai continued to berate them. "Not a storm of arrows, mind you, but a storm with clouds, and thunder, and rain. Rain!"

Someone broke into his tirade, saying, "We were just following your orders, *Chief.*"

La-kaodai whirled around. "Who said that?" He demanded. When no one answered him, he snarled. "When I find the warrior who dares to mock me, I will make him wish that he had kept his mouth shut." He ground out.

As soon as La-kaodai turned around again, the same voice muttered loudly, "He should remember that he is only a regent."

La-kaodai spun around again but saw only tired faces. "When I get my hands on you—" he fumed. He marched to the nearest canopy-covered fire and snapped at the men gathered there, "May I help you?"

The Clanswarriors murmured indistinct replies and slunk away to find a fire with friendlier tenants.

Yonkas away, the storm clouds that so troubled La-kaodai and his warriors were only a shadow in the sky for the small band of warriors crouched in the trees about the Clan's camp.

Rolling Stone and Deep Waters had crept in to reconnoiter the camp one last time before they attempted to rescue Chief Mark-hai. "They have not changed the layout of the camp." Deep Waters reported. "Most of the warriors are asleep in their rackleens. There are a handful of perimeter guards, but they are widely spaced. We will not have much trouble sneaking through them. There are two guards outside a rackleen in the very center, which is where we saw Chief Mark-hai taken earlier."

Swift Arrow digested this information for a moment. "Strong Oak, take the two best archers to the far side of the camp. You will be our distraction, if necessary." He ordered.

Strong Oak nodded. "Yes, Sire. I will take Deep Waters and Running Eagle."

"How will we know if you need us?" Running Eagle's brow creased.

"Chieftess?" Swift Arrow prompted.

"I thought perhaps we might need a signal, so I came prepared." Zephyr removed a long red ribbon from a beaded pocket on her quiver. "I will tie this to an arrow, and, if we need you, I will shoot this into the oak tree on the far side of the clearing."

Running Eagle nodded but did not speak.

"Strong Oak, go now. We will give you a few minutes before we move."

"Yes, Chief," they all chorused, including Zephyr.

As the archers moved off, Swift Arrow leaned over to whisper in his wife's ear. "You know, you can call me Swift Arrow.

Zephyr suppressed a smile. "You know that I would never do that. It might damage your reputation with the warriors."

Swift Arrow shook his head and chuckled. "We will have to finish this conversation later."

"Oh, dear. Now I am regretting that I said anything at all." Zephyr sighed dramatically as she pulled an arrow out of her quiver and began tying the ribbon to it.

Rolling Stone broke into their quiet conversation. "We might have a problem."

Swift Arrow moved to Rolling Stone's side, and that warrior pointed. Beneath them, a group of Clanswarriors was walking into the trees, torches held high, as they scanned the trees for any movement.

"Up," Swift Arrow hissed. Zephyr grabbed the branch above her head and quietly pulled herself up. The Clanswarriors marched beneath them without ever looking up.

"What are they doing?" Rolling Stone whispered.

"No time to find out now." Swift Arrow said. "Zephyr, do they have the archers?"

Zephyr took a deep breath, cocked her head, and listened. A breeze started blowing through the camp towards them. This was something that she had been working on recently.

She shook her head. "No."

"Let us go," Swift Arrow gave the ground beneath them a quick scan before dropping to the ground, looking around again, and then motioning for Zephyr and Rolling Stone to follow.

Zephyr fitted the arrow with the ribbon tied to it to her bow and pointed it at the ground as the trio crept towards the camp, as they snuck past the guards and to Mark-hai's rackleen.

They came up behind the rackleen where Mark-hai was being held. Swift Arrow drew his kameiz and slit the leather wall in half. "I am not paying for damages." He murmured. Zephyr put her hand to her mouth to smother a giggle.

Mark-hai was laying on a pallet in the middle of the small rackleen, his ankles tied to the center post.

Swift Arrow gently shook his father-in-law awake. "What?" Mark-hai mumbled groggily.

"Quiet," Swift Arrow warned. "We are here to rescue you." Rolling Stone cut the Chief's bonds, and Mark-hai, now fully awake, stood silently.

Zephyr, standing by the entrance that Swift Arrow had made, heard footsteps coming toward the rackleen. She waved the three warriors back from the hole and snatched Rolling Stone's kameiz from his confused hands.

She slit the door flap from top to bottom and pulled her father outside. The other two warriors followed, dumbstruck by her strange behavior. They watched as she refitted the arrow to her bow and raised it. Inclining her head forward to give the arrow more speed, she sent it flying over the camp.

Zephyr grabbed Mark-hai's hand again and dragged him behind a nearby rackleen. "I heard the guards coming." She whispered. "They cannot know he is gone yet."

Just then, shouts rang out from the far side of the camp. "Archers in the trees! Rouse the camp! Defend the malekua!"[30] The Clanswarriors who had been guarding Mark-hai rushed past the hidden Tribesfolk.

Swift Arrow glanced at his wife and then led the way back to the trees without the wasted time of more words. By the time they reached the trees, Strong Oak, Running Eagle, and Deep Waters were waiting for them.

"Are you up for going through the treetops?" Chief Swift Arrow asked Chief Mark-hai.

Mark-hai looked up. "I suppose so," he said doubtfully.

"We will help you, Sire." Strong Oak assured him from above.

Swift Arrow and Rolling Stone helped Mark-hai up, and once they were all in the trees, Running Eagle asked, "Straight home, Sire?"

Swift Arrow shook his head. "No, not yet. A group of Clanswarriors headed into the forest right after you left. They looked as if they were searching for someone.

---

30 This is a word often used by Clanswarriors. All historians consulted agreed that this word could refer to the commander, the flag, the camp, the prisoner, or the shoes.

We need to see what they are doing. Rolling Stone, Deep Waters, go ahead and find them. They were headed east when we saw them. We will follow you."

The two warriors moved off quickly. Zephyr, Strong Oak, and Running Eagle climbed ahead through the trees, while Swift Arrow followed behind at a slower pace with Mark-hai. Mark-hai watched as the warriors and Chieftess moved confidently across the limbs, carefully putting his feet wherever they did.

Deep Waters appeared in front of the two Chiefs a short while later, startling Mark-hai. "We found them, Sire." He said briskly. "Rolling Stone is keeping an eye on them.

Swift Arrow nodded. "Strong Oak," he called. "Help Chief Mark-hai while I go look."

Mark-hai watched with slight alarm as Swift Arrow and Deep Waters moved away even before Strong Oak had reached him. Zephyr followed the warriors, staying behind them. Soon, they found Rolling Stone.

Rolling Stone wordlessly pointed at the clearing beneath them. A large group of Clanswarriors held an only slightly less large group of Tribeswarriors captive.

"Can we help them?" Zephyr whispered.

"Yes, we can, and we will." Swift Arrow whispered firmly. "Are you up for a challenge, Ze?"

Strong Pine was a tolerable shot with a bow and arrow. Certainly not as good as his brother, Strong Oak, but fair enough. He had served Chief Mark-hai and the Tribe for thirty years. He refused to let it all end like this.

As he faced his Clanswarriors captors, he considered what advantages were on his side. In a way, they had numbers on their side, since there were only a handful more Clanswarriors than there were Tribeswarriors. The Clan, however, had weapons, and they were not nearly as tired as the Tribeswarriors were.

Strong Pine was understandably shocked and more than a little confused when an arrow came singing out of nowhere and embedded itself in the shield of one of the Clanswarriors. Another arrow came from the opposite direction and hit one of the Clanswarriors on the arm.

Three more arrows came out of nowhere before a sudden gust of wind blew out all the torches. Then, everything went dark. At least, in that part of the clearing occupied by the Clan.

The stars still twinkled merrily down on the Tribeswarriors, even as the Clanswarriors fumbled around in the dark, all the while crying out in terror, as broiling clouds blocked out the night sky, and a gale came roaring through the clearing.

Strong Pine and the other Tribeswarriors looked around, unsure what to make of the freak weather or even what they should do. Four warriors dropped down into the midst of the Tribeswarriors.

"I am Chief Swift Arrow of the Wind Tribe." One of the men spoke, a stray breeze ruffling his sandy-colored hair. "Follow us," he led the way *up* into the trees.

"Would it not be faster to travel on the ground?" Strong Pine said to no one in particular.

"Perhaps, but it would not be as safe," a voice said from behind him.

Strong Pine turned, a smile stretched out his face. "Peace be on you, brother."

Strong Oak hugged his brother as if they were standing on solid ground and not a limb five feet off the ground. Pine almost fell out of the tree when they stopped hugging, but Oak reached out and caught his arm.

"I missed you, Pine," Oak said, his smile matching Pine's.

"Come, brother," Pine said, clasping Oak's hand. "Show me how to walk in the trees without falling to my doom."

Oak laughed. "Gladly, and then I shall help you regain your home."

"Let us be off!" Chief Swift Arrow called, and the rescuers and former captives made their ponderous way through the trees, leaving befuddled Clanswarriors in their wake.

CHAPTER TWENTY-FOUR

The Chief and Chieftess of the Wind Tribe stood on a large branch with Bark and Fast Rain over-looking the village. Chief Mark-hai and his newly rescued warriors were in the Gathering Rackleen, eating a well-enjoyed meal.

"La-kaodai's men set up camp about four and a half yonkas away," Bark said.

Fast Rain continued. "There has only been one Wind Tribe casualty, and that was because Bark does not know how to use a cooking pot properly."

Zephyr choked back a laugh and began intently studying her fingernails.

"Our scouts estimate that about half of La-kaodai's force has injuries, but we do not know that happened. We certainly did not cause them." Fast Rain finished.

"Why not?" Swift Arrow asked, puzzled.

Bark replied. "We ambushed them last night from the treetops, but they immediately raised their shields. Shortly thereafter, it began raining, so we returned to our camp, leaving a scout behind."

"And our allies?"

"Will be here within the hour."

Swift Arrow smiled. "Well done, Bark and Fast Rain!" He exclaimed. "Which direction is La-kaodai headed this morning?"

"West," Bark promptly replied.

"Let us recall the warriors and allow everyone to get some rest in his own rackleen. Have the scouts rotate out. The Chieftess and I will greet the Forest Tribe, and then we will be in our rackleen, getting some rest ourselves."

"Yes, Sire," Bark and Fast Rain turned away, but Swift Arrow called after them.

"And, Bark?"

"Yes, Chief?"

"Make sure that the head warriors get some rest, too."

Bark smiled. "Yes, Sire." The two head warriors climbed out of the tree and headed across the village.

"May I laugh now?" Zephyr asked, looking at her husband.

Swift Arrow turned to look at her, brow creased in confusion. "Laugh? Laugh at what?"

A giggle broke through Zephyr's careful control. "Bark burning his hand."

"Oh, that, yes, that is fine." Swift Arrow responded offhandedly, adding to his wife's tired merriment.

La-kaodai was in a fine, raging mood. "I hope you realize," he growled at his warriors as they slowly wandered back to their base camp. "That you have been chasing shadows all morning."

"We have been following *you,* and *you* have been chasing shadows all morning!" The same mocking voice from yesterday called out, followed by soft laughter from some of the warriors.

La-kaodai started, his hand straying dangerously close to his kameiz. "Crow Hunter!" He bellowed.

Crow Hunter, the head warrior the Chief of the Clan had given La-kaodai, elbowed his way past warriors until he was standing next to La-kaodai's side. "You bellowed, Sire?"

"You know these warriors better than me," La-kaodai said quietly. "Who was that mocking me just now?"

"Well, Sire," Crow Hunter began respectfully. "I believe it was the warrior who mocked you yesterday."

"Do not tell me what I already know!" La-kaodai snapped, annoyance coming off him in waves.

Crow Hunter could not resist. "I am doing my utmost to only tell you what you do not know, *Chief.*"

The way Crow Hunter said "Chief" sent bells clanging in La-kaodai's brain, and a slow smile spread across his face.

Crow Hunter grinned back, glad the regent was good for a laugh, even if he wasn't about to admit to mocking him, but his grin faded to fear in a flash when La-kaodai whipped his kameiz out and held it inches from Crow Hunter's face.

"You had best learn to show proper respect for your Chief, or I will be forced to take action." La-kaodai had dropped his voice to terrifying effect. The rest of the Clanswarriors froze, riveted by the spectacle in front of them.

"Rest assured," La-kaodai continued. "I will deal with you myself." La-kaodai moved his kameiz 'till it was just touching the head warrior's nose. "Do I make myself clear?"

Crow Hunter gulped and took a hasty step backward. "Yes, Sire, perfectly clear." He nodded his head nervously.

"Good." La-kaodai also took a step backward and pointed with his kameiz in the direction of the camp. "Lead the warriors back to camp." He stood still, letting the Clanswarriors, now mysteriously back in formation, pass him.

La-kaodai fell in step with his band, the warriors he had recruited before all of this Clan business. "I want you to take care of Crow Hunter tonight before he becomes anything worse than a nuisance. Unfortunately, the Wind Tribe does not even spare our head warriors."

As La-kaodai moved back to the front of the column, wanting to keep an eye on his head warrior, his band grinned evilly at each other.

"You look exhausted," Cornflower said compassionately, dropping an arm around her friend.

Zephyr yawned. "I am, I was up all night, but I am waiting for the Forest Tribe to arrive before I go take a long nap."

"We need scouts on La-kaodai's camp. We need to know as soon as he returns." Swift Arrow was checking in with his head warriors a few steps away.

A scout came running up just then. "Chief, Chieftess, the Forest Tribe has arrived."

Swift Arrow and Zephyr, followed by Cornflower, Fast Rain, Bark, Running Eagle, and Strong Oak, crossed the village with as much haste as they could muster to meet the large group of warriors, each carrying a large, round shield with a yna tree embossed on it.

"Chieftess Ivey Flower!" Zephyr was so delighted to see her old friend that she could not contain her excitement. "I am so glad to see you!"

Ivey Flower hesitated for half a moment, as if unsure of what was expected of her, before speaking. "My husband, Chief Running Stream, is ill and unable to lead our warriors in battle. I humbly ask that you consult my head warrior, Far Sight, in all matters concerning the attack." She motioned to a young man who stood beside her.

Swift Arrow bowed his head in acknowledgment of the Chieftess' wishes. "Far Sight, we have food prepared in the Gathering Rackleen and beds where your warriors may sleep before we attack tonight."

Far Sight bowed his head. "I thank you, Chief Swift Arrow." Soon all the warriors had gone, leaving only the two Chieftesses, Cornflower and a young lady who stood quietly by Ivey Flower's side.

Ivey breathed a sigh of relief. "The Protector certainly did not place me on this world to lead warriors." She stepped forward to embrace Zephyr. "It is good to see you, old friend."

Zephyr warmly returned the hug. "Is your husband alright?"

"Oh, yes, the Healers say he will be fine in a few days, as long as he rests. This is my oldest daughter, Laughing Brook."

"Laughing Brook, it is a pleasure to meet you at last. It seems you have grown up since your mother used to tell me tales of her energetic daughter." Zephyr smiled. "This is our best healer, Cornflower."

Laughing Brook smiled and dipped her head. "It is an honor to meet you both."

"Brook has become my right hand." Ivey Flower said proudly, laying a hand on her daughter's shoulder. "I did not wish to travel with so many warriors alone, so she cheerfully gave up her own plans to come with me."

"I am afraid that all of our own women and children have been sent away for safety," Zephyr said, somewhat apologetically, "so there is no reward for your sacrifice here."

"Is it really so dangerous here?" Ivey Flower asked seriously.

"To defeat La-kaodai and win back the Tribe's village, we will need every available warrior," Zephyr explained. "There will be no one to protect the village, and we shudder to think what La-kaodai might do if he learned of our defenseless state and slipped by us."

"Now, however," Cornflower said. "With all of the warriors around, there is no place safer on The Continent."

Ivey Flower nodded, obviously relieved.

"When will we attack?" Laughing Brook asked.

"Not until after dark," Cornflower answered, since Zephyr was waging an unsuccessful war to hide a yawn behind her hand.

"Please excuse me," Zephyr finally managed. "I have been up all night."

Ivey Flower smiled back. "As have we."

"Well then, follow us." Cornflower smiled.

"Do you think they are lost?" Bark asked conversationally.

"Quite possibly. We might have to go find them." Fast Rain returned, settling into a comfortable position.

"I do not understand how La-kaodai is so lost." Strong Oak said from the branch above Bark and Fast Rain. "It is not as if he has never been to our village before."

"The Protector is on our side." Fast Rain responded with quiet conviction.

The three head warriors were on scout duty above La-kaodai's camp, waiting for the Clanswarriors to return. Swift Arrow made his way down the branch to join his warriors.

"Any sightings?" The Chief asked in the slowly gathering gloom.

"No, not yet—" Fast Rain began, but Strong Oak interrupted him.

"Look, there on the right." The other warriors looked, and sure enough, a few Clanswarriors were beginning to straggle through the undergrowth and trees.

"Time to disappear." Swift Arrow murmured, and the four warriors melted into the trees.

When they returned to the village, Swift Arrow immediately began giving orders. "Fast Rain, prepare the warriors. Strong Oak, pass the word to Far Sight. Running Eagle, Bark, you two are with Zephyr and I."

The Sixth War between the Tribe and Clan was about to begin.

"I was lost," La-kaodai murmured under his breath as he watched his weary men rekindle the fires they had put out ten hours before. Publicly and loudly, La-kaodai would place all the blame on Crown Hunter's shoulders. After all, La-kaodai *had* ordered him to lead the men back to camp.

The truth of it, though, was that La-kaodai had been just as lost as his warriors, and he hadn't the faintest clue how it had happened. He had found the Wind Tribe's village with ease before, and now he could not even find Swift Arrow's defenses.

La-kaodai lifted his face, both to study the setting sun and to hide his perplexity, and froze. Swift Arrow was standing on a branch, high off the ground, unarmed and unarmored.

"Surender, La-kaodai!" Swift Arrow's voice was unnaturally loud, filling the whole clearing and startling warriors. "You cannot win!"

La-kaodai laughed scornfully. With movements made smooth and swift by decades of practice, he drew his bow and sent an arrow sailing right at his most hated enemy.

Swift Arrow did not so much as blink, and at the last second, the arrow swerved to the side and plowed into a tree with a dull thud.

La-kaodai acted swiftly to forestall panic among the highly superstitious Clanswarriors. "A freak of the wind, boys!" He called. "Show him what Clanswarriors are made of."

Swift Arrow stood calmly, arms crossed over his chest, as a veritable storm of arrows assailed him. Meanwhile, La-kaodai watched with rising panic as not a single arrow came anywhere close to its mark.

He scanned the trees around Swift Arrow until he finally found her. Perched even higher than her husband, and flanked by two warriors, sat Zephyr. As she redirected each arrow, she looked as if she were doing nothing more than shooing away an annoying skeeterfly.

Raising his bow again, La-kaodai took aim at the woman he had almost pledged his life to protect six years ago and fired.

Zephyr caught sight of the arrow and waved her hand dismissively, sending it crashing back to earth at La-kaodai's feet. The Clanswarriors had no idea that Zephyr was in the trees, nor had they seen La-kaodai fire, but every single one saw the arrow come back down.

That did it. The warriors turned and began pushing to get out of the clearing. Crow Hunter was the first to reach the edge of the clearing, but an arrow from La-kaodai silenced him forever.

"No one leaves." His voice was deadly. "Do you fools not understand? It is a trick! The Chieftess of the

Wind Tribe controls the wind, and she is sitting up in a tree, making you panic like a tabby of flowercats."

The warriors looked where La-kaodai pointed, but Zephyr and her escort had vanished from sight. Before La-kaodai had a chance to speak again, Swift Arrow's voice rang clear and sincere.

"You cannot win, for you fight against what is good and right. Remember the battle cry of the Wind Tribe!" Instantly, the cry seemed to come from a thousand throats all around them.

It sounded like the howling of the west wind, rising and falling unpredictably, making the hairs stand up on the necks of the most battle-hardened warriors. The Clanswarriors huddled together in terror, not daring to run for the trees, fearing both La-kaodai's wrath and the Wind Tribe.

Up in the trees, Swift Arrow joined his wife and her escort.

"Well done, all." He said. "That might have been the best battle cry I have ever heard."

Running Eagle and Bark grinned at each other. "Thank you, Chief, but we cannot take all the credit." Running Eagle said.

"It really was the Chieftess," Bark added.

"It was nothing." Zephyr said with a smile.

Swift Arrow put his arm around her. "All the same, it was well done. By the way," he added with a twinkle in his eyes. "Thank you for not letting me be shot."

"Bark found me a good viewpoint." Zephyr frowned. "I did not expect La-kaodai to shoot me. It scared me a bit."

"I did not expect it either." Swift Arrow said, all merriment gone. "It scared me, too. It did seem to convince the Clanswarriors, though, yes?"

"It did," Bark agreed.

They tree-walked until they reached the line of trees where the rest of the army was waiting. Zephyr joined Ivey Flower, Laughing Brook, and Cornflower, who would all wait in a tree for the first battle to end.

Just before the warriors left, Swift Arrow stopped to speak to Zephyr. "La-kaodai is dangerous. We watched him kill one of his own warriors today, and this attack is bound to make him angry. Promise me that you will be cautious in the extreme until La-kaodai has been arrested and his judgment meted out."

Zephyr held his eyes with her own. "I promise."

CHAPTER TWENTY-FIVE

The battle, if it was even deserving of that name, was over before it began. When Wind Tribeswarriors, standing in the trees surrounding the clearing where La-kaodai's men were camped, sounded their battle cry, and sent a flurry of arrows downward, the Clanswarriors panicked.

The invaders fled toward the trees, only to be accosted by a line of avenging Tribeswarriors. Many of the Clanswarriors immediately threw down their weapons and surrendered; however, La-kaodai and his thugs managed to rally a small portion in the center of the clearing.

Within minutes, it was clear that the Tribe and Wind Tribe would win, and La-kaodai made a break for the trees with his band on his heels.

When they saw that their leader had abandoned them, the last pockets of resistance evaporated. Within half an hour of the beginning of the attack, the clearing was calm.

"That would have ended very differently if La-kaodai had not killed his head warrior." Swift Arrow said soberly, surveying the clearing full of leaderless warriors.

A soft, feminine voice spoke at his shoulder. "How many wounded?"

Swift Arrow turned to greet the women, and the two warriors he had sent to escort them to the clearing left without a word.

"Twenty-seven. Seven of ours, and twenty of theirs. They are over there under that canopy." Swift Arrow motioned, and Cornflower immediately headed in that direction, her satchel of healing supplies bouncing against her hip.

"Where is Far Sight?" Ivey Flower asked. Worry danced in her eyes, despite her best efforts to conceal it.

Swift Arrow wordlessly pointed to the place where Far Sight stood talking to a few of his warriors, and Ivey Flower and Laughing Brook walked away.

Swift Arrow stood facing Zephyr, weariness etched on his face in that moment of unguarded privacy. "The easy part is over." He said. "Now we have to chase Lakaodai to the Tribe."

Zephyr closed the gap between them and wrapped her arms around his waist. "You will find him." She whispered. "You will free the Tribe."

The number of warriors had swelled, joined by more Tribeswarriors who had heard the battle cries and materialized from their many hiding places. The army now moved off towards the Tribe's village, taking their many prisoners with them.

The allies now had to give up every advantage they had enjoyed before. The Tribe's village was in the middle of a clearing, which prevented the Wind Tribeswarriors from effectively fighting from the trees. They also could not sneak up and surround the village.

They would have to simply march up to the village and face these Clanswarriors who were forewarned and not frightened. Added to all this was the news, reported by scouts, that they could not spy La-kaodai in the village.

"Pine Oak, take a detail of warriors to guard the prisoners." Far Sight ordered.

"I do not think we can spare warriors for that." Fast Rain interposed skeptically.

"I do not see that we have a choice." The young head warrior said evenly and with composure. "If they escape, all they must do is return to the clearing and gather their weapons, and then they are in the perfect position to ambush us from behind. Besides, Chieftess Zephyr, my mother, and my sister are waiting in the woods, and I see no need to compromise their safely."

Fast Rain found himself momentarily without words, if only because he had forgotten Far Sight's relationship to the Forest Tribe's Chieftess and because he had entirely forgotten about the women.

"You are right," Fast Rain said after a moment's thought, albeit a bit ruefully.

Far Sight smiled, but there was no condescension in it. "Go, Pine Oak."

In the end, the allies decided to divide. The Tribeswarriors would attack in the center, the Forest Tribeswarriors on the right, and the Wind Tribeswarriors the left. The Sixth War Between the Tribe and Clan had begun in earnest.

Zephyr sat on a branch a half yonka away from the village, accompanied by Cornflower, Ivey Flower, and Laughing Brook. Nearby, a handful of warriors were watching the Clan prisoners.

"What will happen to the prisoners?" Laughing Brook asked.

"Daughter," Ivey Flower rebuked softly. "That is none of our business."

"Unfortunately," Zephyr said. "It is none of mine either. We are helping the Tribe, so just as any prisoners that your warriors capture are the Wind Tribe's, all prisoners of the Wind Tribe are, in truth, the Tribe's."

"The River Clan kills all their prisoners." Laughing Brook said sadly.

"I do not believe Chief Mark-hai will allow these men to be killed," Zephyr reassured her.

Laughing Brook's eyebrows met in a frown. "I heard that his wife was killed by the Clan. Would that not be cause for retaliation?"

Zephyr sighed. "Yes, my mother was killed by the Clan. It was the most needless battle ever seen on the Continent. The Protector commands us to protect life, however, not destroy it. One sin is not just cause for another."

"What happened?" Ivey asked quietly.

"My father used to allow her to go hunting with him. It was unorthodox, as the Tribe has strong traditions, but she loved it; so he humored her, for he loved her very much. One day, they went north to hunt, unaware that the Clan had once again claimed more land while failing to inform the surrounding Tribes and Clans. Clanswarriors attacked the hunting party without mercy. Only my father and a few other warriors escaped."

"How awful," Laughing Brook breathed. "How can men be so evil?"

"I do not know." Ivey Flower put an arm around her daughter and pulled her close. "I do not know."

A heavy silence descended on the branch for several long minutes. Then Cornflower's eye caught movement below them. "Zephyr," she whispered urgently. "Do you see that large branch with the locolata[31] vines hanging from it?"

---

31 A deep brown vine, with beautiful, vibrant, green blossoms.

Zephyr nodded, and Cornflower went on. "Can you move the vines? I thought I saw someone behind it."

Zephyr moved her foot, and a breeze pushed the locolata vines aside for a second. Cornflower inhaled sharply. "I saw at least three warriors."

Zephyr nodded decisively. "Could you see if they are ours or not?"

Cornflower shook her head. "No."

Zephyr rose. "Only one way to find out, then." She stepped around the other three ladies and drew her bow.

"I have arrows." Ivey Flower offered quickly, seeing that Zephyr did not even have a quiver, much less an arrow.

"Thank you, but I do not need one."

Cornflower smiled. "This is fun to watch."

Zephyr raised her bow and carefully sighted along it. She pulled back on the string, and in the space where the arrow should have been, the air shimmered.

Laughing Brook gasped. Zephyr released, and a second later, the branch and its vine came crashing down, revealing La-kaodai's thugs.

"She controls the wind!" Laughing Brook exclaimed. "Did you see that, Mammy?"

The thugs looked up and snarled at the women high above them. "Cornflower?" Zephyr asked, already preparing to fire again.

"Going," Cornflower swiftly began climbing to the other side of the tree.

Zephyr's next shot sent a bolt of air slamming down in front of the men, knocking the smallest one flat on his back. Ivey Flower stood up and added her arrows to the rather one-sided fight.

Before the men could get more than two shots off, which Zephyr easily brushed away, three warriors came running around the base of the broad tree. Seeing them, La-kaodai's men turned tail and fled. The warriors pursued them for a few minutes before returning.

"Thank you, Chieftess!" They called up. They were all Wind Tribeswarriors and clearly understood exactly what part Zephyr had played.

Zephyr waved and sat back down. Laughing Brook turned to her excitedly. "How long have you been able to do *that?*" She exclaimed.

Zephyr's laugh rang out on the summer breeze.

"Where are the prisoners?" La-kaodai demanded impatiently when his men crashed into view. Of the five men that he had begun with, only three remained. One had been killed and another had been wounded in the leg and ridden ahead to the Tribe's village to warn the commanding warrior.

"We could not get to them. Some meddling woman, in a tree of all places, shot down the branch we were hiding behind. Then some warriors showed up and chased us away." The first thug said, shoving aggressively past La-kaodai to get to his llama.

The smallest thug spoke up. "It was like she was shooting bolts of wind at us!"

"Oh, shut up, Raven." The third thug said while mounting his llama. "Do not be stupid, if you can at all help it. She was doing nothing of the sort."

La-kaodai rubbed the bridge of his nose. "Imbeciles!" He shouted. "That was Chieftess Zephyr. I warned you about her!"

"Oh, right," the first thug said lazily. "That was right after the weird stuff with the warrior in the tree. I stopped listening."

"You stopped listening to me?" La-kaodai was livid. "How *dare* you stop listening to me?"

"You sounded as superstitious as the Clanswarriors." The thug said, lifting his shoulders in a shrug and turning his llama away. The first thug followed suit.

La-kaodai sprang forward and grabbed the bridles. "Where on Hereth do you two idiots think you are going?" He asked, incensed.

"To find better employment, Chief. This has become a ridiculous quest for revenge. We are done." The thug pulled his kameiz out and took a swipe at La-kaodai.

La-kaodai was a good deal faster and sprang backward, escaping the blow but allowing the men to escape. He stood there panting for a moment, frustration pouring out of him. "Come on," he said shortly to Raven. "Let us go."

He mounted his llama and waited impatiently for Raven to do likewise. La-kaodai was irate and disgusted. He had failed once again, and now, instead of returning to the Clan as a defeated warrior who had lost the battle and the village, but had still managed to rescue most of his followers from imprisonment or death at hands of the enemy, he would have to flee for his life. As they rode, he considered his options.

The Forest was not an option, due to an unfortunate incident a few years ago. Prokaryota might be an excellent place to begin again, but the distance was too great. His original plan would be best. He was headed to Eulgaria.

CHAPTER TWENTY-SIX

The sun burst golden and free over the horizon, shedding its light on three disparate scenes. Wives, mothers, and sisters tearfully reunited with men they had feared were forever lost. On the other side of the Tribe's village, a burial detail somberly went about its grim work. Several yonkas away, two men rode their llamas as hard as they could, fleeing from the fields of the battles that had ended just a few short hours ago.

Zephyr made her way through the familiar streets of her homevillage,[32] dodging tight groups of people. She reached a rackleen whose door flap was tacked wide open, letting the sun shine in on two women who were cleaning as if their lives depended on it.

"Crab Apple?" Zephyr called gently. "May I come in?"

---

32 This is the equivalent of saying "her hometown."

Crab Apple was bent over a pot hanging above the fire, but now she straightened up and smiled. "Of course, Chieftess, come in."

Zephyr smiled back, relieved that she had not been rebuffed by the wife of La-kaodai. "It smells wonderful in here."

"Thank you. Mammy has been slowly teaching me her cooking secrets, and now that those horrid Clanswarriors are gone, we felt like celebrating."

"Cleaning, too?"

"Yes, and cleaning." Crab Apple agreed with a merry laugh. "Please, will you sit down?"

"I will, thank you" Zephyr sat down and measured her next words carefully. "I need to ask you both about La-kaodai."

Crab Apple glanced at her mother-in-law before sitting down and folding her hands in her lap. "We thought you might. We will tell you whatever we can, but it is not much, I am afraid."

"Whatever you *can* tell us will be exceedingly helpful," Zephyr assured her. Last Spring came to stand behind her daughter-in-law, hands resting on Crab Apple's shoulders. "Has La-kaodai returned since he left to fight the Wind Tribe?"

Crab Apple shook her head. "No, he has not. One of his thugs rode into the village to warn the head warrior here, but I could not even get into the healing rackleen to ask him about La-kaodai."

Last Spring shook her head. "That no good son of mine married the sweetest girl in the Tribe just to have sons and then ran off and left her without a farewell! I still say the village is better off without him."

"Mammy, please." Crab Apple said wearily. "I *did* choose to marry him."

"Some choice it was." Last Spring snorted. "I do not know anything more than she does, Chieftess." She added before turning back to the fireplace.

"Do you have any idea where he might be going?" Zephyr asked gently.

Crab Apple hesitated. "Eulgaria," she finally said confidently. "He is going to Eulgaria."

"Are you sure?" Zephyr pressed, needing to understand her friend's confidence.

"Yes. I overheard La-kaodai talking to his men one night after he thought I was asleep. He told them that if something were to 'go wrong,' they would all meet in Eulgaria. The next morning he left to go 'hunt down those troublesome exiles,' and I have not seen him since."

"Can we be sure that he is going to Eulgaria?"

"Yes, there is no reason for him to change his mind. Prokaryota is too far for him to hope to make it, and he cannot go to the Forest because, a few years ago, La-kaodai was quite rude to the Elvish ambassador, and it did not end well."

Zephyr rose. "Thank you so much, Crab Apple. One of the warriors will come inform you as soon as he has been arrested."

Crab Apple stood and smiled faintly. "*If* he is arrested, Chieftess, *if*."

"You do not believe our warriors can find him?" Zephyr asked, raising her eyebrows.

"I believe that they can find him. I do not believe that they can keep him." Crab Apple waved her hand in dismissal. "It does not matter what I think, though. I am sorry that I could not be of more help."

"You were most helpful," Zephyr assured her. "May peace follow both of you today."

"Peace, Chieftess." Crab Apple echoed quietly as Zephyr walked out of the rackleen.

Zephyr found Swift Arrow watching a group of warriors herd the prisoners out of the village. He turned when he heard her footsteps. "Chief Mark-hai has ordered the Clanswarriors be escorted off our land without their weapons."

"That sounds familiar." Zephyr leaned her head against Swift Arrow's shoulder and smiled. "He is copying the best Chief that I know."

Swift Arrow smiled back and dropped his arm around her. "Did you talk to Crab Apple?"

"I did," Zephyr confirmed. "La-kaodai has not been back, but it seems that he is fleeing to Eulgaria."

"Can we trust her?"

"You should have seen them, Arrow. Last Spring and Crab Apple, I mean. Last Spring has no good feelings in her heart for her son, and it is clear that there was no lost love between Crab Apple and La-kaodai when he abandoned her."

"Thank you, darling. Bark has gathered some warriors, and I am going with them."

Zephyr nodded and fought the urge to cry. "I know. Please, Swift Arrow, be careful. He hates you more than me."

"I know." Swift Arrow turned, pulling her close, and held her tight for a long time.

When they finally parted, Zephyr saw that Bark and the other warriors had gathered nearby, faces discreetly turned away from the Chief and Chieftess. Far Sight, Bark, Fast Rain, Strong Oak, Running Eagle, and two Tribeswarriors that she did not recognize were all mounted on llamas.

Bark was holding the reins of an eighth llama. Swift Arrow walked over and mounted it in one smooth motion.

Strong Oak spoke, lightly touching the bow slung across his back. "Do not worry, Chieftess. We will protect him."

Zephyr managed a grateful smile at her head warrior as the warriors waved and rode away.

291

"Chieftess Zephyr?"

Zephyr turned and saw her father standing behind her. "Yes, Chief Mark-hai?" A smile sprang to her lips. It was the first time her father had ever addressed her by her rightful title.

"May I speak to you in my rackleen?"

Zephyr looked around. "One moment, please. Rolling Stone!" She called. Mark-hai waited patiently.

"Yes, Chieftess?" Rolling Stone asked.

"Choose six more warriors and go escort the women and children home from The Fortress."

"Immediately, Chieftess." Rolling Stone moved away with alacrity.

"What is it?" Zephyr asked, although there was no impatience in her voice. Mark-hai started walking to his rackleen, and she fell into step beside him.

"The Fortress? I had no idea that it was real." Mark-hai said, obviously content to wait until they were at his rackleen to get to the heart of the matter.

"Yes, it is, and it is beautiful," Zephyr said softly. "We happened upon it three years ago, and it became our secret."

"Was anyone living there?" Mark-hai asked in an almost reverent tone.

"Mm, no, not anymore," Zephyr said, "but there used to be a great civilization living there, of that we have no doubt. It took months of hard work to clear all the debris out and make it fit for people to live there again."

"Did you leave caretakers there?"

"We did," Zephyr confirmed. "You only need a handful of warriors to defend it, really, so well-suited it was." They had reached the Chief's rackleen, and she sat down on a bench outside, looking expectantly up at her father.

Mark-hai hesitated in the doorway for a second, clearly surprised, but then he accepted her choice and joined her on the bench.

"Many years ago," Mark-hai began without preamble. "La-kaodai's father was accused of terrible things by four warriors. You know as well as I that the Protector teaches that if there are two or more witnesses, a statement is to be believed, and since no one came forward to contradict the claim, La-kaodai's father was executed.

"I learned, far too late, that it was all a lie, that his neighbors were fed up with the way he treated everyone and so sought to get rid of him since milder forms of punishment had done nothing to reform his habits. I was determined not to make the same mistake and went too far in the other direction.

"I closed my ears to all rumors about La-kaodai, and, in the process, I closed my ears to the truth. Your mother was not around to set me straight, and—have you ever heard your mother's last words?"

Zephyr shook her head.

Mark-hai picked up her hand. "It will be alright, my love."

"Choose a good husband for her."

"I will, I promise." Tears pricked at his eyes as he watched his wife.

"La-kaodai—don't—" her words trailed off. One more breath, and she was gone.

Mark-hai closed his eyes for a moment as the remembrance of that horrible day came rushing back. "First, your mother asked me to find a good husband for you. Then, she said two more words, 'La-kaodai' and 'don't.' For years, I assumed, although I now believe I was wrong, that she meant that I was not to let La-kaodai get away. Now, I think she was trying to warn me not to let him marry you."

Tears filled Zephyr's eyes. With her last words, her mother had tried to protect her beloved daughter. Although, in the end, the attempt had met with failure, the act meant more to Zephyr than she would ever be able to say. It was a truth that she would treasure in her heart for all her days.

"Oh, Zephyr," Mark-hai said. "I never thought that Swift Arrow was a lesser man. La-kaodai was my first choice, and I thought he was your mother's choice. After I saw the Wind Tribe with my own eyes and was no longer relying on La-kaodai's reports, I thought that perhaps it was time to pardon you all and allow you to return home."

Mark-hai scoffed. "All along, it was I who needed to be pardoned, not you, or Swift Arrow, or any other person who was banished."

Mark-hai sighed. "I am sorrier than I can truly express. Will you—can you—ever forgive me for all the suffering I have caused, for my pride, and for my anger?"

Zephyr could not stand the distance between them any longer, and she hugged her father. "Oh, Father, I forgave you long ago."

"Zephyr," Mark-hai said hoarsely after a long moment. "I have no heirs. Would the Wind Tribe ever consider becoming one with the Tribe again?"

Zephyr's brilliant smile made Mark-hai regret that he had not done this years ago. "We have always said that, if given the chance, we would rejoin the Tribe." She paused and thought for a moment. "Although, perhaps two villages would be in order."

Mark-hai smiled. "Yes, yes, indeed. Only they must not be so far apart as our villages are now." His smile faded, and he added earnestly, "I have no deSire to strip you and Swift Arrow of your titles. I am ready to step down from being Chief."

Zephyr laid her head on her father's shoulder for a moment, just as she had used to do when she was younger.

"Was it hard for you to accept them as your people, to see past the fact that they were exiles?" He asked after a short pause.

"In a way, I suppose. When I first saw them come streaming into our tiny clearing, all I could see were hurting people who needed someone to minister to them, and I recognized that I could be that someone. I still struggled to think of them as *my* Tribe, and then Swift Arrow said, 'These are your people now, and they need you.' It was eye-opening, in a way."

"Are you worried about Swift Arrow?"

"I am trying not to be." Zephyr's gaze drifted to the horizon. "I know that he is surrounded by good and loyal warriors who will give their lives to protect him if need be. I also know that Swift Arrow will not take unnecessary risks."

"He is a wise man." Mark-hai agreed.

"It is what I do not know that scares me," Zephyr said softly.

"What do you mean?" Mark-hai asked.

"I have no idea what La-kaodai will try next, and that terrifies me."

CHAPTER TWENTY-SEVEN

"Which way now?" Swift Arrow reined in his llama at a crossroads and waited for Bear Claws, a tracker on loan from Chief Mark-hai, to respond.

Bear Claws swung off his llama again to study the tracks more closely, as he had done a half-dozen times in the last two hours. "Left," he said after a brief moment.

Swift Arrow waited for the other warrior to mount before leading the way down the left path. Suddenly, Bear Claws called a halt.

"What is it?" Strong Pine asked his fellow Tribeswarrior.

"The tracks end." Without dismounting, Bear Claws pointed. "No tracks."

Swift Arrow's brow furrowed. He hadn't noticed and probably hadn't had a shadow of a chance to notice from astride his llama. "What happened then?"

"One moment, please, Chief." Bear Claws wheeled his llama around and galloped back the way they had come. Less than five minutes later, he returned.

"La-kaodai covered his tracks up for a distance on the right path and had someone ride back this way. That is why these tracks look strange."

"Well done, Bear Claws!" Swift Arrow exclaimed, turning his llama, impressed by the tracker's skill once again. "The right path it is."

They rode down the right path for an hour before Bear Claws called a halt. He hopped off his llama and studied the ground, walking around. "There is one other person with La-kaodai." He said after a long moment.

"The llamas got tired and laid down. La-kaodai and his companion went off on foot. At some point, the llamas wandered away, possibly after they heard us coming."

"I hope someone finds them before the big cats do," Bark said, running an affectionate hand down his llama's neck.

Bear Claws remounted his llama and looked at Swift Arrow. "We are getting close."

La-kaodai crouched in a tree, one steadying hand on the trunk and the other balancing a sharp rock. He watched Swift Arrow sit on his llama, watching Bear Claws study La-kaodai's tracks.

Bear Claws straightened. "One set of tracks goes due north and the other seems to disappear."

"I was told La-kaodai would go due south, not north." Swift Arrow said thoughtfully.

"And what happened to the second set of tracks?" Bark asked. "I suppose we should search around here. Either La-kaodai or his companion might be hiding near-by."

Swift Arrow dismounted, but before he or any of the other warriors could respond, a crashing sound in the undergrowth to the north caused them all to turn and draw their kameizs.

"Who are you, and what is your business here?" Swift Arrow demanded.

"My—my name is Raven. I was with—with La-kaodai." The warrior stuttered.

Swift Arrow sighed and slid his kameiz back into his belt. "I would not do that, Chief," Bark warned, eyes on Raven. "I do not trust anything he says."

Up in his tree, La-kaodai smiled and hefted his rock. La-kaodai, while not the best archer, had excellent aim, and now that Raven had moved Swift Arrow in the right direction—

Swift Arrow grunted and stumbled backward into his llama, causing the startled animal to trot away, and reached for his forehead. His hand came away red.

The warriors all looked up at the same time to see La-kaodai standing triumphantly on a tree branch with a drawn bow.

"I am going to enjoy *this* victory more than all the others, Swift Arrow." His smile was entirely vitriolic. "I will finally have all the things that *you* denied me. I only became head warrior because you turned the position down. You had the respect of the warriors. You had Zephyr. You had the admiration of the Chief."

"Do not be silly, La-kaodai." Fast Rain called out while Running Eagle inched closer to Swift Arrow. "You banished us all, you married Crab Apple, and you even ruled the Tribe for a time."

"*For a time,*" La-kaodai repeated mockingly. "Swift Arrow received everything of lasting value, but no more. I am going to have my freedom and my life, and you, Swift Arrow, will have neither."

Running Eagle put a hand on Swift Arrow's arm and called out boldly, "You will not get away with this, La-kaodai."

"Oh, really?" La-kaodai asked, amusement pouring from him. "I think it is obvious who has the upper hand."

"You are right; it is." Fast Rain said with quiet confidence.

"And it is not you." A firm voice spoke in La-kaodai's ear. La-kaodai turned to see Strong Oak standing perpendicular to him, bow drawn.

Fast Rain had been the one to tell Strong Oak to climb the tree, and he had also been the one to tell Running Eagle to stand next to Swift Arrow.

La-kaodai howled in rage and let loose the arrow he had aimed straight at Swift Arrow's heart. Running Eagle jerked his Chief to the side milliseconds before the arrow sped through the air where Swift Arrow had been and embedded itself in the heart of a tree.

La-kaodai gave vent to his frustrations with a wild yell, and the warriors turned their heads to see that La-kaodai was now on the ground, a throwing knife raised in the air.

There was no time for anyone on the ground to react, but Strong Oak had a much clearer view of all that was happening.

The twang of an arrow leaving its bow filled the air, and La-kaodai's face filled with surprise. He staggered a few steps and then fell, an arrow protruding from his back.

Strong Oak stood in the tree, looking sadly down at the warrior he'd just been forced to kill.

Raven whimpered, and Bear Claws and Strong Pine hurried forward to prevent him from running away. "Someone help Chief Swift Arrow sit down." Running Eagle said, hastening to his llama.

Bark and Fast Rain eased their Chief to the ground beneath a tree. "Cornflower sent some healing supplies with me." Running Eagle said, removing a satchel from his saddlebag and coming to Swift Arrow's side.

Swift Arrow winced as Running Eagle began washing the gash. "You are in charge, Bark." He ground out.

Soon, the warriors and one prisoner had ridden off, and the only trace of the tragedy that had occurred was the fresh mound of dirt beneath a single sentinel tree.

"Swift Arrow! What happened? Are you alright?" Zephyr cried when the warriors rode back into the village. She had been crossing the village with Mark-hai when they spotted the cloud of dust kicked up by the llamas.

Swift Arrow grimaced as Fast Rain and bark helped him off his llama. "I will give you one guess," Bark said darkly.

"I will get Cornflower." Mark-hai offered quickly. Bear Claws and Strong Pine led Raven away to a holding rackleen.

"You did not even capture him?" Zephyr asked.

"No, we captured him." Fast Rain said quietly. "He is dead."

"Oh," Zephyr said softly. "Come along, let us get Swift Arrow to Chief Mark-hai's rackleen.

Zephyr and Running Eagle followed the other three warriors to the Chief's rackleen. Zephyr quickly pulled out the mattresses and made up a bed. By the time they had Swift Arrow settled, Cornflower had arrived.

Running Eagle and Bark stayed to tell the women what had transpired while Fast Rain left and made his way to the far side of the village. He reached Crab

Apple's rackleen. The door flap was still tacked open, but he knocked anyway.

Crab Apple looked up from her sewing and came to the door with a smile. "Peace be on you, Fast Rain."

"Peace be on you, Crab Apple."

"Mammy is not here, but she will return shortly."

"I am not here to see Mammy. Not now, at least."

"He is dead." It was a statement, not a question.

Fast Rain nodded somberly. "We had no choice. I am sorry, Crab Apple."

"It was not your fault. La-kaodai made his own choices." Crab Apple said simply. She moved to a bench outside the rackleen and choked back a sob. "Now what will I do? My father was killed by the Clan, and my only brother is younger than I. What will I do? I am all alone."

"You are not alone." Fast Rain blurted out before his brain could catch up.

"Really?" Hope shone in her eyes through the tears.

He sighed. "Truly." He moved to sit beside her, careful to keep a proper distance between them. "I told myself that I would wait until the time of mourning was over, but the truth of the matter is that I love you, Crab Apple, and I have for years. Six years ago, I was just biding my time 'til I was old enough to ask for your hand. Then I was banished and lost all hope."

"When you were banished, _I_ lost hope." Crab Apple broke in. "I married your brother because I had no other options, but six years ago I prayed every day that the Protector would see fit to bring us together."

"And now He has." Fast Rain added. "Would it please you, Crab Apple, if I were to speak with the Chief about contracting with you?"

Crab Apple's smile seemed as though it would escape from her face. "Yes, yes, it would."

Zephyr sat on the floor next to Swift Arrow's bed. Cornflower had ordered him to stay down for at least the next few hours. "I miss our bed at home." She said with a smile.

Swift Arrow smiled tenderly back. "When we move, I will build you a new one."

"What do we do now?" She asked suddenly. "Lakaodai is gone. We are free to rejoin the Tribe. Everything we have worked for over the last six years has come to fruition. Where do we go from here?"

"I do not know for sure." Swift Arrow said wisely. "I do know, however, that we will continue doing what we have always done, faithfully doing whatever the Protector has for us. I believe that He still has a task for us."

"Why do you believe that?" Zephyr asked quietly.

"Running Eagle pulled me out of the path of a speeding arrow today. The arrow was not deflected with a shield; *I was pulled out of its path.* How can that not be a sure sign of the Protector's favor?"

Zephyr smiled. "You are right. The Protector has blessed us mightily. I cannot wait to see what He has for us next."

FIFTEEN YEARS LATER

"You are late, Zephyr." Sunblossom chided with a smile. "My girls refuse to be satisfied until you have given them a tour of the old village." Zephyr smiled and dismounted her llama, Olivia. She took a moment to survey the busy scene before her.

Now twenty, her oldest Ziph, was deep in conversation with his same-age cousins Keilah and Kelian. Jattir, now nineteen, was chatting with her anlacs Cornflower and Crab Apple, as well as her cousin and Crab Apple's daughter, little Zephyr.

Sunblossom's girls, Dancing River, Running Brook, Sparkling Waterfall, Starry Night, Smooth Pond, Lilly Heart, and Swan laughed at the other girls' antics.

Cherryblossom and Caloundra, Zephyr's daughters, were pretending to fight off Snowblossom, Sweet Apple, and Yna Vine, Cornflower's daughters, using flowers as kameizs.

Zephyr's youngest son, Maon, was shooting bow and arrows with the warriors and his cousins little Strong Oak and Walking Eagle, both Cornflower's boys.

Jattir glanced up and saw her mother. "Mammy!" She called excitedly. "Come here, Cornflower's baby is kicking, and I can feel him!"

Zephyr took a step in her daughter's direction but found herself surrounded by little girls before she could go very far. "Will you show us where you lived now?" Lilly Heart asked excitedly.

"Go gather everyone else, and then, yes." The Chieftess replied. After everyone was gathered, Chief Swift Arrow and Chieftess Zephyr showed the children the old Gathering Rackleen, which was still standing many years later, the Chief's rackleen, and the Healer's rackleen. "That is the place where Ella scared Anlac Sunblossom and I." Zephyr pointed.

"Who's Ella?" Sawn asked, leaning against Zephyr's leg.

"Ella was my llama."

"Your llama is Olivia." Swan pointed out helpfully.

"Olivia is Ella's daughter. I do not have Ella anymore." Zephyr explained.

Swan seemed satisfied and ran off to play with her sisters and cousins.

The adults walked the children around the old village and promised them a trip to The Fortress. As the summer afternoon drifted to a close, Zephyr greeted a group of young people who materialized at the edge of the forest.

"Azal, I am so glad that you could come!" Zephyr greeted them.

The redhead embraced Zephyr. "Thank you for inviting us, Chieftess."

"Of course. You used to play with Jattir, and Kelian all the time when we lived here. They are looking forward to seeing you."

"You know my brother Ekro and his wife, Thebes, and our friend, Shaphir." Azal began, motioning to each in turn. "You do not, however, know my husband-promised, Kannauj. His family is from Prokaryota."

"Husband-promised?" Zephyr smiled. "That is wonderful. Not many people wait after they sign the contract."

"We have not known each other as long as most," Azal smiled.

"When is the claiming then?"

"In six months." Azal smiled up at Kannauj.

"If there is ever anything that Chief Swift Arrow and I can do for you, please, just tell us. We would love to help."

Azal smiled, although it was clear to Zephyr that the girl could not foresee any such need. "Thank you again. Where are the girls?"

Zephyr pointed them out with a smile, and the young people moved off. Swift Arrow walked up just then and put his arm around Zephyr. "You look tired."

"Tired, but happy. I was just thinking, Arrow, that we have done it. Everything we have done has been so that no one would ever have to be banished again. Look around! We have raised a generation of leaders who will honor the Protector and show mercy to their people."

"The Protector has used us mightily." Swift Arrow agreed, smiling down at Zephyr. "I cannot wait to see what the next fifteen years have for us."

EXCERPTS FROM
DEBSTER'S DICTIONARY

Acaidia /ə-ˈkā-dē-ə/ n. an ancient city, the first center of Continental learning and arts.

anlac /ˈȯn-läk/ n. means *aunt*. A common term of respect was used to refer to family friends as well.

balankn /ˈba-lən-kin/ n. a small, cake-like dessert.

coe /ˈcō/ adv. a very common word throughout Hereth, it means "clearly." See Dr Brain's *Words and Where They Come From, Probably* for a detailed discussion.

Crown of Thorns Porridge - made with whole branches from the Crown of Thorns bush, wild honey, oats, llama milk, and a dash of truffle oil.

Elves - the people group that occupies The Forest. Every Elf controls a Gift.

Eulgaria /lo͞o-ger-ē-ən/ n. a country to the south of The Continent. It is on a peninsula, just south of The Forest.

Gifts, the - Fire, Ice, Water, Sound, Earth, Light, Rock, and Nature.

kameiz /kam-ˈmīz/ n. a long, curved dagger. The first kameiz was given directly to the Chief of the Tribe by the Settlers.

kamina / ka-ˈmə-nə/ n. Eulgarian term for the Gifts.

Kgbjrkeoowkay - a very complicated, impossible to pronounce word which roughly translates to *kitchen staff.*

locolata /ˈlō-kō-lä-tä vines - a beautiful deep brown vine with vibrant green blooms. It is found on The Continent, in The Forest, and in the Royal Gardens of Eulgaria.

malekua /ˈmə-le-küə/ n. This is a word often used by Clanswarriors. All historians consulted agreed that this word could refer to the commander, the flag, the camp, the prisoner, or the shoes.

"Offending Tradition" - a common phrase on The Continent that is used by young people everywhere and refers to ignoring or rebelling against tradition.

Prokaryota /prō-ˈker-ē-ō-tə/ n. a small country to the northeast of The Continent and home to the most inventive people on Hereth. Prokaryota: A History of Inventions by Senator Dumah and published by Presidential Presses is a good resource.

rackleens /ˈrak-lēns/ n. six-sided buildings used on The Continent. The name comes from two Eulgarian words, *rack* meaning *live* and *leen* meaning *family*.

Spiderfly - a small, pesky insect. It looks like a spider with wings.

sparking tea - a lemongrass tea made with sparkling water from the Golden Springs. The Golden Springs were discovered by Mahli's great aunt in 0005 OT (Olden Times).

Swamp Raiders - a vicious people that live in the swamps of The Continent and are known for their cruelty.

The Forest - a country to the south of The Continent. It is a large forest populated by the Elves.

tiffin /ˈtif-fin/ n. Eulgarian term for the noon meal.

tock /ˈtäk/ v. means *find her, find him, find my sock*. It is considered a Eulgarian word by most.

unlac /ˈəŋ- lak/ n. means *uncle*. It is a common term of respect given to family friends.

whatancta /wä-chä-chä/ pn. means *whatever* or *I am done talking to you, but I don't want to be rude so I'm going to say whatancta.*

wolfurnut / ˈwoolf- ər- nät/ n. a dog-like animal that walks or runs on four legs. Wolfurnuts are extremely empathic and can be taught to climb trees. Pronounced ˈwoolf- ər- nät (*u* makes an *ə* sound when preceded by *n* and followed by t).

yna /ˈnyə/ adj. The bark of a yna tree is streaked with purple. The leaves of this flowering tree are heart-shaped, and the flowers and leaves can either be red, orange, or purple. Yna trees belong to the class evercolor, as their leaves do not fall off in winter.

yonka /ˈyäŋ-kə/ n. a Continental unit of measure, equal to two mikás, three miles, or seven tonkowdas. (A miká is a Eulgarian unit of measure and a tonkowda is a Prokaryotan unit of measure).

BIBLIOGRAPHY

Note: These resources have been translated into Eulgarian, Prokaryotan, and the five southern Continental dialects only. My apologies to those of you who are from the northern Tribes and Clans.

Brain, Dr. Steveonus. *Words and Where They Come From, Probably*. Eulgaria: Spoon of Power Publishing, 0097.

Debster, Shem. *Debster's Dictionary, Abridged Version*. Far Countries: Words, Words, Words, 0087 OT.
[**Note**: This 2,000-page book was brought by the Settlers into the Continent and surrounding lands. Everyone is scared to know how thick the unabridged version was.]

Dumah, Senator. *A History of Inventions*. Prokaryota: Presidential Presses. Prokaryota, 0092.

Flower, Ivey. *Cooking on The Continent*. Continent: Waterfall House, 0091.

Queen Raychal. *Tapestries; What We Can Learn About Our History*. Eulgaria: Royal Library Press, 0060.

Unknown. *The Legend of The Hill.* Continent.

[Literally any wandering bard can tell you this legend. You just have to ask and be prepared to listen to six hours' worth of ballads].

Vine-agar, Hosie. *Hosie's Notes on Continental and Eulgarian Insects.* Eulgaria: Vine-agar Vintage Design Studios, 0098.

ACKNOWLEDGMENTS

Eulgaria would not have been possible without the awesomely amazing people that God has placed in my life. This list is a mere handful, and I am sure that I will spend this entire series thanking new and entirely different people.

Thanks to my research and idea team (Aka Mama and my siblings, mostly Felicity, Micah, Josie, and Sophie) for all the ideas, suggestions, edits, and for listening to me ramble.

Thanks to Daddy and Mama for letting me write, slogging through my first couple of attempts at writing (Mama) and giving me my laptop in the first place (Daddy).

Thanks to my siblings for being my best friends in the whole world and letting me tickle them.

Thanks to Emma Bean, my absolutely amazing friend, for the free (!) cover and wonderful artwork.

Thanks to Ella Hoy for reading my second, third, *and* fourth drafts (and being excited for every one) and for giving me feedback.

Thanks to Mr Dave for taking my photo and generally being awesome.

Thanks to Gigi and Grammy for telling me the story about Pawpaw's pet cow. Even though I didn't know it at the time, I'm glad I named a wolfurnut after his cow.

Thanks to Mrs. Amanda Blizzard for reading and editing my book, and thanks to Miss Rose Ann Futoran for also editing my book and explaining semicolons.

Finally, it feels appropriate to end this first book as I began it, thanking my LORD and Master for the Gift of writing and for the entire world of Hereth. Onward to Eulgaria!

ABOUT THE AUTHOR

Abigail Jeanne is seventeen and a recent high school graduate. She loves reading and writing fiction with a Christian message, and her favorite genres are biographies, fantasy, and historical fiction. She has four sisters, and six brothers, all younger than she is. Abigail looks forward to exploring all the stories that Eulgaria holds.

Made in United States
Orlando, FL
22 June 2023

34418190R00200